THE LAST WORD

Susan knew that her mother had brought her to the ball to attract the wealthy, eligible, supremely boring Lord Buxford. Susan was therefore not surprised to see her mother shocked when Susan snared Captain Camberley for the supper dance.

"Really, my dear," her mother said in a low voice. "You need not be quite so obvious. The Captain is not an eligible, you know. You must get over this ridiculous infatuation."

"What ridiculous infatuation?" Susan said with dignity. She avoided her mother's eyes. "I merely like him. He is a friend."

To which her mother replied, "At your age, Susan, you need more than friends."

Which left Susan wordless . . . since a friend was all that the Captain seemed determined to be . . .

MARGARET WESTHAVEN is a native Oregonian. She is married and has a young son.

SIGNET REGENCY ROMANCE
COMING IN AUGUST 1992

Anne Barbour
A Talent for Trouble

Patricia Rice
Artful Deceptions

Sandra Heath
A Country Cotillion

Georgette Heyer
Lady of Quality

TOWN
FOLLIES

by

Margaret Westhaven

A SIGNET BOOK

SIGNET
Published by the Penguin Group
Penguin Books USA Inc., 375 Hudson Street,
New York, New York, 10014, U.S.A.
Penguin Books Ltd, 27 Wrights Lane, London W8 5TZ, England
Penguin Books Australia Ltd, Ringwood, Victoria, Australia
Penguin Books Canada Ltd, 10 Alcorn Avenue, Toronto, Ontario, Canada M4V 3B2
Penguin Books (N.Z.) Ltd, 182-190 Wairau Road,
Auckland 10, New Zealand

Penguin Books Ltd, Registered Offices:
Harmondsworth, Middlesex, England

First published by Signet, an imprint of New American Library,
a division of Penguin Books USA Inc.

First Printing, July, 1992

10 9 8 7 6 5 4 3 2 1

In my time, the follies of the town
crept slowly among us, but now
they travel faster than a stagecoach.

—*She Stoops to Conquer*

1

Captain Vincent Camberley was strolling the perimeters of his park when his glance lighted on an airy Grecian summerhouse just across the paling in his neighbor's garden.

In recent years the captain had been more at home on the seas than in places as peaceful as the Surrey countryside, and thus he could be forgiven for not noticing some of the less significant details of his landlocked environment. Still, he was struck at once by something out of the ordinary about the summerhouse.

A female's white skirt was visible between the columns of the little structure. The woman appeared to be standing on top of something, for her head and shoulders disappeared into the dome of the temple. What was more, she looked to be struggling.

Camberley did not hesitate. Years spent in command on a ship of the line had given him lightning-quick reactions. He crossed onto the other property and approached the folly.

Standing just outside, he continued to observe the female, or what he could see of her. She was perched upon a rickety garden chair which was in its turn placed on a low stone table that looked to be a fixture in the center of the summerhouse. Small kid slippers stood on tiptoe. The head and shoulders were indistinct, for they were inside what appeared to be a kind of attic opening in the summerhouse dome. Unlike most domes, the interior of this one was not rounded, but had a flat ceiling.

A sound of frustration came from within this ceiling.

Camberley cleared his throat and drew nearer. "Madam, may I be of help?"

The figure froze. "Oh!" came a soft voice. There was a moment's pause. Then, "Whoever you are, sir, do go away."

"But, ma'am, every chivalrous instinct tells me that you could be in some difficulty."

"It's nothing. I've merely lost something," the voice said.

Camberley looked about him and spotted a book upon the table. "This book, perhaps?" He lifted it. The binding was moldy, and he opened the cover curiously. The familiar title of a famous French novel of the last century leapt out at him. *Des Leçons dans la Vie,* by an anonymous lady of the court. Salacious reading, this, for a young creature. He judged the female young by her voice and also by the muslin gown.

"For heaven's sake, sir, do not look at it," the voice commanded in a shocked tone.

He snapped the volume shut. "By no means, though I confess to having glimpsed the title. I've already read it, ma'am."

A gasp, and another pause. "You have?"

He smiled. "Won't you come down, ma'am? I'm your new neighbor from Royce Park, by the way. Camberley is my name."

"You are Captain Camberley! How do you do, sir."

Her tones betrayed that she had heard of him. She would naturally know of his naval victories, he supposed, for they had been sufficiently puffed in the press. He felt a pang of disappointment. He would have liked to banter with a country lass who didn't know who he was.

"My pleasure, ma'am," he answered politely, then stood where he was and waited. But the young woman didn't move, nor did she offer her name—and the strange intimacy of this situation would certainly seem to make an exchange of names proper. Perhaps he should go away, for she was evidently embarrassed to be discovered in whatever furtive act she was about.

"Sir," said the young woman after a long moment of silence, "perhaps you could help me."

"At your service. What do you require?"

"I . . . I'm stuck."

"Stuck?"

"My sleeve is caught on a nail inside this opening, and I'm afraid to tug on it for fear I'll fall."

"I can't say I blame you, ma'am. Here." Camberley mounted the table and matter-of-factly put his arms around the young woman's waist—a supple, slender waist, he could not help noting. "You may rip away now and be quite safe."

She stiffened perceptibly under his hands. "Thank you, sir," she said in a shaky voice. Then she tugged.

The violence of her movement surprised Camberley, and before he knew it the female had slipped from the chair and was looking up at him from the circle of his arms. He found himself gazing into a delightfully pretty face. Wide blue-green eyes, thickly fringed with dark lashes, stared up at him with a dismayed expression. A tumble of golden-brown curls, bound simply with a ribbon, fell back from a slender white neck.

Camberley swallowed hard and hastily revised his opinion of the social diversions likely to be found in his new neighborhood. Further inspection revealed the creature in his arms to be exquisitely formed and trembling gently.

He smiled. "If I had needed to be shown that I'm no longer on the deck of a ship, this experience would be a sure indicator."

She looked at him in confusion for a moment, then smiled in appreciation of his joke.

He helped the girl to stand upright and assisted her down from the table. She gave him a hasty curtsy, then turned away and ran down the steps of the folly.

Amused but indignant, he called after her, "Unfair, ma'am! After involving me in a delightful mystery, you owe me some explanation. Your name, at the very least."

The girl hesitated and turned back. "You're right, sir. I am Susan Danvers."

The daughter of the house? he wondered. Camberley had heard that Pilgrim Court, the estate he was trespassing on at present, was owned by an elderly eccentric. He had heard nothing about an angelic beauty; but then, he was only just come into the neighborhood. The girl's speech and even her simple muslin dress, unadorned though it was, revealed her to be a young woman of quality. She couldn't be a servant, and looked too young to be a companion.

"And who is Susan Danvers?" Camberley asked with a smile. He had already scanned her left hand for a ring and found it bare; he never remembered doing such a thing before, let alone feeling relief at the likelihood that a young female was single. He was surprised to be granted her given name on such short acquaintance—this bespoke a less-than-expert knowledge of society and its ways. "I hope you have not scratched your arm," he added, indicating the torn muslin sleeve in the hopes that this would initiate a friendly exchange.

"Not at all, Captain Camberley," Miss Danvers replied, glancing at her sleeve. She smiled. "As to who I am: what a very curious question! I am myself, of course, and no other."

"What a very curious answer." His tone was gently mocking. "Are you the daughter of this estate that I'm so blithely tramping through?"

"Mrs. Palmer is my grandmother."

He surmised, then, that Mrs. Palmer was the old eccentric who owned Pilgrim Court. "And I won't even bother asking what you were doing in your late predicament, Miss Danvers. It would be ungentlemanly of me to press you."

She smiled, a lovely smile showing even white teeth. "But you are curious, aren't you, sir?"

He bowed in answer.

She picked up the French novel which had surprised him earlier. "I was trying to hide this book until I can find time to read it further." Her smile displayed a dimple in her cheek, and Camberley resisted with difficulty the urge to reach out and touch it. "This is my usual hiding place for books. You must know, sir, that my grandmother doesn't approve of reading."

He nodded. "Many elderly ladies, I believe, grow to distrust novels."

"Not only novels." She sighed. "Grandmama disapproves of reading altogether."

"Curious! Isn't it the fashion for young ladies to be greatly accomplished?" So Camberley's sister often advised him, though Drusilla, as a bluestocking, never failed to disparage what passed for learning with young ladies of quality. He added, only half in earnest, "It would seem to me that a course of serious reading would be part of that goal."

"Grandmama is a little singular," the girl said.

"Did your grandmother bring you up?"

Miss Danvers nodded. If she was surprised at his curiosity, she gave no sign. "I'm afraid she's done a less-than-creditable job from my point of view. For though I can spin and knit and keep bees, I know nothing of the pianoforte and the globes and modern languages and all those other things that young ladies must know.''

He laughed at the list of accomplishments which so nearly matched his private prejudices. It was an affectionate laugh. She appeared startled, and he sobered his expression instantly. ''You must know something of French, to be reading *Lessons in Life*. It was translated recently, you know. That is its English title.''

''Indeed?'' Miss Danvers brightened. ''Then perhaps I could find a copy. I fear that my French is self-taught—there was a grammar in the attic—and there is much that I don't understand. Although,'' she added in a confidential tone, ''if I'm not much mistaken, this is a rather coarse tale in places.''

He laughed. That was an understatement. ''In its time, the novel caused a scandal. Such a subject as a courtesan's career, to be undertaken by a lady, even an anonymous one! But you must know, Miss Danvers, that some also say this was a political tract. Its plot foretold the revolution: the court life shattering, Paris in anarchy. And so its author, if she—or he, for there's really no telling about anonymous authors—could be found, would be hailed as a sort of minor Voltaire.''

''Voltaire?''

Her look of puzzlement suggested that she had never heard the name before. He forbore to insult her with a lecture on French letters and turned the subject back to what she did know. ''Never mind. Are you enjoying the book?''

''I'm only as far as the place where Zephyrine is being transported to Paris concealed in a giant pumpkin,'' she said eagerly. ''So she is to become a courtesan! How delightfully improper. But Grandmama wishes me to spend the rest of the day churning butter, and so I'm forced to stop.'' She looked up at him with a worried expression. ''You won't betray me, will you, Captain Camberley?''

''Betray you! How could you even suggest such a thing, Miss Danvers?'' Camberley drew himself up to his full height and tried to look severe. So attracted was he by this young lady, and so amused, that the attempt was a dismal failure.

He caught himself staring at her face, at a light curl that was brushing one ear, at the calm lines of her brow. ''Did you say you were to churn butter?'' he asked, bemused. He must have misheard her.

"Grandmama is more than a little singular,'' Miss Danvers replied with a nod and a curtsy. "And so, good-bye, sir. Many thanks for your aid.'' She looked shyly at him. "I hope we meet again.''

"Surely we will,'' he exclaimed. "We are neighbors, and I take my neighborly duties very seriously.''

Her answer was another of her bright smiles. Then she turned and walked out of the little temple. She soon disappeared around a turning of a brick path lined with privet.

He stared at the book in his hand. She had forgotten all about hiding it. With a shrug and a smile, he hoisted himself up to the table and thence to the chair.

Once his head was poking into the hole of the summerhouse ceiling, he could see in the shadows a pile of books laid on a piece of cloth. He brought them out to look at them. A meager pile, all ancient and in disreputable condition. Miss Danvers must have ferreted them out in the corners of her house that her nonliterary grandmother hadn't thought to purge. There was a history of England, a couple of books of poetry by Thomson and Cowper, a bound edition of *The Rambler*, and some volumes of *Tristram Shandy*—the first four.

Camberley replaced the books, added the French novel to the stack, and fitted in the square board that concealed the opening. He leapt lightly down from his perch just as Miss Danvers appeared again, out of breath, her bosom rising and falling in a most distracting manner.

"Oh.'' She came to a halt as she saw him, then glanced above to the now-innocent-looking ceiling. "Thank you so much, Captain. You are certain you won't betray me?''

"I have already sworn never to do so,'' he replied in his best formal style, his hand on his heart.

She gave him another curtsy and a twinkling grin. Once again he watched her away, admiring the lightness of her step, the grace of her retreating figure.

Descending the steps of the summerhouse, Captan Camberley found himself whistling a sea chantey he had thought he would never wish to hear again.

* * *

Susan hurried through the gardens of Pilgrim Court, following the brick pathway under waving lime trees, then leaving the bricks for another path of stone flags. In a short time she arrived at her grandmother's model dairy, a thatched and tidy structure. Susan could remember when the dairy had been surrounded by velvet lawns and visited only to churn butter and skim cream as a sort of play. The place was now given over to the trampled mud usually associated with the habitation of cows. Grandmama's mania for the natural had finally led her to turn the pretty model into a working dairy.

As Susan approached the cowshed, she was thinking, not of the dairy and her duties there, but of Captain Camberley. Sheltered she might be from the neighborhood as a whole, but she had heard stories from the servants about the noted sea captain who had let Royce Park.

Odd, thought Susan, that none of the stories had mentioned what an attractive man the captain was. Perhaps—a smile played across her features—his attractions were most clear at close proximity. She had never been held in a man's arms, and was still tingling from the unexpected contact.

''Ah, there you are, child!'' Grandmama looked up from her station on a milk stool as Susan entered the cool stone building.

Susan paused to pat the warm brown side of Amabel, the cow. ''I'm sorry I'm late.''

''Some mischief, I'd wager,'' Grandmama said, speaking over the rhythmic squirt of milk into the pail. She eyed Susan's torn sleeve. ''There's a mending job for the evening. But what can one do with children, Miss Camberley?''

Susan whirled around and saw that there was a lady seated in one corner of the shed, in the only chair the place boasted, a rough wooden one judged too rickety for the kitchen.

''You don't look like your brother.'' Susan made this observation before she could stop herself.

''You have met my twin.'' The words were spoken with a wise look.

The lady stood up and smiled, and then Susan did trace a likeness to Captain Camberley. Other than the smile, though, and a certain gleam of intelligence in the eyes, the captain's sister looked nothing like him. Whereas he was tall and lanky, with straight brown hair, she was small, and her raven hair curled even more wildly than did Susan's own tresses. Miss Camberley's eyes were light blue and sharp behind a pair of little square spectacles. Her brother's eyes, on the other hand, were dark and melting. Miss Camberley, like the captain, was not in her first youth, Susan could see by the bright morning light coming through the shed's window. Well, she had said they were twins.

"Nonsense, Susan, you can't have met her brother." Grandmama's irritated voice was muffled by Amabel. "She came to call by herself."

There would be no hiding the meeting, Susan supposed, and she answered honestly. "I did meet him, near the border of Royce Park, and we exchanged a few words only."

"Ah," Miss Camberley said.

"Hmph," came Grandmama's snort, over the sound of milk shooting into the pail.

"How do you do, ma'am?" Susan, who had so forgotten herself on first seeing the lady, determined to repair her hoydenish first impression. Grandmama was evidently in no mood to do the polite. "I am Mrs. Palmer's granddaughter Susan Danvers."

"How do you do, my dear?" The other's voice was kind, and she came forward to take Susan by the hand.

"The churning, Susan, the churning," Mrs. Palmer said.

With an apologetic smile Susan seated herself on a tall stool near the butter churn and began the steady motions up and down, long habit making her movements fluid. She indicated that Miss Camberley should reseat herself, and was gratified that she did so rather than give up on these strange neighbors and leave the shed.

"You must have found it strange, ma'am, to be shown into a dairy," Susan said as she worked, one eye on the cow. Grandmama would probably rise up in disapproval any moment, but Susan was determined to salvage some remnants of the social amenities, even from the seat of a churning stool, and thus perhaps to make a friend of Captain Camberley's sister. "You must know that Grandmama allows nothing to disturb her schedule.''

"The cows won't wait," Mrs. Palmer grumbled.

"I think this a quite delightful experience," Miss Camberley said. Susan wondered if politeness would have allowed her to say anything else under the circumstances. "Do you . . . churn often, Miss Danvers?"

"Country skills, country virtues," Mrs. Palmer said from behind the cow.

"Yes," Susan added with a wink at their visitor.

"Her education," Mrs. Palmer said, "has been most exacting."

"Grandmama means I churn well," Susan said with a demure casting down of lashes.

Miss Camberley allowed a snicker to escape her.

Mrs. Palmer chose that moment to stand up in majestic dudgeon from the milk stool. A stately woman, she was clad in a brown worsted gown and an apron. The large cap she sported was adorned with black ribbons—she had never laid off mourning for Mr. Palmer. Grandmama had seen about seventy summers, but Susan had always thought she looked much younger than her years despite her gray hair. Under the cap which covered this, keen gray eyes in a finely boned face settled on Susan in disapproval.

"Granddaughter," Mrs. Palmer said, "you forget yourself."

"I'm sorry, Grandmama." Susan's tone managed to convey that, although meaning every respect, she was not sorry at all.

"The girl has a sense of humor," Mrs. Palmer told their guest. "An unfortunate quirk which I can't seem to tamp down, no matter how I try."

"Grandmama, you speak as though I had a contagious malady," Susan said with a laugh. She smiled apologetically at Miss Camberley. "You must think me as intolerably pert, ma'am, as my grandmother finds me. Will you forgive me? May I take you into the house for a glass of wine?"

"Thank you, I have already had some new milk," Miss Camberley said, indicating a glass on the floor by her chair. She rose again, cast a speculative glance around, and continued, "And there is nothing to forgive. I am amazed to find such delightful neighbors. I thought country society would be a dead bore.''

"I'd wager you'll find it so," Mrs. Palmer said darkly. "Don't think I haven't heard of you, miss. Flitting all about London like a butterfly. We welcome your friendship, but I warn you now that I won't have Susan corrupted by any modern town notions.''

There was a gasp from Susan, and their new neighbor stood still for a moment. Then she laughed, a pleasant sound which somehow reminded Susan of her brother.

"Oh, Mrs. Palmer," Miss Camberley said with a rueful shake of her head, "if you knew me better, you wouldn't have issued me what sounds like a challenge.''

Susan relaxed. She had been afraid that Miss Camberley would stalk from the room in as much stateliness as her tiny form could muster.

As for Grandmama, she nodded at the visitor in something like satisfaction. "You are not a milk-and-water miss, at any rate," she said. "Well, you could hardly be so, a woman of your years.''

"Nor have I flitted about London like a butterfly," Miss Camberley said, appearing to fight back another laugh. "You've been misinformed, madam. I am what is termed a bluestocking. I can't even remember the last ball I attended, and I am much past the age for social follies.''

"There are other, more insidious paths to corruption than balls and drums," Mrs. Palmer proclaimed with another grim stare. "Blue, are you? Then the country air is more necessary than I thought. It will cleanse you, my dear, if you but give it leave to do so.''

"Grandmama," Susan said with a pleading look at Miss Camberley. The woman still seemed to understand the situation; her good humor didn't diminish.

"I must bid you good day, ladies," she said with a brisk nod. Susan was sure she saw a mischievous look on the lady's face as she added, "I am most eager to begin my study of the Roman remains in the south meadow of Royce Park.''

"Disturbing the treasures of antiquity," Mrs. Palmer exclaimed in evident disgust.

"Really, Grandmama," put in Susan, who was wide-eyed at the thought of a female who would have a serious interest in ruins. "Miss Camberley said she was going to study them, not dig them up."

Susan's eyes met those of Miss Camberley, and they both laughed. Nodding pleasantly in farewell, the latter lady left the shed.

When they were alone, Mrs. Palmer looked severely at her granddaughter. "One day, my dear, you will go too far. Now, what is this about meeting the woman's brother?"

"It happened quite by accident." Susan's lips twitched at the thought of what a very undignified accident it had been.

"I cannot say whether those Camberleys will be troublesome or not," Mrs. Palmer went on, her suspicious eye on Susan's torn sleeve. Evidently she preferred not to mention it again for fear she would hear something she did not wish to know. "I am quite willing to lend my counsel to young people in need, but as you know, we do not go out socially."

"I am most sensible of that, Grandmama," Susan said with a sigh.

"Silly of her to call," the old lady grumbled.

"I'd wager she was curious. She would have waited many a long day for us to call on her," Susan said thoughtfully. "Wouldn't that have been the proper form, Grandmama?"

"What do you know of proper forms, miss?" came the snappish reply.

"Nothing, to be sure, ma'am." Her lack of training in common manners had become a source of great trial to Susan as she reached years of discretion. All she could do about it was to copy the few gently bred people she saw, and she saw them at such rare intervals.

"And we shall keep it that way," Mrs. Palmer said, fixing a shrewd glance on Susan. "Back to your churning, young lady. You have fallen sadly behind on your chores already. Where have you been keeping yourself since breakfasttime?"

"I was in the garden. Communing with nature," Susan said, knowing that answer would please her grandmother. Mrs. Palmer indeed nodded in approval.

Susan began to churn energetically, thinking over the lively bits of the French novel that had really claimed her morning's attention. She had planned to so engage herself all during the day's work, but somehow puzzling out the bawdy adventures of the heroine was not such an intriguing prospect as she had expected.

Resigning herself to the inevitable, Susan gave herself over to the contemplation of another vision: that of a certain strong-featured young man with lively brown eyes.

2

Susan sat in the gloom of falling evening, a quill in her hand. Paper was spread out before her on Grandmama's delicate French escritoire, an inkpot was open, but Susan couldn't concentrate on the letter to Papa in faraway India. As usual, she had nothing to report and was racking her brain for something, anything, to say. And this time her reticence had another cause than simple lack of material. Her mind was full of the impressions of the day. And there were some impressions in particular that no girl would be comfortable writing of to her father.

Captain Camberley was a fine figure of a man. Susan had never thought to meet such a noted sea captain, one who had been so feted in fashionable circles after his triumphs in the Mediterranean and more recently in the Atlantic.

She had heard of him, of course. Grandmama disapproved of newspapers as heartily as she disdained books, feeling both to be corrupting influences. But Susan was a friend of Blenkinsop, the butler, and he, quite against his mistress's wishes, received the London papers secondhand from his comrade the village innkeeper. Susan was free to peruse these whenever she could snatch a moment.

Her gaze, which had begun to wander about, fell upon the only jarring ornament in an otherwise flawlessly decorated drawing room. Grandmama's commemorative Trafalgar jug, in the shape of Nelson's head. It was an ugly piece and didn't look in the least like Nelson, but Grandmama was most fervently attached to it and quite vocal in her support of the Royal Navy. She must harbor some soft feelings for the new neighbor, at least from a patriotic motive. Why else would she have received his sister at all? She was never at home to callers.

Susan's musings had not progressed much beyond this point,

and her letter had not got past the salutation, when the drawing-room door was flung open and Blenkinsop announced in a hearty but surprised voice, "Lady Delafort."

Susan dropped her pen and spun round, upsetting her velvet-covered gilt stool in the process of rising to her feet. "Mama!" she cried, staring at the woman who had entered.

"Good heavens," the lady responded, her eyes wide. These eyes were blue-green and thickly lashed and remarkably similar to Susan's own. Lady Delafort was dressed in deep blue sarcenet and lace, and a magnificent hat sat atop her dark curls. She held a silver-wrapped parcel in one gloved hand. The package dropped to the carpet.

Behind Lady Delafort there appeared the foxlike visage of a bald man with side whiskers. A glass was affixed to one eye, and he leered at Susan benignly before advancing into the room to stand at his lady's elbow. He was a foppishly dressed individual, tall and solid-looking. Susan, in her inexpert way, judged him to be above forty years of age. Quite ancient, in fact.

As for Mama—she hadn't changed.

The last time Susan had seen her mother, she had run to her in a childish enthusiasm quite unbefitting her fourteen years and had been rewarded by a startled order not to tumble Mama's gown.

Now she was eighteen, and she did not run. She merely stood and looked, glad that she had put on her only good gown this evening for the usual early dinner tête-à-tête with Grandmama. Since Mama was so very beautiful and fashionable, she deserved to have a daughter who would do her credit.

Only to herself would Susan have admitted the reason she had wanted to look her best this evening. She had dressed for Captain Camberley, though logic told her she would not see him. It was not as though the gallant gentleman might be strolling on the lawns of Pilgrim Court and pass by the windows. Nevertheless Susan had persisted in her design. Her choice was easy, for though her wardrobe was restricted for the most part to the drabbest of cottons and woolens, she did have her birthday dress.

On Susan's last natal day Grandmama Palmer had had to admit that her granddaughter was a grown woman, and she had let Susan have a gown made up to order. Susan and the dress-maker in the nearby village had designed a shell-pink silk, low-necked and slightly off the shoulder, with sleeves that puffed to the elbow, then were made tight to the wrist, where medieval points covered the tops of Susan's hands. The style was not in the common way and was doubtless not the latest thing. But Susan had always felt like a captive princess, and she wanted, for once, to look like one.

Grandmama had laughed at Susan for ordering the dress, lectured her for a good three-quarters of an hour on the folly of vanity, and finally shaken her head and let Susan keep it. There had been a faraway look in Grandmama's eye for the merest instant as she made this great concession to her ordinary rules for simplicity in dress.

Lady Delafort was groping for a chair. Still staring at her daughter, she sank down onto the rose brocade Louis Quinze settee near the small fire. The blaze, an uncommon luxury in summer, had been kindled against the chilling mists which had come on in the afternoon.

"How are you, Mama?" Susan asked, for she really wished someone would speak.

The man with the eyeglass followed Lady Delafort and stood behind her seat. "So this is the little girl, Jenny?" he said with a braying laugh. "I might think again about the present you brought her."

Lady Delafort nodded weakly.

"A present? For me?" Susan couldn't keep the childish delight out of her voice. When last had her mother remembered her with a gift?

Looking much amused, the gentleman crossed the room again to the doorway and retrieved the dropped parcel. He presented it to Susan with a flourish. She thought his sharp gaze lingered too long on her bosom. Or was she only being oversensitive about a feature no gentleman had seen uncovered before? Then he walked back to her mother's station and placed himself again in a protective attitude behind the lady.

Susan, dimpling with pleasure, opened the package.

A doll! She held up a gorgeous creation of painted wood. It was dressed in a most delicate and doubtless fashionable gown of white net and sparkling stones. "I should like to have it, Mama, if I may," she said a little timidly.

Her mother's stricken gaze lit on Susan, then continued down to the Aubusson. Susan recognized the problem on the spot; indeed, she had known it for some time, ever since Mama's last visit. Lady Delafort simply couldn't admit to having a daughter of Susan's age. Knowing that there was nothing she could do about the problem, Susan was willing to understand and even to forgive. Mama was so very beautiful, and she didn't grow old. How lowering it must be to have a great girl to remind her of her own mortality.

"If you like it, my dear," Lady Delafort said with a sigh. "Fitz is right, of course; you are much too grown-up for a doll."

"But it will be the very thing for my chamber," Susan said. Grandmama's regulations for simplicity in all things extended even to bedroom decor. Indeed, the ornate French drawing room was the only room in the house that was not ascetic to the point of discomfort. Susan's virginal cell followed the grand plan of simplicity, with its narrow white bed and plain walls, the only ornament a pastoral picture of lambs done in worsted work by Lady Delafort in her seminary days.

The doll would sit upon a certain small table by the window and remind Susan of her mother. Indeed, Susan thought, looking at the doll's sweet face and painted raven hair, there was a certain resemblance.

"Susan, I must present you to Lord Fitzalbin," Mama was saying.

Must you? Susan wanted to respond, disliking the man's foxy demeanor more than ever. She held her tongue as the man approached her to grasp her hand and eye her figure once more, then hurried back to Lady Delafort. What was he doing here with Mama, and acting as though he owned her? Susan bobbed what she hoped was a passable curtsy and forced a smile.

Then she went to sit opposite her mother. Her eyes shifted away from Lord Fitzalbin, who most definitely peered down her bosom from his standing position, as she voiced the question uppermost in her mind. "What are you doing here, Mama? You never stir from town."

"We are on our road to the Duchess of York's, as it happens, and Jenny couldn't pass by without stopping to visit her mother. And her lovely daughter, of course," Fitzalbin answered before Lady Delafort could open her mouth.

"Yes," her ladyship assented, with a vexed look at her escort.

"Oh." Susan nodded pleasantly. She had set the doll aside, and now her hands were folded in her lap. She looked down at the laced fingers, wondering what next to say. Mother-and-daughter confidences, even had there been any to exchange, would be out of place as long as Lord Fitzalbin was in the room.

The door opened before the atmosphere grew any less comfortable, and Mrs. Palmer paused on the threshold. Her matronly figure attired in the rusty black and voluminous cap she wore for evening, she made a daunting sight, especially when one looked into her snapping gray eyes.

"Susan, I do wish you wouldn't wear that ribbon round your throat. Reminds me of Paris in the nineties."

Susan touched the bit of deep green velvet. "But, Grandmama, I have no jewels, and I felt—" What she felt was that the green velvet turned her eyes to green in a most flattering manner, and that since she had really dressed for an imaginary encounter with Captain Camberley, she would have wished him to see her looking her finest. She cut off her words, quite unable to admit to such a jumble of feelings.

She needn't have distressed herself. Mrs. Palmer was not in the mood to continue haranguing her granddaughter when she had better game in the room. "Well, Jeanne-Jacqueline," she next said in an acid tone, "so you've decided to say how d'ye do to your old mother as you breeze by on your way from one den of depravity to another. I've already spoken to your coachman; I know you're not stopping the night. And who"—her eyes rested on Fitzalbin in the same manner they might have surveyed a bramble in her garden—"is this?"

Lady Delafort hastily made introductions. Mrs. Palmer, after seating herself with a flourish and a thump of her gold-headed cane, stared Lord Fitzalbin down for a few moments and then suggested, in the smoothest tones in the world, that his lordship might find a breath of air most refreshing on such a close night.

"But it's been raining, Grandmama," Susan said.

"Good for the constitution," Mrs. Palmer said with a wave

of her hand. "Especially night rain. Takes years off the complexion."

"Well, madam, I daresay I might confer with the coachman," Fitzalbin said, clearing his throat. He definitely looked insulted. "We must be on our way shortly, you know."

When the door shut behind the man, Mrs. Palmer snapped, "Have you lost what little is left of your mind, Jeanne-Jacqueline? Why is that macaroni trailing behind you? If you must play your husband false, the least you could do is to keep it quiet."

"No one has said 'macaroni' in thirty years, Mama," Lady Delafort said with a toss of her head that set her plumes to waving. "Nor has anyone called me by that dreadful name you insisted on saddling me with. It's Jenny, if you please."

Susan noticed, with a twinge of uneasiness, that her mother hadn't precisely denied Grandmama's accusation of infidelity.

"I was but this moment writing to Papa," she said brightly, in an effort to dispel some of the tension in the room; then realized that she could have said nothing that would make her mother less easy.

Lady Delafort evidently decided that a total change of subject was the remedy. "Fitz is escorting me to Oatlands," she said, ignoring her daughter's statement. "There is to be a grand party. I am to recite the prologue in a little play the duchess is getting up. And I have ordered the prettiest gown! If I can but manage to flog my dresser into a nice sense of her duties. Angleton fancies herself allergic to dog hair, and you must know there is nothing else at Oatlands." She interrupted the flow of bright social chatter to look at her daughter earnestly. "The duchess has above a hundred dogs, and one is quite forced to caress them and make much of them, and then of course one's clothes become the veriest mess of—"

"Dog hair," Mrs. Palmer said in a tone of flat disgust. "You come to visit your daughter for the first time in four years and you choose to ramble on about dog hair?"

"Mama!" Lady Delafort looked hurt.

Susan felt a sudden protective surge. "My mother is so very busy, Grandmama. You can hardly expect her to spend time buried in the country. We correspond, you know. I write to her almost as often as I write to Papa."

"And does she write back?"

This was indeed a sore point. In sudden embarrassment, Susan looked down at her shoes.

Lady Delafort reached out to touch her daughter's face. Susan was delighted to look up and find her mother smiling at her. "I was shocked this evening, my love, deeply shocked to find you grown up and looking so lovely," Lady Delafort said. "But now I am reminded of my duty. You must be presented next Season. You will be what—seventeen?"

"By next spring I'll be nearly nineteen."

"Impossible! Mama, didn't you even teach the child to count?" Lady Delafort let out a tinkling laugh. "I was eighteen when she was born, and I am only . . ." Her words trailed away, and she rose suddenly to look into the Venetian glass over the chimneypiece. A flash of dismay crossed her lovely features.

"You, Jeanne-Jacqueline, are a woman of six-and-thirty," Mrs. Palmer said dryly. "And I'll have no foolish talk of presenting this child. You know the agreement you made with me when you left my roof. I was to bring Susan up as I pleased, and you, in exchange for your freedom, engaged not to interfere. I do not choose to expose Susan to the giddy foolishness of life among the *ton.*"

Susan felt a little pang. Her heart had lifted momentarily at her mother's mention of a presentation, but now it sank. Grandmama would win. She always won.

Lady Delafort turned back to face her mother and her daughter. "No, Mother, this time you won't wear me down," she said. "When she turns eighteen—since you insist she is eighteen—Susan's care reverts to me. Don't you remember the agreement? You demanded to have it in writing, and I, foolish and dissipated though I was, kept my head enough to ensure my daughter's debut in society."

Mrs. Palmer's sullen silence had the effect of confirming these words. Susan's excitement began to build once more.

Lady Delafort caught Susan's hands and raised her up. She turned her daughter to the mirror and surveyed both their faces in pleasure. "We will cut the veriest dash, I assure you, my dearest creature—my dearest daughter. How very lucky that your hair should be light! We will be perfect foils to one another." She turned from the glass to scrutinize Susan's gown. "That dress, child—who made it?"

"Miss Porter in the village. She and I designed it."

"Admirable! It is a very strange cut, but it works, my dear, it works. You will be a beauty, mark my words, and a beauty needs taste almost more than she needs good features."

"Oh, Mama." Susan kissed her mother's rouged cheek. "I can hardly wait until spring."

Mrs. Palmer frowned at the two. "I tell you, Jeanne-Jacqueline, you will regret it all your life if you expose this innocent child to your depraved world. I've raised her following the strictest principles of Rousseau—my version of Rousseau, which tempers French enthusiasm with English restraint and acknowledges that a girl may be raised upon the same system as a boy."

Grandmama's method, which she had spent years in developing, was a great source of pride to her, Susan knew. She had grown to comprehend her grandmother's enthusiasm, but in her less charitable moments she harbored some resentment that the elder lady had practiced upon her quite as though she were a fallow field or an untrained household pet.

"And I've taught her every country virtue, from early rising to beekeeping," Mrs. Palmer was continuing. "You'll ruin her in a moment."

Lady Delafort exchanged an amused glance with her daughter. "You need not remind me of your theories, Mama. I'm only grateful Papa kept you from inflicting this *belle sauvage* mania upon me. Susan looks a sensible young lady to me. She won't be ruined in any sense of the word. She will be too clever for that."

"I will write to Lord Delafort by the next post," Mrs. Palmer warned, thumping her cane. "He will take my part and forbid this nonsensical idea. A Season, indeed! Unravel all my careful work in a week or two, will you? We'll see about that. My son-in-law has learned the hard way what tragedies a life of dissipation can bring."

"Really, Mama, it is hardly tragic that Delafort is making me rich in India."

Mrs. Palmer didn't dignify this flippant statement with an answer.

Susan eventually spoke into the silence. "Grandmama, I'm not a piece of knitting. Nobody will unravel me."

"You, miss, are a pert and forward piece."

Mrs. Palmer turned on Susan, who could see from the gloom of the elder lady's expression that her grandmother was seriously overset.

She was instantly contrite that she had spoken up. "Forgive me, Grandmama."

Mrs. Palmer rose majestically and addressed Lady Delafort. "I will be in my dressing room, daughter, if you wish to bid me good-bye before you continue on your latest hey-go-mad start. Oatlands indeed! Dog hair! As for you, Susan, you mean no harm. But I have no idea where you got your unruly tongue."

"From me, of course," Lady Delafort said with a twinkle when her mother had left the room. She and Susan sat down together on the rose-colored settee. "Now, tell me, my dear girl, have you any admirers here in the back of beyond? With your looks, you simply must."

"We see no society, Mama," Susan said.

"Oh, that's right. Then there's no one you can practice your wiles upon?"

Susan laughed. "I don't have wiles. But . . . ." She hesitated, and the urge to say something about the subject that had been driving her thoughts all day overrode all her more careful feelings. "I did meet someone today."

"Who?" Lady Delafort asked eagerly.

Susan was charmed by Mama's manner. She was quite like a young girl. How delightful that the years had not made her cynical on the subject of men. "Captain Vincent Camberley," she responded with conscious pride in uttering the well-known name. "He has taken the estate next to here."

"The sea captain. The hero," Lady Delafort said thoughtfully. "I know nothing about him, child, but I have my sources. Do nothing to encourage him until I find out his prospects."

"Prospects?" Susan laughed. "Some say he is the greatest naval hero since Nelson."

"And what family does he have? What title?"

"I've read in the papers that he graciously refused the offer of a title. He has great natural modesty," Susan said, hoping her mother would not ask why her knowledge was so extensive. She had spent the afternoon surrounded by the butler's hoarded old newspapers in the cellar, gleaning them for any mention of the fatal name. "Anyone else would have been called ungrateful and impertinent for turning down a title, so the papers relate, but Captain Camberley charmed the Regent into thinking more highly of him than ever."

"Greatest of follies, to refuse a title!" Lady Delafort shook her head. "Don't let your head be turned, Susan. There is little danger of that, with my mother's insistence upon shutting you away from society. I daresay Captain Camberley will be snapped up this winter by one of the desperate damsels in this neighborhood."

Susan's face fell.

Her mother saw the look and pinched her cheek. "Never you mind, my dear. There are plenty more fish in the sea." Her laugh rang out once more. "A particularly apt comment on a sailor, don't you think?"

Susan managed a weak nod.

Lady Delafort, satisfied that she had given the best of motherly advice, soon got up in a swirl of perfume and ostrich plumes and said that she and Lord Fitzalbin must be on their way if they were to reach Oatlands before evening's end. In a remarkably short time she was gone, and but for the trace of scent and the beautiful doll resting on a satin pillow, her visit might have been a dream.

Susan returned to the desk and took up her pen with a renewed energy. She would write to Papa that Mama had visited and been most kind. She would warn him that a crotchety letter from Grandmama would be arriving by the same post and beg him not to forbid her debut.

But somehow, though she now had so many things to write about, her pen was no faster than before.

Despite Mama's warnings, perhaps because of Mama's

warnings, Susan was still stubbornly thinking of Captain Camberley. The prospect of next spring in town was nothing compared to the thought of meeting him by accident again in the garden. She knew she would haunt the boundary between their two estates for the rest of the summer.

3

"I call it absolutely shameful," Drusilla Camberley said with a rueful shake of her head. "The poor child has been raised to be ignorant as a newborn lamb. Rousseau, indeed!"

Vincent smiled, a slow smile which many ladies thought devastatingly attractive.

His sister had known him too long to be charmed. "Do you laugh at me because you call it a good thing for a woman to be ignorant as a . . . as a post?"

"I thought it was a newborn lamb you compared Miss Danvers to," Vincent said. "I would not call her either one. She is, quite simply, an angel."

His sister stared at him, and a smile, the feminine twin of Vincent's, played about her lips. "You in love, Vincent? And on such short acquaintance? The sea air must definitely have pickled your brain."

Vincent recalled the stange encounter with his new neighbor as he might a dream. He had clasped a young woman in his arms, and she had felt mysteriously right there. Was that such a rare experience? It happened to be so for him, but surely any man would have felt as much in the face of such innocent temptation. "Love!" he scoffed, as any right-thinking brother must in the face of such an accusation. "Who said anything about that? I barely met the young lady."

"Whom you refer to as an angel," his sister said tartly.

"I found her intelligence to be evident, and her accomplishments are quite intriguing."

"Do you call churning butter an accomplishment?" Drusilla said in scorn. "Did you notice the butter at breakfast? That was her gift to me."

"I have never before seen butter in the shape of a cow, but I forbore to laugh at it for fear it was the loving work of some one of the servants. Then Miss Danvers has a fine sense of humor. That's another accomplishment,'' Vincent said. ''Did she send you butter, then, knowing how infuriated the intellectual Miss Camberley must be by a simple child of nature and her bucolic pursuits? This proves to me that she is more knowing than perhaps you realize.''

''It's her grandmother who angers me, not the girl,'' Drusilla said. ''Miss Danvers is quite a sweet thing, and she knows nothing about what would infuriate me. Now, hand me that spade.''

Vincent was assisting his sister in the south meadow. Drusilla was determined to uncover more of the Roman ruins which had led her to hit upon Royce Park as the perfect house for them to let.

The Roman ruins had their place in local lore. In theory there had been a villa on the site, but in practice, there were a few stones which, Drusilla convinced herself, looked quite exotic.

Her zeal to get at the ruins had rested while she and her brother settled into the long-vacant house, minor seat of some impoverished peer, and while she received some calls from neighbors eager to cultivate the well-known Captain Camberley through his sister. Mrs. Palmer she had called on out of curiosity, for the old lady had been the only one in the neighborhood not to pay her compliments to the Camberley family.

Social duties could only divert one for so long, though. This very morning Vincent had seen his sister's small, determined form marching across the lawn, followed by a gardener's lad who piloted a wheelbarrow full of tools. Vincent had gone after the procession out of a slight curiosity for the project.

Once in the south meadow, Drusilla had dismissed the lad and informed her brother that he would do quite well to help her. ''Indeed, as you pass for an educated man,'' she added now, ''you will be bound to be more careful than that clumsy boy. I would hate to have any of these stones disturbed.''

Vincent looked down his nose in mock anger. ''My dear, it does you little credit to remind me that my education has been mostly self-inflicted. They don't teach the finer points of anything but sailing at the Royal Naval Academy.''

Drusilla looked contrite, and Vincent saw that she didn't know he had been teasing her. His twin was subject to lapses of this sort; though she possessed a fine sense of humor, she could often be a little slow when the laugh was directed right at her.

And she might well have felt a pang of guilt, thought Vincent, for their scholarly father's knowledge had been at her sole disposal after Vincent had gone off to the academy at the tender age of twelve. Not many eldest sons of the gentry were so constrained; the navy was more the dumping ground for younger spawn of the gentry or the clergy. But the Camberley family was poor and for patronage possessed only a distant admiral cousin.

Vincent had not gone to sea from any love of it, but he had soon come to enjoy his career and to be thankful that his family's connections hadn't included bishops and barristers. He would have cut a poor figure in the pulpit or at the bar.

"I didn't mean for you to feel guilt-ridden, sis," he said in a teasing tone. "However my learning came about, I did get it."

"Which is more than we can say for poor Miss Danvers." Drusilla returned to their previous subject with a shake of her head. "Oh, blast!" (as her spade struck something hard.) "I suppose I've broken a mosaic."

Vincent looked. "Merely a token of a later passage than the Roman's," he said, turning over the earth carefully while Drusilla hovered. He took a fiendish pleasure in handing his sister a rusty cow bell.

When she had gotten over this disappointment, Drusilla pushed her spectacles up her nose, took the spade in hand again, and continued to talk of Susan Danvers. "I intend to do something about that poor girl's situation," she said. "If she has the capacity for learning, I will ferret it out and minister to it."

"But her grandmother is said to be against all such practices."

Drusilla shook her head at the memory of Mrs. Palmer. "She is indeed—that will make it all the more satisfying to foil the old lady. Mrs. Palmer is truly a strange woman. When I visited, she was working in a dairy and lost no time in informing me that she had no patience for any but country pursuits and disdained everything about the wicked metropolis—including, by implication, myself. Yet something did not fit."

"Perhaps it is only Pilgrim Court which did not fit your image of its owner," Vincent suggested. "It's a perfect small Palladian manor, though the gardens do tend to an Elizabethan formality—except for the Greek folly, to be sure." He smiled.

Drusilla looked at him sharply. "You are certainly well conversant with the estate. Have you been visiting there without my knowing it?"

"No. I've merely had a good view of it over the park palings. That, and my one encounter with Miss Danvers near the folly."

Drusilla shot him another suspicious glance. "Men! Always attracted to ignorance."

Vincent shrugged and gave another mischievous smile. "You may think Miss Danvers ignorant if you wish. But I believe it will fall out, Drusilla, that she's sharper than you on certain subjects. There is something about her eyes."

Drusilla found herself rendered less than comfortable by the idea that her twin might be interested in Miss Danvers, in however idle a way. Vincent had never, to her knowledge, been attracted to any young lady in all their thirty years. But, Drusilla had to admit, she had scarcely been in a position to observe her brother's career in the arena of love—had there been one— any more than she had been on the spot for his naval battles.

Armed with a pencil and a pad of paper tucked into her large and sensible reticule, Drusilla chose the next morning to pay a call at Pilgrim Court. Miss Danvers had managed to convey, in a note which she had sent with the butter, that though she was not allowed to pay calls, Mrs. Palmer could scarcely refuse to allow her to receive respectable female visitors who were neighbors.

Drusilla noted the unformed childish hand of the message and realized that her work was cut out for her. When, upon arrival at Pilgrim Court, she was shown into what was described as Miss Danver's dressing room and found the young lady seated before a large spinning wheel surrounded by piles of carded wool, she fell back a pace in astonishment.

"Do excuse the sheeplike smell of my surroundings, Miss Camberley," Susan said, coming forward with outstretched hands. "How kind of you to take my hint and visit me. Grandmama is out with the bees, as it happens, and we can be quite private.''

Drusilla spent some moments in trying to envision which neighbors the B's were before she recalled that the rustic Mrs. Palmer was likely concerned at the moment with the hives of buzzing honeymakers. "You really spin, my dear?" she said in barely concealed horror.

"Not very genteel, is it? But Grandmama says, 'When Adam delved and Eve span, Who was then the gentleman?' ''

"John Ball," Miss Camberley said with a nod.

"Besides, it's not so bad," Susan went on with a twinkle in her eye. She pulled a chair close to the wheel for her visitor and sat back down. "I believe it induces serenity and makes my thoughts flow faster." She began to twirl something and to pump her foot, and Drusilla watched in fascination as a fine thread came off the wheel and was rolled onto a spool with the aid of Susan's nimble fingers.

"I came to find out, my dear," Drusilla said, speaking in a slightly raised voice over the noise of the wheel, "if you would accept my aid in a certain project."

"What project is that?" Susan asked, head to one side. "Oh, I quite forget my manners. Callers are usually offered something to eat and drink, aren't they? Let me ring."

She took care of this matter, cautioning Blenkinsop, when he arrived, to include some of the new honey cakes on the tray.

Despite her shocked reaction to the specter of a young lady of quality engaged in the homely task of spinning, Miss Camberley was honest enough to admit that Miss Danvers' dressing room had a certain charm. It was evidently the permanent resort of the spinning impedimenta and had little other furniture. But the proportions of the chamber were elegant, no surprise in a Palladian mansion, and the friezes around the ceiling were most attractive. Susan's stool and Drusilla's chair were of the same rough-hewn wood as the furnishings in the cow shed.

Drusilla's imagination was always fired by classical subjects. She remembered that Homer's Penelope wove on a loom—surely close to spinning—and felt herself transported back to ancient Greece or Rome. The furniture would have been better in the ancient times she envisioned, but aside from that detail the picture was quite complete. Susan Danvers, sitting so serenely at her wheel in a simple white gown, could have been a maiden of ancient Attica. Somehow—it must be a trick of the light—the calm lines of her face betokened a rare wisdom.

Drusilla caught herself. An ignorant young girl wise? She was allowing the strange atmosphere of the room to play tricks on her. "Pardon me if this question is of too personal a nature, my dear," she said, pulling her mind back from the world of dreams, "but did your grandmother perhaps reject the corruption of civilization at some point? This rusticity"—and she shifted uncomfortably on her hard chair—"seems too determined to be merely the result of habit."

"I know little of Grandmama's life before she began to raise me," Susan said, "but there is the drawing room. It doesn't match Grandmama in the least. The furnishings are French, and I know my grandparents spent much time in France before I was born. They were even there after the revolution."

"Ah. Yes." Miss Camberley had been shown into the drawing room on the occasion of her first call, while the staff ascertained whether Mrs. Palmer was to be found in the dairy or in one of the fields. At the time she had not been at all surprised by the sight of an elegant and richly furnished room adorned with the most opulent fixtures of the *ancien régime*. After she had met Mrs. Palmer, though, and especially after seeing this room and the barren corridors one passed through to get to it . . .

"Perhaps Grandpapa loved ornate furnishings, and my grandmother keeps the room in memory of him. Or in memory of happy times in Paris with him," Susan suggested. "I've been able to think of nothing better. And Grandmama won't respond to a direct question on the subject."

"Indeed, your reasoning makes perfect sense. I am told that females are inordinately sentimental at times when it comes to a question of men's whims," Drusilla said, thinking of her late mother. Mrs. Camberley had had upwards of ten thousand excuses for her husband's tedious and unending renovation of the family home in Yorkshire, which had left her housekeeping in a shambles for all their married life. Now that Vincent was rich on prize money, he was finally seeing that the estate was completed—from a distance, for he had never been fond of the unfinished state of their home. Drusilla didn't expect him to settle in Yorkshire until every last fitting was in place.

Susan was looking most thoughtful at Miss Camberley's diagnosis of her grandmother's feelings.

The girl's air of wishing to learn whatever she might reminded Drusilla of what had brought her to Pilgrim Court. "My dear," she said, withdrawing the pad of paper and the pencil from her reticule, "as I mentioned a little while ago, I would like to help you. Now, shall we begin? Tell me what you have read."

"What?" Susan's eyes widened.

Drusilla noticed how large and thickly lashed those eyes were. Vincent might well have been captivated by such a little beauty. Well, if Vincent's interest should be serious, he would have his sister to thank if his bride were not an ignorant bumpkin. "The books you have read. From what I am told, there can't have been too many."

"I . . . Why would you wish to know?" Susan looked very wary.

"I propose, my dear, to further your education," Drusilla announced with an emphatic nod. "I know your grandmother disapproves of the wisdom to be found in books, for so she told me. She was quite proud of having kept you untainted by such. But I say she has forgotten that you must someday enter the world. And a female cannot be too educated."

"Really?" Susan kept spinning, but she leaned forward eagerly. "I have sometimes felt the same, but experience has taught me that the opposite would be true. My mother is not bookish, but she is the toast of London."

"Indeed?" Drusilla had no idea who Miss Danvers' mother was, but she didn't intend to be contradicted. "My dear young creature, you might never use one-quarter of the knowledge I intend to impart to you, but it will be there, in the back of your mind, for you to draw on."

"I don't think I'm particularly bookish myself," Susan was musing. "I like books very well, and I've read a quantity that Grandmama doesn't know of, but I get stuck on Mr. Hume's philosophy, and I am quite puzzled by the Latin parts of *Tristram Shandy*."

"You have read *Tristram Shandy*?" Drusilla said with a gasp. "I can hardly credit that, my dear. It is a novel, and I didn't come here to talk of novels. They are . . . well, if I were an Evangelical, I would call them the devil's work, but suffice it to say that they are too frivolous and sentimental, most of them, to be worth one's time. There is so much else to read."

"Like Mr. Hume," Susan said with a sigh.

"Indeed, and I am fascinated to find that you have heard the name," Drusilla said, leaning forward in her turn.

"And of course *Robinson Crusoe,*" Susan said. "Grandmama said from Mr. Rousseau's point of view, that was the only proper book for a young person to read—even though it is a novel."

"Fancy that!" Drusilla was amazed, not being acquainted herself with Rousseau's recommendation for the adolescent Emile.

The conversation was interrupted at this point by the return of the butler bearing a tray on which reposed a decanter of cordial, two glasses, and a plate of honest-looking brown cakes.

The wheel spun to a halt, and Susan did the honors, bringing forward a small table from somewhere (she brushed a pile of yarn from it) and pulling her stool up to face Miss Camberley's chair. "I had hoped," Susan confessed when she had helped her guest to cordial and a cake—both of her own making, she stated proudly—"that you would perhaps be able to help me get the latest novels. There is a circulating library in the village now, you know. Mrs. Monkton runs it out of her cottage. But I have no pocket money, and I couldn't manage to subscribe in any case. Grandmama would hear of it."

"How do you know the neighbors," asked Drusilla, "if no one calls on you?"

"I go out from time to time in the company of the housemaid," Susan said with a shrug. "I have from childhood. Grandmama believes in children running wild, but as I am a female she couldn't let me run wild by myself, and so a maid has always accompanied me. She hasn't seemed to consider that I might one day leave off swinging from vines, or whatever she pictures me doing, and go into the village to see a little life."

Drusilla had been to the village, and she had found that little resembling "life" could be found in it at all, from her more sophisticated point of view. She had dutifully admired the duck pond and deplored the lack of gentlemens' houses. Susan Danvers, though, might see the little hamlet as a bustling place.

"Well," she said, hiding her indignation at the poor girl's misspent life, "so you have heard of Hume, Defoe, and Sterne." She noted the names on her pad. "Who else?"

Susan said in a tentative voice, "This is most kind of you, ma'am, but I can't say I would be successful if I were to read a lot of heavy tomes. I merely read out of curiosity."

"Nonsense, that is what education is. And you are simply unware of the treasures that await you," Drusilla said briskly. "Now, what else have you read?" There was a note of determination in her voice which was well-nigh irresistible.

Susan, at any rate, was unable to fight it. Carefully omitting the French novel she had found in an odd corner of the house, she mentioned all the rest of her reading. Since Grandmama had sold off the library after Grandpapa's death, Susan had found her small store of books in attic corners and forgotten chests.

Miss Camberley scanned the short list on her pad and observed that though it wasn't much, it was a good solid start.

"I'm glad to know that," Susan said, gratified. Perhaps when she came to make her debut she wouldn't seem so hopelessly simple as she feared to do.

Miss Camberley soon went away, promising to return the next day with a selection of good solid books: whatever she could fit into her reticule. "Perhaps you can conceal them beneath some of this wool," she suggested, casting an eye around the chamber. Then she sailed off, quite satisfied with her errand of mercy.

Vincent was not quite so sanguine. "What the devil have you done?" he demanded.

"I told you," Drusilla said in a calm tone. "I quizzed Miss Danvers on her reading, and I am making up a list now of volumes she would find most enlightening. You ought to be flattered that I've asked for your help, for you have no experience with educating females."

"You mean," Vincent said through clenched teeth, "that you swept over the poor girl and doubtless made her feel as though she must bow down to the superior knowledge of the London bluestocking. Really, Drusilla. It is unforgiveable."

"But, Vincent . . ." Drusilla began, then stopped. Her normally placid brow furrowed, as though she were thinking over the approach she had taken. "Perhaps I might have been a bit schoolmistressy in tone, but I meant it only for the girl's good."

"Doubtless," Vincent said, rolling his eyes. He marched out of the room, leaving his twin sister to ponder over exactly how attached he was to their ignorant little neighbor.

Vincent stopped to collect his hat and a large Newfoundland puppy he was training to heel. Then he went on his way to Pilgrim Court by the road so that he might go in at the front gates. He didn't want to startle the ladies by appearing at their windows.

As he walked, he whistled to the dog from time to time and wondered what he could possibly say to Miss Danvers. He hated being put in the awkward position of making excuses for Drusilla's rudeness. Dash it all, by the age of thirty she ought to be able to distinguish the social amenities from downright officious prying.

At Pilgrim Court the butler gave him a startled look and showed him into the drawing room.

Vincent cooled his heels, hoping that the dog would be manageable tied to that outdoor post, and that Miss Danvers would arrive soon. He had made sure to ask for Miss Danvers only, but he feared that her grandmother would be lurking nearby and would intercept the butler. A request to see a young lady without mention of her chaperon and guardian was surely most improper. Still, Vincent didn't regret his visit, or the coin he had pressed into the servant's hand as a discretionary measure. He could hardly communicate his apologies in front of Miss Danvers' termagant of a grandmother.

The fates did not favor the captain's mission. Mrs. Palmer happened to enter her drawing room through the French windows before Vincent had completed his second circuit of the room.

"Lud!" the old lady exclaimed, dropping a basket which contained rhubarb and asparagus. The vegetation, in all its bucolic glory, seized upon the carpet with tendrils of roots and grime. Mrs. Palmer looked at the stuff in exasperation and then fixed the same order of stare upon Captain Camberley.

Vincent was taken aback. The only thing that occurred to him was to bow, which he did, in his most ingratiating style. As he rose from this obeisance his eye happened to light on the Trafalgar jug.

"I hope you will forgive me the liberty of calling, madam," he said in a serious tone. "I am Captain Camberley, your neighbor. I have heard much of the support you showed for his majesty's navy during the late war, and especially for our late lamented Lord Nelson. I cherished hopes that you would welcome me for his sake." He invented quickly, wagering that the ugly jug denoted patriotism and was not merely some aberration: put there to frighten the cats from climbing onto the furniture, perhaps.

Mrs. Palmer was disarmed by this unexpected hit at one of her secret weaknesses. She had followed Nelson's career with interest, forgiven him Lady Hamilton, and had never been the same since the great man's death in 1805. But she soon came to her senses. This young man might have won a few victories, but he was not Nelson. She had heard he was retired, or some such nonsense. A young man of his age, and with his astounding record, might have risen high in the admirality if he had only stuck to a thing. She had no patience with dilettantes.

"How kind of you to call, Captain Camberley," she said in her most majestic tones, which contrasted strongly with the simple country clothes she wore. "You have perhaps not heard that I am not in the habit of receiving company."

The captain bowed again. "I hoped to see your granddaughter, ma'am. On a matter of some importance. A message from my sister."

"Your sister is mighty free with her communications, young man. She was here only this morning. Do you think I'll alow her to monopolize my granddaughter, to fill her head with foolish town notions?"

"You need have no fear of that, madam. I have reason to

suppose that Miss Danvers is well able to hold her own with my sister. But—''

"Aha!" Mrs. Palmer interrupted. "I know you chanced to meet Miss Danvers in the garden or some such—prowling about my gardens, and for what reason? Mischief! I'll not tolerate any trifling, sirrah, and that is final. Susan knows nothing of the ways of men.''

"She can hardly be expected to end her life in that condition, ma'am, if I may be so bold,'' the captain said smoothly. "She is much too lovely to go through the world unadmired. And admiration leads to contact of some kind, sad though the fact might be.''

"Susan will go through the world however I say she will,'' Mrs. Palmer stated in a flat tone. She looked Camberley up and down. "I know what this is about!" The look became a glare. "Miss Danvers is a young woman of excellent family, and you're out to better your obscure origins.''

The old lady's remarks seemed almost erratic, and certainly had no basis in fact, Vincent observed to himself—yet she could hardly be expected to know anything about his family. He made some soothing sounds of leave-taking and did the best thing for his hostess's mood that he could do—he made an immediate exit.

Mrs. Palmer was a veritable dragon, he was thinking as he untied the Newfoundland from the post and went on his way back home. On impulse he decided to walk through the gardens and exit through the paling near the Grecian folly—supposing that his unwilling hostess did not set the dogs on him. Ah, well, he could retaliate with his own. He scratched the domed head of his new companion. There was much to be said for living on shore. One would hate to raise a puppy amid the confines of a ship, though many sailors did have their whole families with them, not to mention pets of sundry sorts.

The puppy lumbered ahead of Vincent under an archway and into a walled rose garden heady with the scent of multicolored blooms. And there stood Susan, a wide-brimmed hat on her head, a large basket on her arm as she gathered roses. She was dressed as Vincent had seen her before, in white muslin.

The Newfoundland bounded up to her, tail wagging, and Susan immediately knelt to hug him and have her ears licked.

"Are the two of you acquainted?" Vincent asked, coming up to the pretty tableau.

"No, but I love dogs," Susan said. "What is this one's name, sir?"

"I'm trying to choose. What do you suggest?"

Susan frowned in thought. "I really cannot say, Captain Camberley. Names are such personal things, and he is your dog."

"Yes, it is nice to have such a fine animal for my own," Vincent said in satisfaction.

Susan looked at him closely, seeming to see him for the first time. "What are you doing here, sir? Never tell me Grandmama received you."

"She almost did," Vincent said with a rueful smile. "I surprised her in her drawing room, and as you may observe, I managed to escape with my life. I came to see you."

"Me?" Susan was all innocent confusion and bright interest.

Vincent couldn't help contrasting this honest attitude with the simpering insincerities the sophisticated young ladies who had stalked him in the past would have come up with in the same situation. "Yes, you," he said with a tender smile. "I wanted to apologize to you for my sister's behavior. She visited you this morning, I understand, with the intention of making you her latest project by inflicting a reading list on you. She's not very worldly wise sometimes. She is well respected in her bluestocking circles in town, though, and she may feel that gives her a certain freedom she certainly ought not to take."

"Oh, sir, don't give it a thought," Susan said, blushing. "Miss Camberley was merely trying to correct my ignorance. I fear she never can."

"Don't tell me you approve of her scheme? You can't want to be prodded into her image of the educated young woman. I assure you, some of Drusilla's ideas are every bit as odd as what your grandmother might preach."

"You are saying that though Miss Camberley wouldn't have me collect petals for rosewater in the heat of the day, she might set me to cataloging the bushes?" Susan asked. Then she laughed.

Vincent found it a contagious laugh and joined her. "No, Drusilla would be more likely to have you digging dirt out in her beloved south meadow."

"Oh, yes, the ruins. I've seen them and think them fascinating, but Grandmama says they don't amount to much."

"Let us keep that a secret between us. I have a feeling that I'll be much indebted to the ruins for many precious moments alone. Unless"—and Vincent gave a rueful shake of his head—"Drusilla decides to muster every able man in her household to uncover what she is certain is an important villa."

"In any case," Susan said, showing her delightful dimples again, "you mustn't worry over your sister's behavior to me. I'll simply take what she brings and read or not, as I please. She will soon despair of making me into a genius, and there will be an end to it. And I will be very glad to have seen the books."

"You are very wise, ma'am," Vincent said. "Has anyone ever told you—that is, I assume they haven't, as you live out of the world—you're delightful as you are, Miss Danvers."

Susan blushed even deeper and looked immeasurably pleased.

Vincent regretted greatly that he couldn't stay longer. A memory of their first meeting rose to haunt him. How natural it would be to take her in his arms . . . but unless she stumbled into them, or fell from some precipice, he had no right to do so. "I must leave," he said. "I don't want to bring your grandmother's wrath down upon you."

"Or you," Susan replied. How he looked at her! Would all men do that, caress one with the eyes, or was Captain Camberley being too bold? She wished he would be bolder, and, even as she had the audacious thought, knew that he would do nothing to compromise her. He was a gentleman.

He went on his way, preceded by the nameless puppy.

Susan looked after him wistfully, charmed by the admiration of such an important man. A naval hero. A man of the world. An educated man who had known the history of that French novel she had been struggling to decipher.

She looked down at herself: basket, rustic gown, the picture of imbecilic rural virtues. She could never hope to meet with

Captain Camberley on equal ground, no matter how many of his sister's books she might read. Why, then, did he seem to be so attracted to her?

"Impossible," she muttered aloud as a thought struck her. "He can't like me because I'm stupid."

But the more Susan considered this new and unwelcome idea, the more likely it seemed.

4

Time passed, and with it all hopes Susan had nourished of beginning a romance with her neighbor at Royce Park.

Trusting that her youth and inexperience would excuse a wealth of unsubtle behavior, Susan haunted the Grecian summerhouse and made sundry excuses to wander near the estates' boundaries as the summer wore on. On a very few occasions she was lucky enough to encounter Captain Camberley and the growing Newfoundland puppy, who was soon settled with the name of Neptune. But their conversations were brief, thanks to the extra vigilance every servant at Pilgrim Court seemed suddenly to be according Miss Danvers. Mrs. Palmer's staff was not large, but both the gardener and the housemaid took to dogging Susan's footsteps as they never had before.

Vincent tried to call with his sister, but on these occasions Miss Danvers was denied them. Miss Camberley was grudgingly permitted to see the young lady; her brother was not.

From Susan's point of view, there was nothing to be done. She had never before been allowed to visit in the neighborhood and could not go to see Camberley without raising a general alarm. She had no way to inform Captain Camberley when she made an excursion to the village. And though she rode out regularly on the one aging farm horse Mrs. Palmer's stable housed, there was no chance for a romantic equestrian encounter, for Susan always took her exercise on Grandmama's land.

A lifetime of trying to circumvent this or that severe rule of her grandmother's had given Susan the dubious habit of leaving many things unsaid—for example, she didn't mention that Miss Camberley sometimes hid a book in her reticule when she paid a call—but she had never indulged in outright lies. Already dissatisfied with her own deceiving nature, Susan drew the line

at blatant falsehoods and could no more have met Captain
Camberley clandestinely than she could have stolen a loaf from
the baker's.

The situation worsened as the year wore on. The Camberleys
took to spending as much time in London as they did in Surrey.
This had always been their plan, the easy distance from Royce
Park to London having been one of the house's major attractions.
As the autumn passed and the weather grew wet and unpredict-
able, Drusilla spent less time poking at her ruins or visiting
Susan, and more time longing for the comfortable literary salons
of her particular circle of town friends. Vincent escorted her
to London for many a visit, and they kept the Christmas there.
For Susan it was as bleak a Yuletide as she could remember.

"Why so glum, dear brother?" Drusilla asked, on one winter
morning when she found Vincent, broad shoulders slumped,
nose pressed against a library window at Royce Park. "There
is nothing out there but snow and more snow. Is that the reason
you've been such a bear recently?" A mischievous gleam
appeared behind her spectacles. "Or is it that your imprisoned
beauty is even less accessible to you now? One can hardly expect
Miss Danvers to be wandering in the snow, though perhaps I
shouldn't say that. Mrs. Palmer might well think such exercise
most healthy." She shuddered.

Vincent turned and gave a rueful smile. "A sight of Miss
Danvers would brighten up this gloomy day," he said, "but
I'm not thinking of the young lady."

"Oh." Drusilla studied him a moment, then made a guess
which was perhaps not so insightful, considering that the two
were twins. "Give over thinking of the war, dear brother. It's
over, and you have given quite enough for king and country,
thank you. You never liked the sea; you were pushed into the
life."

"But I have much to be grateful for. The honors paid me
whether I deserved them or not, the prize money—"

"You've received another letter, haven't you?" was
Drusilla's matter-of-fact diagnosis.

Vincent nodded. The letter from the admiral had arrived the
day before, urging Captain Camberley to come out of a

premature retirement and take another ship. But he had seen quite enough—not of the world, perhaps, but of death and the horrors of war. No peace could be lasting, and navy ships were meant to fight.

And was he being cowardly, he who had come back whole from his dangerous missions to be feted as no moral man deserved? Sea battles were no easier than land ones. He sometimes woke up in the morning amazed that he had escaped with a few trifling scars. Many others had not—so many others.

"You need something to put your mind to. Some project." Drusilla spoke up brightly, hating to see her brother so dejected.

"But as you say, Miss Danvers would hardly be walking about in the snow," Vincent replied. Under the influence of only a little more bantering, the twinkle returned to his eye.

On the other side of the park palings Susan, in a dismal mood because of the dull weather and her duller life, decided to focus her hopes on her coming Season. Her mother actually wrote to her to encourage her in this project. Lady Delafort counseled application to accomplishments and said that she herself would fill in the gaps in Susan's education with the aid of a dancing master when her daughter came to town.

Her mother's advice sounded reasonable to Susan; young ladies were supposed to be accomplished, and, with the summer gone, she was not spending so much time as formerly in keeping bees and gardening. She practiced upon the harp. Grandmama had never allowed her a master, but she hadn't objected to Susan's teaching herself to pluck the strings of the ornate instrument in the drawing room, considering it nature's plan. Susan also surreptitiously read the books Miss Camberley managed to pass to her in her large reticule. These, regretfully, were a very dry lot. Miss Camberley had a scholarly taste which Susan could not share, no matter how she might long to prove herself as intelligent as a certain man's sister.

Aside from drawing a very little—another natural bent which had gone untrained—Susan really had no other accomplishments to practice in anticipation of her debut. Spinning and carding wool, she judged, would not be sought-after talents in London.

Would the Camberleys be in town for the Season? They

seemed to spend so much time there already. Would it not be ironic if she and Captain Camberley could further their acquaintance in the metropolis when they had not been able to do so living side by side in the country?

These thoughts could not help sneaking their way into her consciousness; yet Susan was making an honest effort not to dwell on the captain. She refused to lose her heart to someone she barely knew and scarcely ever saw. To give herself something else to do, she wrote even more often to her father. Lord Delafort had sent her an encouraging letter, telling her not to worry over Grandmama's disapproval of a Season. Susan had no idea what answer he had returned to Grandmama, but that lady went about looking grim and determined whenever London was mentioned. Evidently Lord Delafort had chosen not to forbid the visit.

"Since you must go to town against my wishes," Mrs. Palmer said to Susan one sharp day in early spring, when the two were outdoors trimming the roses, "I would have you behave properly."

"Yes, Grandmama," Susan said, tugging at a stubborn cane. She betrayed no sudden interest in the topic. While relieved that her Season was an established fact in Grandmama's mind, she did not like to see the old lady distress herself by dwelling on it.

Without further encouragement, Mrs. Palmer explained what she meant. "Do not let your mother ruin herself in clothes for you. A young girl should dress simply at all times, in white muslin. And as for your manner, you must speak only when spoken to, and then say as little as possible."

Susan decided that to nod agreement and later to arrange things as she wished would be the simplest course to take with Grandmama. The poor dear lady would worry if she knew that Susan planned to enjoy all the pleasures of town, including dress and conversation, that fell in her way.

"Take care that you do not keep late hours," Mrs. Palmer continued. "It will be a simple matter to return home early from any parties your mother takes you to. She won't want to leave, mind you—not that one!—but you may properly go in the care of a servant."

Susan nodded, trying to imagine what it would be like to attend a party.

"Since you will be going up next week, for heaven knows what silly reason of your mother's, you will need to pay more heed to my words than you do. I know that faraway expression, young lady."

"Next week?" Susan's admittedly wandering thoughts pulled back in sharply, and she stared at her grandmother. "But it's not yet time for the Season."

Grandmama's face softened for an instant, and Susan was certain she could see a glimpse of a much younger woman, perhaps one who had also gone to town for the first time, full of hopes and dreams. "Be careful, my dear," Mrs. Palmer said, and held out her arms.

Susan gave her grandmother a hearty hug while the old lady murmured about this visit being a true test for the precepts Susan had been taught since infancy. When the two women finally separated, Susan saw tears on her grandmother's cheeks.

"Of course I'll be careful, ma'am," she promised.

The great day of Susan's trip to London arrived—and then it passed. Susan, who had been poised for flight all during the daylight hours, with her cloak ready to hand and her small trunk corded, went to bed soothed by the cheerful predictions of her grandmother.

"I'll wager that flibbertigibbet of a daughter of mine has forgotten all about you."

"Please, Grandmama, don't crow."

"I beg your pardon, my dear. But if this is a sample of your mother's care of you—"

"She will be here tomorrow," Susan said stoutly. She went to undo her valise for what she hoped would be the last night in a room which was looking strangely stripped and bare since Susan had packed up her mother's doll to take with her.

Midmorning of the following day did bring an elegant post chaise emblazoned with the Delafort crest. Susan ran to the window as the vehicle swung into the front sweep and halted with a flourish. Outriders in livery! Fancy that.

As Susan watched, a severely dressed lady of indeterminate age and very slender build alighted from the carriage and marched, spine stiff, to the front door of Pilgrim Court. Susan kept looking at the carriage door, expecting to see Mama emerge, but the footman put away the steps and shut up the carriage, which then rattled off to the stables.

Susan hurried into the hall just as Blenkinsop was showing the unknown lady in.

"How do you do?" Susan came forward with her hand outstretched. "I am Miss Danvers. Will my mother be arriving later?"

The slender lady inclined her head and dipped a curtsy. "I am Angleton, her ladyship's abigail," she said from under the concealing poke of her bonnet. "I have come alone, ma'am, to chaperon you to town."

"Oh." Susan was a bit crestfallen. Though her grandmother had mentioned no details of the proposed trip, Susan had imagined her mother would travel down to bear her company. Upon reflection, though, she could see that such a notion had been childish in the extreme.

"I am a day late, for which I beg pardon," the abigail went on, "but Lady Delafort mistook the date."

"I am quite as ready today as I was yesterday," Susan said. "You will want refreshment while I prepare myself. Blenkinsop?"

The butler acted as guide to Miss Angleton—at least Susan presumed she was a "Miss"—while Susan ran upstairs to inform her grandmother of her imminent departure.

Since her trunk was ready, and she had replaced her nightdress and toilet things in her valise at dawn in determined optimism, she had only to hurry into the stout traveling dress she had worn all the day before. This morning she had not wished to face Grandmama's derision.

Almost before Susan knew it, she was standing on the front steps, receiving Mrs. Palmer's last dire warnings.

"Do not let the town corrupt you, my child." Grandmama enfolded Susan in a final embrace.

"By no means, Grandmama," Susan said in her most dutiful

style. Then, with an unbecoming eagerness, she followed her mother's dresser into the carriage.

The carriage was bowling out of the gates of Pilgrim Court when Susan cried, "Wait!"

Angleton, who was sitting backward, hastily pulled the checkstring.

The chaise rattled to a halt. "I'm sorry," Susan said sheepishly. "I . . . I have never been away from home before."

Angleton gave her an inscrutable glance from under long eyelids as Susan took one last long loving look at Pilgrim Court. The whole front of the house could be seen from the carriage window. Its pure lines, which Susan had often thought were cold and unwelcoming, seemed infinitely dear now—especially since Grandmama still stood on the front steps.

Angleton assisted Susan in letting down the glass. Susan waved her handkerchief out the window, then nodded to the maid.

"Drive on!" Angleton shouted out the window in a startlingly unladylike voice. Then she snapped the glass up into place and retired to her seat, where she folded her gloved hands in the most refined way in the world.

Susan hid her amusement and concentrated on arranging the hot brick at her feet.

The drive of twenty miles into London was made without incident. Susan soon discovered that it was not proper to talk to ladies' maids. At least, Angleton gently rebuffed Susan's every foray into conversational waters.

Unfortunately, a foggy night had fallen by the time the post chaise entered London. Susan looked this way and that, trying to discern something in the gloom. Lamps were being lit, but their glow provided only the occasional tantalizing glimpse of a building or bridge. On the pavements shadowy figures passed by—more people, Susan was certain, than she had ever seen in her life, if only she might have seen them properly.

"Are we nearing Portland Place?" Susan asked the abigail. She could hardly feature that she was about to set foot in Papa's town residence, the house that had been only a street direction to her all these years.

Angleton's lined features relaxed for an instant, and she said, "Yes, madam," in a not unfriendly tone.

Eventually the carriage came to a stop, and a footman ran to open the door. Susan arranged her simple cloak around herself, touched her close bonnet, and stepped down.

A tall, narrow house stood before her. The brick structure was attached on either side to other houses and looked quite modest to Susan's eyes, used to the Palladian grandeur of Pilgrim Court.

A butler appeared at the door and swept a bow. "Miss Danvers?" he queried as Susan mounted the steps. "Her ladyship has been expecting you."

"Take me to her at once, please," Susan said with a bright smile.

"Ma'am, I regret that Lady Delafort is out for the evening. A long-standing engagement. She has told us to expect you, though, and to see to your every comfort."

"Oh." Susan couldn't hold back a disappointed frown.

"Your dinner will be ready as soon as you have refreshed yourself in your room," the butler went on. He was evidently trying to cheer her up. Susan saw him exchange a glance with Angleton, who had come sailing up the steps armed with Susan's homely valise, which she carried as though it were a jewel case. "I am Bland," he added.

Susan started at such a brutal self-estimation coming from a stranger, then realized she had just been given the butler's name. He certainly seemed to fit it, being middle-aged, middle-sized, and quite colorless from his mouse-colored eyes to his highly polished shoes.

"I am pleased to meet you, Bland," Susan said with a pleasant nod. "And I would delight in seeing my room. What a pretty house this is!"

"Lady Delafort likes everything in the first style," Angleton put in, bustling up. "I shall show you to your room, Miss Danvers. Lady Delafort had me make everything ready."

The trunk and valise had already disappeared up the stairs in the care of some footmen. Susan looked with pleasure at a gracefully curving staircase whose inlaid mahogany banister was polished to a high shine. An expensive-looking carpet, in misty shades of rose, green, and blue, covered the stairs and was echoed in the hall carpet at Susan's feet. In the entryway some painted porcelain vases were filled with flowers. Hothouse flowers! Susan had never seen any before, nor tasted any hothouse fruit. Grandmama thought succession houses and conservatories flew in the face of nature.

Susan's room was up the stairs and down a prettily papered hall. "Lady Delafort redecorated it just for you, ma'am," Angleton said with a note of pride. She threw open the door, then stood aside to let Miss Danvers pass.

Susan stepped into a fairy's chamber of white and silver. Later, when she had leisure to think about it, she would find her new bedroom a touch too ruffled, too busily feminine for her taste, but at first sight she cried out with pleasure. Such a change from her room at Pilgrim Court was most welcome.

Angleton, with a satisfied smile at Miss Danvers' reaction, helped the young lady off with her outdoor things and soon left her to rest. Dinner could be brought up to the bedroom or, if Miss Danvers preferred, be served to her in the dining room.

"The dining room, please." Susan preferred to see over the entire house as soon as possible. When she was left alone, she knelt before her trunk and drew out her favorite dress, the one Mama had said good things about.

Attired in the shell-pink silk, Susan descended with a hesitant step to the main floor and inquired of a hovering Bland the way to the dining room. The house being a town dwelling of more modest proportions than Pilgrim Court, the room was easily reached behind one of the doors that opened off the hall.

Susan dined in lonely state, surrounded by attentive servants with interested expressions. She smiled at them all, asked their names, and soon came to see that she was being too casual in her manners. The dinner consisted of one course, and more food than Susan could have consumed in a week: a roasted pheasant, fried soles, a ragout, amd a dozen side dishes. Used to a simple country supper of bread and cheese, she was quite overwhelmed and picked at the food with a good will but without much appetite.

Whenever her fork clicked on her plate, Susan became aware of the echoing silence. She had never dined alone before, except on the rare occasions when Grandmama had thought fit to punish her and send her to bed with bread and milk.

Where was Mama? Susan's loyalty stretched thin as she considered this question. Should Lady Delafort not make time from her engagements to greet her only daughter on the occasion of that daughter's arrival in her home?

Dinner over, Susan drifted from drawing room to library. In the latter room she paused before a painting of her father, taken at his coming of age, which hung over the mantelpiece. How she did miss him! Or, if not him precisely, she missed the idea of having a father. She barely remembered Lord Delafort; only a vague impression of a laughing young man tossing her high into the air came sometimes to haunt her dreams.

Viscount Delafort had spent fifteen years in India. He had gone there to make money, and he had been making it steadily for years now. This pretty house, supplied with every luxury, was testimony to that. Susan knew that when Papa had left for foreign parts, the Portland Place house had been much out of repair. It had been shut up and would have gone under the hammer were it not part of the entailed estate of the Delafort family.

Susan had heard her grandmother's tales and drawn some conclusions on her own, but the gist of the story was that her parents, as newlyweds, had been sadly extravagant young care-for-nobodies. By the time Susan was three years old, they were outrunning the constable. Lord Delafort's gaming and expensive taste in horses and carriages were matched by his lady's dress-makers' and jewelers' bills. Finally they ran out of luck and into the hands of the moneylenders.

The Delaforts woke up one morning to find an execution in the house and their life of fashionable heedlessness a thing of the past. Lord Delafort, to everyone's surprise, did not shoot himself in the head or fly abroad without a word. He made a tardy metamorphosis into a model of rectitude. Swearing to repay every penny he owed, he took ship to India. Many of his set scoffed at his resort to trade, but he stood firm in his decision.

As for Lady Delafort, she could not be persuaded to follow

her lord to the end of the world and into a frightful climate. And Susan was much too delicate. To take a little child to India would be signing her death warrant. Her ladyship, chastened for the moment, retired into the country to live with her parents.

The years went by. Soon Lord Delafort had his debts paid, for he discovered a latent talent for business, and everything he touched turned to gold. He put his energies next into feathering his family's nest. He earned money for the benefit of the Delafort country seat in Derbyshire, which Susan had never seen. Then the house in London was refurbished.

Lady Delafort, the instant she became the proud possessor of a new and lavish allowance from her husband, fluttered from her severe parents' nest to the renovated town haven. And there she stayed, with most infrequent visits into Surrey to see her daughter.

Nobody knew when, or if, Lord Delafort would come home. Susan believed that making money was such a thrilling challenge to him that he might well stay abroad forever. The frequent letters he sent his daughter gave no hint of a homecoming. And what did he have to come back to? Mama not only hadn't cared to go with him into his exile, Susan would be very surprised if Lady Delafort even thought of her husband from one year's end to the next.

Susan sometimes wondered if she shouldn't go abroad herself to keep her father's house now that she was grown up. She had put forth the suggestion to him in a letter and been roundly refused. India, Lord Delafort wrote sternly, was no place for a young lady who did not have to be there. He could look out for himself very well, though Susan was a dear and loving daughter for asking.

Would she ever get the chance to be a really dear and loving daughter to anybody? Susan looked up wistfully at her father's picture.

"Miss Danvers." Bland poked his head in at the library door, making Susan jump. "I beg your pardon for the intrusion, ma'am, but there is a caller."

"A caller?" Susan was dumbfounded. "Nobody in London can wish to see me, Bland. You see, I don't know anyone."

"A Captain Camberley. He is your neighbor in Surrey, so

he says, and he has a message from your grandmother. Miss Angleton has engaged to remain in the room with you if you wish to see the gentleman.''

Susan was thrown into a flutter. Grandmama would never send a message by Captain Camberley! Would she? Susan smoothed down her gown and hurried after Bland into the drawing room.

This chamber exhibited the Empire style as interpreted by a luxury-loving lady. Susan had noted on her earlier progress through the room the large number of fainting couches it contained. Now she saw nothing but Captain Camberley, who looked very large surrounded by the delicate furnishings as he stood brushing a stray lock of brown hair back from his forehead.

Susan nodded in acknowledgment of Angleton's presence. The maid was frowning over her work in a corner of the room in the most proper chaperon style. Susan then held out her hand to the captain.

He grasped hers in both of his and smiled at her in a way which made her knees quiver. He let go of her hand only after placing a kiss upon it. Susan was amazed that such a feather-light caress could make her wish to throw herself into the captain's arms, and gave stern instructions to her knees, which were weaker than ever.

''Good evening, Captain.'' The knees cooperated for a small curtsy. ''Have you a message from Mrs. Palmer? How very singular. But Grandmama never does the expected.''

The captain's gaze slid to the abigail, then returned to Susan. ''If you wish the truth, I never expected to have the happiness of seeing you at this late hour, ma'am. I had thought to write on my card. The message I bring is somewhat informal.'' His brown eyes twinkling, he added, ''May I say you're looking lovely, Miss Danvers? I've never seen you in such splendor.''

Susan felt her cheeks grow warm. So dreams did come true! Whenever she had put on this gown in the past months, she had wished Captain Camberley might see her in it. Now here he was, and if she was not much mistaken, she was about to act like an idiotish schoolroom miss in front of him.

''I . . . Thank you,'' she said, her eyes downcast. When she lifted her gaze, she was surprised to find his smile had disappeared. "Is something wrong?" she blurted.

"This is difficult for me to admit, Miss Danvers," Camberley said with another glance at the attendant abigail. Lowering his voice, he added, "I have no message from your grandmother. I lied."

"You lied?" Susan said loudly.

Angleton looked up from a piece of mending with an odd expression on her face.

"You lied when you said the message was not important?" Susan tried to retrieve her mistake. She saw Angleton's eyes return to her work. "Is my grandmother well, sir?"

"Mrs. Palmer continues in perfect health," Camberley said. He was smiling again, and his next words were spoken in an undertone. "I had a servant inquire at Pilgrim Court before I started on my road to London, so that I might have a message for you, though I know you parted from your grandmother only this morning and might not be looking for news so soon."

"Did you indeed?" Susan's voice matched the captain's in softness. Angleton looked disgruntled that they were whispering, but the abigail could hardly ask them to speak up. As long as the captain didn't grasp Susan in his arms—Susan's heart lifted at this pleasing fantasy—the proprieties would be observed.

"I hope, ma'am, that here in London we will be able to be neighbors at last, in the finest sense of the word," the captain whispered. "You came to town to go out into society, didn't you?"

"I dearly hope so."

"Then we will meet, which is more than we could do in Surrey," Camberley said in satisfaction. "I look forward . . . well, let us say that I felt myself compelled to come and advise you of my arrival here. My sister is with me, and she will call on you and her ladyship."

Susan gazed at him in fascination. This hero of the realm, this important man who had no peer in her estimation, was indicating in the plainest language that he had an interest in her. "Did you bring your dog?" she asked in a dreamy tone, then could have bitten off her tongue for such an inane statement.

"Neptune is with me. The fellow has wormed his way into

my heart, and we can't be parted," the captain assured her. "Perhaps the two of you will meet in the park one day soon."

"I look forward to renewing our acquaintance," Susan said in what she hoped was a sophisticated, joking tone. If she kept acting like a mooncalf, Camberley would surely repent his overtures to her. And what were these overtures exactly? She could hardly ask Camberley, though she quite wished she could. When a young man arrived at a young lady's house to inform her—late in the evening, no less!—of his arrival in town, what did it mean? Susan wished she were more versed in the social arts. Was this attention more or less than a bouquet of flowers or a verse written in a lady's honor?

"I dare not stay longer," the captain said, raising Susan's hand to his lips once more. "Thank you, Miss Danvers, for receiving me."

"Oh . . . whenever you wish," Susan said. Then once again she cursed herself silently for the artlessness, the absolute abysmal ignorance, of her manner. She might as well fall down at his feet! Some instinct told her that this much honesty was not normally a part of the game between the sexes.

"You are delightful," Captain Camberley said. Susan recalled that he had once used the same words in the rose garden at Pilgrim Court. She ought to remember—she relived that incident every night as she drifted off to sleep.

The captain nodded to Angleton, received a piercing stare in return, and left the room.

Susan stood at the window and watched him mount up into a sporting vehicle drawn by a team of horses. Had he come to her straightaway on his arrival in town?

He had been so forgiving, so amused at her little gaucheries. Susan was afraid she knew the reason why. Captain Camberley was a veteran of war, a mover of men and ships. Such a man could never be interested in a simple countrified miss for any sensible reason. If sense guided his actions, would he not hit upon a sophisticated lady of society, one whose intellect was sufficiently trained to afford him an equal match?

His idle admiration for Susan, if admiration it really was, must be based on her absolute and shaming innocence.

This was a chastening thought. Even more dismaying was

the notion that he didn't admire her at all, for any reason, and was merely being polite, or socially adept, by calling her "delightful" twice now in their acquaintance.

Yet he had followed her to town on the very same day she had come up, had called on her most particularly to tell her of his arrival.

Susan knew she would spend her first night in London puzzling all this out.

"If you will permit me, ma'am, you might find an early night most helpful in restoring your strength," Angleton said, rising and folding the piece of mending, which proved to be an intimate feminine undergarment of so lacy and transparent a style that it had to belong to Lady Delafort. "Her ladyship won't be back until the small hours. She would never wish you to wait up."

"I agree with you. I'm quite longing for my pillow," Susan said at once.

She was more than eager to start on her solitary project of getting to the heart of Captain Camberley's motives—not to mention conjuring up a dream of the man—and turned eager footsteps to the staircase, where she found a bed candle awaiting her on a small table.

Angleton did not know much of young ladies, but she was surprised to see one so new to London go tamely to bed on her first night in town.

5

"There are three words to be said about your introduction to London, my child." Lady Delafort raised her chocolate cup to her lips. "Clothes, clothes, clothes."

Susan lifted her own cup of chocolate in a kind of salute. She was seated beside the bed in Lady Delafort's elegant chamber. This room was done in tones of rose and silver, colors most soothing to the eyes, Lady Delafort informed her daughter, as well as flattering to the complexion. Susan's mother leaned back upon snowy lace-edged pillows while she opened her eyes to the morning. The hour was noon, but Lady Delafort had arrived home at dawn. She was quite proud of herself for rising so early to greet her daughter.

"I have no objection to clothes," Susan said in a serious tone. "But did you not also mention something about a dancing master in one of your letters, Mama?"

"Indeed I did." Lady Delafort gave a sunny smile. "I've found him, too. The most stunning *émigré*—that is to say, he is a very well-looking man, which I consider to be a most important requirement for a person one must actually touch in the line of duty, as it were. My friend Lady Samms used him for both of her daughters. Monsieur Beauclair is a perfect choice, my dear: ugly enough that no green girl would fall in love with him, yet with a certain something—a *savoir faire*, if you will—that a more mature female can quite appreciate."

"Oh." Susan opened her eyes wide. Sophisticated chatter was new in her experience. "Mama, why do I feel you are being more frank with me than a mother usually is with a green daughter?"

"Because I mean you to come on quickly, of course, and pick up some town bronze," was Lady Delafort's instant answer.

"We have years of Rousseau to overcome. Tell me, was your grandmother's regime too, too stultifying?"

Susan considered this for a moment. "Yes and no," she said at last. "Grandmama interpreted Rousseau's teaching to mean that I should run quite free throughout my childhood, and that was most pleasant. But she was disappointed that I taught myself to read so early. Grandpapa's library wasn't sold until I was nine. Once I knew how to read, I did learn enough to know that there were many, many things of which I was ignorant. And that didn't make me happy."

Lady Delafort nodded, replacing her chocolate cup in its saucer and returning it to her tray. "You will learn many of these things before you're much older, Susan," she said with a determined air. "Now, let's begin with what you do know. How are ladies normally dressed for a court presentation?"

Susan let a giggle escape her. She was reminded of another conversation last summer, when Miss Camberley had first quizzed her on her reading. And she was certain that she was about to fall as low in Mama's estimation as she ever had in the small bluestocking's.

"What is so amusing?" Lady Delafort asked with mild interest.

"Oh, I was thinking of a friend of mine."

"Has this friend been to court?"

Susan soon discovered a single-mindedness in her mother's manner that showed her to be the true daughter of Mrs. Palmer. Susan also learned, before the day was over, that hoops were worn at court and would be inflicted on her for the presentation at the royal drawing room which would mark her official entrance into society. She learned that the *real* court of London was Almack's, the exclusive club where weekly assemblies were held during the Season, and that one of Mama's standing would obtain vouchers as a matter of course. And she learned, when Lady Delafort sailed into her daughter's room to peek into her wardrobe, that she had not a rag to her back that was fit to be seen in public.

"Heavens," Lady Delafort said, fingering the fourth white muslin gown, "we must try to get you into some colors. I simply don't care what young ladies wear. You must be bored to death with going about looking like a ghost.''

"White muslin is Grandmama's ideal of simplicity and rusticity and all those things," Susan said with a little smile. "And then there is the washing. She says that if you don't wear colors, they can't run.''

Lady Delafort let out a peal of laughter. "If that doesn't sound for the world like my mother. Well, we must be grateful that she won't be here to be shocked by your extravagant wardrobe. We go to Madame Hélène tomorrow—you must wear a pelisse of mine, and one of my bonnets if this straw coal scuttle is really your only headgear. Madame Hélène, you must know, dresses the most original ladies in the *ton.* ''

The morrow brought not only the visit to the famous modiste but also stops by milliners', glovers', and shoemakers' establishments. Susan, fresh from the country, was amazed at the stamina required to get through such a day of frivolity. She and her mother subsisted on only a couple of ices which their footman brought out to their carriage at Gunter's, the famous pastry cook's.

"Frivolity is hard work," Lady Delafort said when Susan tried to phrase her thoughts in the carriage going home. Susan, as she slid off her shoes to put her feet up on the squabs opposite, had to agree.

As Lady Delafort had done the night before, she dined with Susan *en déshabille,* then made ready for her evening engagements. Susan followed her mother up to her rooms to observe Angleton's magic, as Lady Delafort put it.

"Oh, Mama, you are so very beautiful. There can be no question of magic," Susan protested.

Lady Delafort preened at this and touched her gleaming black hair.

Susan watched, enthralled, as her mother was transformed into a veritable goddess of loveliness under the capable hands of Angleton. A glorious white-and-silver gown, extremely *décolleté;* diamonds "of just the proper size," as Lady Delafort told Susan, neither vulgarly large nor offensively small; a becoming toque. Susan's gaze grew wide when the rouge pot came out, and some sort of paint for the eyes.

"You will not paint, of course," Lady Delafort said, with a severe look and a wink. "You are much too young. Though if you didn't have such a pretty color I would definitely bring up all reinforcements."

Once dressed, her ladyship was most happy to twirl about before the glass to the tune of her daughter's compliments. She caught Susan by the shoulders in her exuberance. "This is nothing, my love. Wait until you are properly gowned. The two of us together—now, there will be something to see." A feathery kiss brushed Susan's cheek; then Lady Delafort drew back from this salute to put her head to one side. "I believe I hear the door. My escort must have arrived." She looked her daughter up and down. "That bedraggled muslin—no, my dear, you mustn't come down, though you ought to meet people as soon as possible. Before the Season really begins is the time to make the first assaults upon the hearts of the unwary."

"Mama, it sounds like war," Susan said, laughing. She was rather glad of her drab state. She would have been frightened to be thrust into society without warning.

Lady Delafort shook her head, smiling. "You shall come down for the callers tomorrow," she promised. "Angleton, see what you can find among my things. You know the style: a proper morning dress, a bit *jeune fille*—and see it doesn't clash with what I shall wear. You two may spend the evening working on the project."

Susan accompanied her mother as far as the head of the stairs, where she waved and blew a kiss. Mama, with a final adjusting of her draperies, put on a serene, regal smile and proceeded down the stairs.

Susan couldn't resist; there was a spot where she might observe from between the spindles of the banister without being seen, as the staircase made a turn. She crouched down and saw her mother descend the last steps into the entry hall.

"My dearest lady! Creature of my dreams," brayed a familiar voice. It was Lord Fitzalbin, whom Susan had had the questionable pleasure of meeting in Surrey the summer before.

"Fair luminary," someone else added, and Susan saw a stalwart-looking man in regimentals close next upon her ladyship's hand, capturing it from Fitzalbin, whose bald dome shone in the light from a branch of candles. At least the military man had hair.

To Susan's surprise, yet another man, this one with a gleaming head of curly black hair and elegant evening clothes, stepped into her line of vision. "Lady Delafort, you overwhelm us poor mortals," a deep voice stated. Despite the timbre of the voice, Susan thought the man sounded young.

As a fourth man stepped up to pay his flowery compliments, Susan realized that her mother had meant "escort" in the military sense. More than ever Susan sensed that this was not play, but war.

"Oh, Mama," she murmured under her breath, "why so many men?" Her first thoughts were for her father. What would he think of Lady Delafort's phalanxes of gentlemen? Well, Mama was doubtless playing it safe by surrounding herself with such numbers. Susan had to admit that nothing like illicit intimacy could take place with so many gentlemen in her ladyship's train.

The next morning continued the military theme as a regiment of callers descended on the house in Portland Place. This was the first day Lady Delafort had received since her daughter's arrival.

Before the visitors were due, Lady Delafort took care to arrange herself and Susan in elegant poses. Her ladyship, dressed in the pristine white Susan was to be spared, reclined upon one of the backless sofas. Susan sat nearby in a deep moss-colored velvet armchair which had been chosen especially to set off her gown of pale green cambric.

"Oh, I think it a famous thing for you to be the young miss and me to wear white," Mama said with a laugh, settling her scarf in just the proper folds. "Angleton is quite a genius. The element of surprise, my dear Susan. Never forget the element of surprise."

First to be announced was a military man, stalwart and sturdy of build, with graying brown hair. Susan could not be sure, but she thought he was the one she had seen from the staircase the night before.

He did not even seem to notice Susan until her presence was

pointed out by Lady Delafort, so thorough were his raptures on seeing Susan's mother. When he was presented to the younger lady, his eyebrows rose.

"Lady Delafort, you cannot have a daughter! That is, I suppose anything is possible, you being a married lady, but . . . Upon my soul! You must have been married right from the cradle."

Such extravagance was much to the taste of his hostess. "General Haverstock, I assure you Miss Danvers is indeed my daughter. Don't you think we shall cut a dash together once the Season begins? I am to present her at the first drawing room, you know."

The general was properly complimentary on the beauties of her ladyship's daughter.

"You need not flatter me to please my mother, sir," Susan said, dimpling. "I know my nose is too short for genuine beauty."

"Susan," Lady Delafort groaned. "One never comments in public on one's physical features. We might have gone all our lives without hearing you disparage your own nose. I have never heard you do so before, and"—here she touched a finger to her own perfect aquiline feature—"though it is different from mine, to be sure, it quite suits your face."

"Indeed, ma'am," put in General Haverstock. "It's a charming nose, if I may say so." The ambiguity of his remark was doubtless meant to satisfy both ladies.

Susan nodded in pleased acceptance of her first compliment out in society, then resolved never to mention any part of her anatomy again. She had much to learn.

The procession of callers continued. More than half a dozen gentlemen, whose various names and titles Susan struggled to remember, professed themselves shocked and enchanted by Lady Delafort's possession of a daughter. Then Bland swung open the doors again to announce, in a surprised voice, "Miss Camberley and Captain Camberley."

He sounded, Susan observed in amusement, as though he had never announced a female in these rooms before.

Drusilla Camberley looked very small beside her tall brother, but at the same time more severe than she ever had. Her sober

walking things and sensible bonnet were in marked contrast to
the other ladies' morning costumes. Her eyes, behind the little
spectacles, seemed to catalog in one sweep every detail of Lady
Delafort's opulent drawing room and its inhabitants.

"Do forgive us the intrusion, my lady," Miss Camberley said
with a curtsy. "We are neighbors of your mother's in Surrey,
and I am your daughter's most particular friend." She smiled
at Susan, who suddenly felt that her green dress was too
frivolous and her hair, done in a new style Mama had recommended, nothing short of ridiculous.

Susan rose to greet her friends, for she noticed that Mama's
welcome seemed a little forced. Then she saw to it that Miss
Camberley took the seat next to hers, which a small foppish
man whose title she couldn't recall obligingly vacated. He hadn't
been talking to Susan anyway. She noted with satisfaction that
Captain Camberley, after the proper obeisance at Lady
Delafort's couch, stuck close to his sister and came to stand
behind her chair, whence Susan had a good view of his stalwart
figure and twinkling brown eyes.

Mama couldn't but be impressed that the great naval hero
was calling on her, Susan reasoned. Still, she thought she
interpreted a flash of annoyance in her mother's eyes before
her ladyship turned away, with the sweetest smile in the world,
to one of her gallants.

"We find you in a much different situation, my dear," Miss
Camberley said with another glance at the rich surroundings.
"I was so surprised to learn that Lady Delafort is your mother!
That is, I cannot believe . . ."

She hesitated, and Susan took the opportunity to laugh. "If
you are about to say, ma'am, that Mama looks much too young
to have a grown-up daughter, you must say that to her face."

Miss Camberley glanced up at her brother, then turned again
to Susan. "What I meant, my dear, is that your mother is one
of society's most famous beauties. Perhaps . . . Was she raised
away from home?"

"Oh, I see what you mean." Susan nodded her understanding.
"You wonder how Grandmama could have brought up such
a butterfly as Mama. Well, the truth is that my grandfather didn't
approve of Grandmama's notions about education. Thanks to

him, Mama was raised in quite ordinary fashion and attended one of the first seminaries.'' She smiled. ''Is Mama really quite well-known? I've read her name in the society columns, to be sure.''

''I assure you her ladyship is indeed a famous character,'' Miss Camberley said in a tone which, without being rude, nevertheless made clear her disapproval of such notoriety.

''And about to become better-known,'' the captain added, ''as the mother of the newest beauty on the scene.''

Susan was momentarily struck dumb by this compliment. Not even stopping to flare up at Miss Camberley in defense of her mother, she smiled at the captain in delight, then caught herself. She had been vapid again, and stupid. A knowing young lady would never react so to a simple courteous comment. She simply must learn sophistication. If only she had rapped the captain upon the knuckles with a fan—but she wasn't carrying a fan—or let out a peal of laughter to draw the room's attention to the flattering remark. Mama would have known precisely what to do.

''I fear to do you a disservice in her ladyship's eyes by calling, dear Miss Danvers,'' Miss Camberley said.

Susan came out of her brown study and looked questioningly at the lady.

''We are hardly people of fashion, my brother and I,'' Drusilla explained.

Susan gasped. ''But Captain Camberley is . . . Surely he must be received everywhere?'' She looked up at him in dismay. What if she didn't meet him at the social events of the Season? Yet how could any society hostess exclude such a man?

He smiled at her. ''I'm most gratified by your confidence, ma'am, and yes, I am received everywhere as a sort of curiosity. Drusilla is trying in her subtle way to inform you that we are only country gentry. Not titled.''

''But you're untitled by your own decision,'' Susan protested. ''And surely a title isn't necessary. Mama has mentioned any number of fashionable names to me, and not all of them have 'Lord' and 'Sir' attached.''

''There are those, dear Miss Danvers, who do not wish to be fashionable. My brother and I number ourselves among them," Miss Camberley said with a little lift of her Roman nose.

Again Susan surveyed Captain Camberley in dismay.

"If having a friend from the country would please you, Miss Danvers, I engage to show myself at any number of those gatherings my sister so charmingly disdains," he said, giving Drusilla a teasing smile when she looked up at him in indignation. "She is come to town for a lecture series on ancient Roman ruins, but I am quite at your disposal."

"Oh." Susan was momentarily deflated. She wondered why she had spent so many hours spinning air-dreams that Captain Camberley had come to London—and coaxed his sister to come with him—for no other reason than to see her. Naturally their plans had been long-standing and had just happened to coincide with hers. Recovering herself, Susan was about to assure Captain Camberley that she would be pleased to see him anywhere, when he was peremptorily summoned by her mother.

"Captain!" Lady Delafort called with a certain teasing note in her voice that, for the first time, set Susan's teeth on edge. "Do come and settle a dispute these gentlemen are having about who is to take me to the opera this evening. You, with your famous reputation for coolness under fire, might escort me yourself and fend off these others."

Susan gasped.

Drusilla Camberley looked at her in what Susan was certain was pity. The younger lady squirmed at her own transparency.

"I suppose Mama thinks she is being kind to the captain," she said with a forced smile. "Her company is so sought-after that she must mean to raise him in the eyes of the *ton*."

Miss Camberley nodded grimly.

The two were approached then by a young earl whom Susan had been surprised to find in her mother's court; for he was more youthful than the other men who surrounded Lady Delafort. His had been the third figure she had seen the night before from her secret place on the stairs. Up close he was a handsome young man with dark curly locks a bit longer than the common mode, and flashing eyes. He seemed fully aware of his attractions. Without any preamble he threw himself at Susan's feet in a negligent attitude that startled both ladies.

Indeed, Miss Camberley looked at him as though he had run mad.

"Miss Camberley, may I present Lord Semerton," Susan said, staring in amazement at the young man.

"Miss Camberley, your most obedient," the earl drawled in a deep, romantic voice with half a glance at the spinster. He gazed up at Susan. "My dear, I had to come to you to tell you that my feelings won't be denied. When I worshiped at your mother's feet, I was but an acolyte awaiting the true goddess. Now I have found her." He grasped Susan's hand and kissed the fingers one by one.

Susan, with her absolute lack of experience in society, had no idea whether this was proper or not. It seemed fairly silly. She threw a desperate glance at Miss Camberley.

"Sir," that lady said, with a severe look, "Miss Danvers and I were in the middle of a most serious discussion."

"Ah, seriousness," Semerton said with a wave of his hand. "The great goal of all conversation, to be sure. Then I must leave you to it. Do permit me, fair goddess"—and he turned back to Susan—"to escort you to the opera this evening."

The opera, where Lady Delafort was angling to have Captain Camberley take her! Susan wished above all things to go, though not under the protection of Lord Semerton. She found him positively unbelievable. "'I'm not really out yet," she said in a mixture of regret and relief. "I don't believe I should attend the opera." She did not voice the objection this young man would most likely have understood, which was that her clothes were not yet made.

"Shouldn't attend!" the young lord exclaimed in horror. Rising with great agility, he kissed Susan's hand once more and winked at her. "I will fix it with her ladyship. Never you fear, fair holder of my heart."

Susan looked in astonishment at Miss Camberley as Semerton moved away. "Can this be in the common way, do you think? His lordship met me only this morning. He said how do you do, went to talk to someone else, and then next thing I knew he was casting himself at my feet."

"You cannot know who that is, my dear, or you would have

given him a set-down," Miss Camberley replied. "Even I have heard of him. That young man is the newest wicked lord. They say he has set out to surpass Lord Byron. He even writes poetry."

"Poetry!" Susan was more shocked by this than anything. "That might explain his silliness. And I suppose he is hanging about Mama because he wishes to be in the fashion. But it doesn't explain his late behavior to me."

"Wickedness, even the self-professed and somewhat perfunctory wickedness which I believe that young man owns, is much attracted to innocence, dear Miss Danvers."

"Then I must be well-nigh irresistible," Susan said with a sigh. "I am finding, Miss Camberley, that I'm much too innocent for my own good."

"Never mind, my dear," Miss Camberley said, patting her young friend's hand. "I have found you possess sense, and that can go a long way in making up for any other deficiencies."

Susan smiled in appreciation of these kind words and wondered if Miss Camberley would possibly approve a match between her brother and such a countrified little chit as Susan Danvers.

The Camberleys soon took their leave. The captain was looking startled, for Lady Delafort had indeed captured his escort for the evening's opera. He had a sheepish smile for Susan as he escorted his sister out of the room.

Still present among the milling gentlemen was Lord Semerton, who, unlike the Camberleys, had no nice notions of the proper length of time for a morning call. He had been with them for at least an hour. "I have made all well with her ladyship," he announced, appearing before Susan once more and casting himself down at her feet in the same disconcerting manner. "She will allow you to go, but she finds me too devilish to be your sole escort and has insisted that I bring my friend Buxford along. Kind of her ladyship to call me devilish! We will be a merry party. Lady Delafort will have that sea captain as well as Lord Fitzalbin at her side, and some of my family may show up. My box will do for us, I think."

"You are most obliging, my lord," Susan said, with so much pleasure that the young earl was encouraged. Susan, however, was thinking with excitement of spending an entire evening in close quarters with Captain Camberley.

As soon as the drawing room was cleared of gentlemen, Lady Delafort rushed her daughter upstairs to her boudoir and summoned Angleton to seek out a suitable gown to deck Susan for the evening. "Semerton's pursuit of you is most encouraging, my dear," she said, watching critically as Susan tried on a white satin gown. "No, Angle, too sophisticated by half. Look at the neck! She is yet to make her come-out."

Angleton nodded and helped Susan out of the gown.

While she stood in her shift waiting for the next garment to be draped about her, Susan said, "Why do you suppose that Lord Semerton was so kind to me, Mama? He met me only this morning, and he is so enamored of you." She did not mention Semerton's talk of acolytes nor his characterization of herself as his true goddess. That was all too silly.

"He has explained that, dear boy, in the most flattering terms," Lady Delafort said with a sigh. "We might even expect one of his wicked poems on the subject. He saw that your eyes were so like mine and fell in love with them. And I am a hopeless case, after all, for I am a married lady."

"I see." Susan felt suddenly forlorn and quite small. She hadn't been comfortable with the idea of Semerton's admiration, to be sure, but his own explanation of his attraction to her had been more palatable than what he had told her mother. Perhaps, she considered in sudden insight, he changed his story according to the person he was trying to impress.

"Besides," Lady Delafort said in satisfaction, "there is no question about it, my dear. You will be much sought after, for not only are you a beautiful girl but also your papa has provided well for you, and you may be certain that I have let that slip. Semerton is quite a wealthy young man, and wealth is drawn to wealth much as beauty is attracted to beauty. Your father and I, dear, were the most attractive young couple in town."

At her mother's expectant look, Susan returned the compliment she supposed was wanting. "You are still the most beautiful woman in London, Mama," she said quickly. Then she added, "So Papa has given me a marriage portion! It somehow never occurred to me that I would be well-dowered."

"You are indeed. It was his first act after paying off our debts of long ago. Everyone will assume you're rich even if they don't know so, for Papa's success in those vulgar business interests has been phenomenal, and all the world knows of them." Lady Delafort sighed. "Thank heaven his lineage is unexceptional. I might have a ticklish time of it otherwise. The taint of trade, my dear," she added by way of explanation.

Susan had always thought her father splendid for making up his mind to recoup the family fortunes and, what was more, actually following through on the project. Her grandmother, too, admired her son-in-law and had never given Susan to understand that trade was a thing to be despised. Susan knew little of business one way or the other. It was a new idea that her father's exploits might need to be apologized for in her mother's circles: a new and unpleasant idea.

Lady Delafort glimpsed her daughter's woebegone face when she glanced up from the jewel case she had been searching for something suitable for a young girl. "What is it, child?"

"I . . . I cannot get used to society," Susan said, lifting her shoulders.

"Heavens, you haven't even seen it yet." Lady Delafort's cheerful laugh rang out. "Do not you worry, Susan. I intend to introduce you to the finest young men in the *ton*. It was no accident that I teased Semerton into bringing his friend Buxford along this evening. Viscount Buxford is richer than you can feature. You will have no time to brood about Captain Camberley."

Susan gave a violent start. "I . . . why should I brood?"

"Because I have done my research on him, my love, and I've decided he is not a suitable *parti* for the only daughter of Lord Delafort. You must be a countess or at the very least a viscountess like your mama. The Camberleys are a landed old family in Yorkshire, it seems, but they were impoverished before Captain Camberley came to the rescue with his prize-money, and they have never been titled or noble. He will be an amusing escort for us, he being such a famous character these days, but he can be nothing more."

"How very cold this seems, Mama," Susan said with a shake

of her head. She knew that no matter what her mother said, she would not give up dreaming of Captain Camberley. He had been easily caught in her mother's net, true, but he had been allowed no opportunity for a civil escape. "I suppose you approve of Lord Semerton."

"Isn't he a dear, though? Of course I approve of him! And don't you fret about his lordship's reputation for wickedness. He is much too young to be really evil."

Susan nodded, her head spinning with all these new ideas.

"I have a theory about Semerton," Lady Delafort went on. "He came down from university not so many years ago, one of a crowd of young men. I believe he wished to be out of the common way and decided that wickedness was his best chance of social success. And so it has proved. He's the darling of every hostess in town, with his devilish smile and fast reputation. But I have never heard any real harm of him, and I know him quite well. He has been writing poems and things to me for . . . oh, above a year now."

"Oh." From mere confusion, Susan's expression turned dazed.

"Angleton," Lady Delafort said, changing the subject briskly, "what do you say to that cream-colored sarcenet that just came home?"

"Your new gown, milady? For Miss?" the abigail gasped.

"Really, Angie, you act as though no mother had ever before made a sacrifice for her child. It is nothing," Lady Delafort said with a sidelong look at her daughter.

Susan was beginning to recognize her mother's hints. She thanked her for the gift with as much gratitude as Lady Delafort could have desired from the most humble of her admirers.

6

That evening, gowned in the fashionable cream-colored sarcenet, with a simple strand of pearls about her neck and matching drops in her ears, Susan realized fully for the first time that she was about to make her first appearance in the fashionable world. Her mother had assured her that there was no impropriety in going about before her presentation to the queen; indeed, who knew if there would be a drawing room soon, her majesty's health being so poor? Society, on the other hand, was waiting with bated breath to make Miss Danvers' acquaintance and must not be disappointed longer.

"Quite as I'd hoped," Mama exclaimed when Susan joined her in her dressing closet. "That gown is a perfect misty background to my costume. I couldn't have planned better had I had days instead of hours." She held out her hand to her daughter, and they stood in front of the silver-framed cheval glass in mutual admiration.

Lady Delafort was attired in emerald satin. The color was perfect with her raven hair, which was curled in a distracting arrangement and shining with red lights that Susan had not noticed before. Her ladyship wore no necklace, and indeed the voluptuous expanse of snow-white bosom looked its best unadorned, Susan thought. Enough emeralds and diamonds glittered on Lady Delafort's arms and at her ears to give proof that her neck had been left bare by design, not necessity.

Susan could scarcely see herself beside her mother's splendor, but when she did focus on her own image she found it not unpleasing. The gown was light-colored, and had been altered by Angleton so that it appeared more virginal than sophisticated, but its rich creamy tone was a most welcome change from the everlasting white prescribed by Grandmama. And Susan was excited to be wearing pearls. She had never had ornaments before, and Mama, on hearing this ingenuous exclamation, had kindly said that Susan might keep these for her own.

The three gentlemen who were to escort them arrived before the ladies were down, which was quite as it should be, Lady Delafort informed her daughter. "Now, let us make our entrance slowly. They will crowd round the bottom of the staircase to see us—silly creatures!—so mind you walk gracefully. Oh, I do wish Monsieur Beauclair had given you at least one lesson. He's said to be marvelous at deportment as well as the waltz."

Lady Delafort went down the stairs first. As she had foretold, Lord Fitzalbin and Lord Semerton sprang to her side immediately with fulsome compliments. Susan, following behind, had eyes for only one man: Captain Camberley, who stood back from the others and gazed earnestly up the staircase at her.

She caught his eye and felt her cheeks reddening. She immediately lowered her lashes, glad that the others had not noticed what she considered to be a private moment.

Then Lord Semerton, Susan's nominal escort, caught sight of Miss Danvers. "Dear angel," he cried out, his hand upon his heart. "You have indeed chosen to honor us with your sweet presence. Ah"—and he kissed Lady Delafort's hand a second time—"it is too unfair, my lady. So much beauty should not exist in one family."

"You are indeed a vision of loveliness, Miss Danvers," Captain Camberley said quickly, before the dramatic earl could begin more raptures. "And you, my lady." He turned to Lady Delafort.

The viscountess appeared a bit disgruntled to be complimented second, and in such an offhand manner, but she took his arm in good humor. "Captain, I am charmed to see you. Now, shall we go? I believe we're as fashionably late as even I wish to be."

Lady Delafort hooked her other arm through Fitzalbin's and sailed out, leaving Susan and Semerton to follow.

The opulent Semerton coach was waiting, and Captain Camberley quickly volunteered to go on the box to keep from crowding the ladies. During the drive to Covent Garden, Lady Delafort kept the conversation lively and superficial, much aided by the two gentlemen.

Susan remained silent, which she supposed was proper for

a young girl in any case, and thought of Captain Camberley on the roof in the gentle spring rain. What luck that he had worn his greatcoat!

He had jumped down off the box and was waiting beside the door by the time the rest of the party was ready to descend. Lady Delafort put her hand through his arm again, while Susan watched with barely suppressed jealousy from her own station next to Lord Semerton. Then, to Lady Delafort's evident amazement, Camberley made his excuses to her and walked swiftly to the side of the building.

Susan noticed for the first time that not only elegantly clad fashionables but also the other side of the social scale clustered around the entrance to the opera house. There were women in oddly brash costumes who were waiting expectantly near the entrance, either that or entering quite as importantly as any of the less vulgar; and there were men with crutches or other infirmities who were begging from the passersby.

The captain approached a ragged man who sat propped next to the wall. The man's face, bony and anguished, was visible in the light of a torch. Susan looked down and saw he had no legs below the knees.

Camberley spoke to the man, then appeared to take out a writing instrument and use it. Something passed from hand to hand, and then the captain rejoined his party, his expression grim. Lady Delafort, on glimpsing the odd scene, had become suddenly interested in settling her opera cloak and other appurtenances. She was ready to move into the lights and face the crowds.

Susan touched Camberley's arm before he reached her mother. "How kind of you, sir," she murmured, feeling tears start to her eyes.

"Kind?" He looked at her, his face so set and cold that Susan hardly recognized it. "That man served on a ship of mine. French cannon deprived him of his legs. No, Miss Danvers, I'm not kind. Luckier than some poor devils, perhaps, but not kind."

Something in his tone of voice made Susan pity him quite as she pitied the legless man. Pity him, and understand more about the late war than she ever had. Before she could say anything else or sort out this odd impression, Lady Delafort called out for the captain, and he moved away.

Susan entered the opera house on the arm of Semerton. The magnificent building could not but dazzle her, though she had had her mind taken off this excitement by Captain Camberley's experience. She had never been inside so vast a building, nor seen so many elegantly clad people. The party ascended the stairs to Semerton's box. Once within and settled on a fine gilt-and-velvet chair next to her mother's, Susan looked about her in awe. The crystal chandeliers, the tier upon tier of boxes like their own—it was overwhelming to one who had spent her lifetime in country seclusion. On the flamboyantly decorated stage someone was singing, but so great was the chatter from the crowd that Susan assumed this wasn't the main performance, but only some minor act.

She looked down at her gloved hands, trying to collect herself so that she would not stare like a country gapeseed.

Semerton's voice distracted her. "Ah, there you are, Buxford. Where are my womenfolk?"

Susan glanced up and saw that a big, burly young man with bright red hair had entered the box. "They're out in the corridor chatting to a pair of old harridans, Semerton," this individual said in a booming voice. Then he rushed immediately to pay his clumsy compliments to Lady Delafort.

Susan was presented to this new paragon, Viscount Buxford, as soon as he could be plucked from Lady Delafort's side, which operation her ladyship performed rather as though she were removing a burr from her sleeve. Susan wished she had the courage to ask Buxford what he meant by Semerton's womenfolk. The young earl's professed wickedness would surely not extend to inviting loose women into a box with ladies? Susan knew all about the muslin company. If nothing else, her careful reading of the scandalous French novel *Lessons in Life* had taught her that there was more to society than simply respectable people meeting together to exchange news.

Buxford was visibly charmed by Susan. "When Semerton told me I'd the job of helping to entertain Lady Delafort's daughter, I expected a miss in leading strings," he said frankly. "Did wonder what such a baby would be doing at the opera.

I'm glad to meet you, ma'am. Now, I'd better go search out the other females, but you're to save this seat for me.'' He dropped his *chapeau bras* on the chair beside Susan, dashing her hope that Captain Camberley, who was still standing, might choose to sit by her.

"What other females?" Susan asked Semerton, who had stationed himself on her other side.

"You'll see," Semerton answered with a would-be smoldering look which did not quite come off. "It's best to confront all these family matters, I say. If you meet 'em now, you can't say later that I hid anything from you."

Susan was quite unequal to responding to this. She simply couldn't believe that a man she had met but that morning, and who was a professed admirer of her mother's, could be planning a future with her.

Soon Buxford entered again and held the door open for two ladies: one a young and lovely brown-haired female with a decided air of fashion; the other a grim-looking dowager in purple and plumes.

Semerton rose to his feet and made introductions all round. "My grandmother, Lady Semerton, and my sister, Lady Emily Forbes," he said with a sweeping bow. "How is it, Grandmama? I'd hoped your gout would let you attend."

"I do not have the gout," the dowager said with a threatening motion of her chicken-skin fan. "Young scamp!"

"Grandmama and I have this little joke together about gout," Semerton whispered into Susan's ear. "She really dotes upon me. Good for a little fortune on her own account and means to leave it between me and Emily if I'm not too wicked, or so she says."

Again Susan was shocked to hear a comment from the earl which would be more properly addressed to a betrothed than to a young lady he had met that morning.

Meanwhile all flirtation was going by the board as Lady Delafort roused herself to greet the Semerton females. The seating was somehow rearranged, Susan thought by old Lady Semerton's devices, so that the ladies were sitting together in a cozy quartet at the front of the box. This left the gentlemen to mill about behind them and scramble to place their own chairs with a leg pointing toward the favored lady. At least Semerton, Buxford, and Fitzalbin played this game, Buxford tenderly trying to smooth his hat, which Lady Semerton had brushed onto the floor and stepped on. Captain Camberley, still looking severe and quite unlike himself to Susan's worried eye, remained standing at the rear of the box.

"I've been so longing to meet you, my dearest creature." Lady Emily Forbes gave Susan's hand a squeeze. She was a couple of years older than Susan and possessed a ready smile and sharp hazel eyes that seemed to see all. "Ever since Semerton told me about you earlier today, I've been dying to see his intended."

"I'm not—"

"Nonsense, my dear, all that is left is crying the banns, and in our set it will be a special license, not dreary old banns," Lady Emily said with a chuckle. "Now, what I wish you will do for me"—and she leaned nearer Susan and spoke under cover of her delicate painted fan—"is to present me to that devastatingly attractive Captain Camberley. I hear you're neighbors in the country. I've seen him at the occasional event, but I've never yet succeeded in throwing myself in his way, and he is so very . . . well, not regularly handsome, of course, but his eyes are beautiful, and his shoulders are magnificent. There is something about him."

"I agree," Susan said with a tender glance at the gentleman in question, who continued to stand detached from the rest of the party. He seemed actually to be giving his attention to the stage. "He is a most unusual man. I would be glad to present you, Lady Emily, when I catch his eye."

Lady Emily shot her new friend a look, as though gauging her for possible rivalry, then laughed merrily. "How lucky you are indeed, my dear, to have captured my brother. The matrimonial prize of the Season, and it has barely begun. We are still in Lent, weeks away from the opening of Almack's. Oh, Miss Danvers, you will be the envy of every young woman in the *ton*."

"I thought your brother was said to be a rather rakish

individual, and I know that young ladies aren't encouraged to attach themselves to rakes,'' Susan said quietly when there was a break in Lady Emily's raptures.

"Oh, his wickedness! It is merely for show,'' Lady Emily informed Susan with a wink, "and it would hardly be a mark in his disfavor were it true. Look at Lord Byron!''

"So my mother says. But if everyone knows Lord Semerton isn't really a devilish rake, why does he keep the reputation?''

"Every Season must have its wicked lord. My brother is filling a necessary place in society.''

"Quite so.'' Susan had not taken her eyes off Captain Camberley during this odd conversation, and now she finally succeeded in capturing his notice. She beckoned him with a smile, wishing privately that she might call him to her for another purpose than to introduce him to a pretty young woman.

A whisper from Susan brought Lady Emily to full attention, a project which involved a slight straightening of shoulders to show off an attractive bosom. A soulful look appeared as though by appointment in the sharp eyes.

Susan performed the introductions, hoping she did not have the order wrong when she presented Camberley to Lady Emily.

"Sir, I have been perishing to meet you this age,'' Lady Emily said. She was evidently not one to beat about the bush. "I dare swear I've read every account of your thrilling victories. You are my hero as well as the vulgar public's, you know.''

Though she did not know why, Susan considered this line of talk to be particularly ill-judged in light of Captain Camberley's exchange with the maimed sailor outside the theater. Lady Emily, of course, could have no way of knowing this, and no way to interpret the flash of annoyance which crossed Camberley's face as he bent to murmur the proper thing over her hand. Susan had no indication that Lady Emily had ever noticed the fleeting look; the young lady was occupied in surveying the house as though to see who was near enough to observe her triumph of capturing Camberley.

"Lady Emily, you do me too much honor,'' Camberley said.

"Heavens, no, sir. Who could do that? Tell me, have you met my grandmother Lady Semerton?''

Hearing her name mentioned, the old lady turned from her

conversation with a bored-looking Lord Fitzalbin and surveyed the captain. "Ah! The sailor. Emily has been panting to meet you, young man. And no wonder! You're a handsome devil."

"I am really nothing out of the common way, ma'am," Camberley protested. "You ladies will turn my head with your kind compliments."

For the first time, Susan thought with a private smile of self-congratulation, she had not been one of the ones to fawn on him! She had had to bite her tongue to keep from assuring him that he was indeed most handsome.

The dowager intrigued Susan mightily. Used to her sober grandmother, she was interested to observe another style of eccentricity. Lady Semerton seemed to have taken the privilege of age to heart and to consider herself now allowed to say all the things she might have left unspoken in her earlier years. Susan was speechless with admiration as she listened to the lady banter with Camberley.

She couldn't avoid noticing that the irritating Lord Fitzalbin, who was still hovering about her mother, paused in his flirting from time to time to cast a raking stare at the daughter. Though chagrined by this situation, Susan had no idea what to do about it. The smallest notice from such an unpleasant and worldly older man alarmed her more than the raptures of Lord Semerton.

Suddenly Lady Semerton turned to Susan. "You, gel. You write to your grandmother, I hope?"

Had a discussion of young people's lazy letter-writing habits been going on without her noticing it? Susan resolutely stopped worrying over Fitzalbin and allowed that she did write to Mrs. Palmer.

"Then send her a message from me," Lady Semerton said with a smile which revealed a fine set of false teeth. "Tell her Livvy calls her a naughty minx."

"Livvy? Minx?" Susan repeated blankly.

Captain Camberley was looking on and appeared much amused. "Do I take it that your ladyship's name is Olivia, and that your ladyship and Mrs. Palmer are old friends?" he asked.

Lady Semerton nodded.

"Oh. I understand." Susan smiled. "Has Grandmama not

kept up her correspondence with you, ma'am? I'm sorry. She lives much out of the world, you know.''

"I know, more's the pity, and the world is the loser," Lady Semerton said. "We were at the seminary together, you know, centuries ago it seems now. And we were both in France as young matrons, back in the days when the court there was something to see. How I do miss Cassandra's jokes and odd starts. She has no excuse for not writing, miss. She knows that if there is nothing going on in her life I would be quite as happy to read a fabrication."

Susan exchanged a laughing glance with Captain Camberley. "I'll tell her so, ma'am," she promised.

"See you do. Now, from the way this large boy is poking me in the ribs, I gather he wishes to talk to the new beauty. There you go, Buxford. Camberley, your arm. I've a fancy to promenade in the gallery."

Lady Semerton, assisted perforce by the captain, moved out of the box. Lady Emily lost no time in seizing her brother's arm and tugging on it. Semerton was drawn from his soulful gaping at Susan to escort his sister into the corridor too, "for," as the crafty young lady said, "you know Grandmama will wish our company."

Susan knew whose company Lady Emily wished, but she said nothing, merely sat quietly wondering what would happen next. She had been at the opera for a long time already, and she had yet to hear any songs.

Buxford, with a sheepish smile, sat down in the place next to Susan.

"Dashed good of the old . . . of her ladyship to leave us some time for a word together, ma'am," the young man said with a hearty grin. "I won't waste it, either. What do you say to riding out in the park early some morning?"

This sounded vastly more amusing than Lady Delafort's habit of lying abed until midday. Susan had spent some lonely mornings rattling around the house, for country hours had followed her to town despite her best efforts at lolling.

"But would such a thing be proper? I riding out with you, I mean to say."

"Couldn't be more so," the young viscount assured her. "I'll mount you, and there'll be a groom of mine along. One of yours too, if her ladyship desires it. Can't be too careful with you young things. I know that much." He laughed heartily.

"Well, with Mama's permission, I would love to go with you," Susan decided. Buxford was a most congenial young man after all. She was sorry she had thought him bluff and loud. And she was certain that the proprieties could be maintained from the back of a horse—two horses. That, and the fact that Buxford's manner toward her was more comradely than loverlike, made her quite look forward to the outing.

Lady Emily, when she returned, was most eager to secure Susan's company as well. The two young women made plans to shop and read and stroll together. Susan suspected that Lady Emily had been pressured by her brother into cultivating Miss Danvers' company, but a friend on any terms was something nearly new in her experience, and she was glad to promise Lady Emily almost anything.

"Now, if I may, Lady Emily, I would like to ask something of you," Susan said when her new friend had noted every date they planned to be together into her pocketbook with a little gold pencil she kept for that purpose. Her ladyship was much more organized than Susan would have imagined a young lady of fashion could be.

"Anything, my dearest creature," Lady Emily said with the extravagance of new affection.

"Well, it is this." Susan straightened her shoulders. "Why does nobody listen to the opera? From the snatches I've been able to make out, it would seem to be very beautiful, but it is so hard to hear over everyone's talking."

Lady Emily's peal of laughter served to add to the general noise. "My dearest Miss Danvers, one doesn't come to the opera for that! At least, so long as no famous singer is appearing. Nobody is to sing tonight, you know." She had to raise her voice a little, for one of the nobodies were engaged in an impassioned aria at the moment. "And so we come mostly to see each other and to chat. A famous system, is it not, for we have a chance to get into our best and newest things and have charming conversations, and the singers are paid whether they are listened to or no."

"I see," Susan said, though she really did not. She didn't want to display her ignorance overmuch, though, and so kept silent.

Captain Camberley had not yet come back to the box with Lady Semerton, and so Susan made a real effort to concentrate on something besides the hope of his return. Lady Emily, too, seemed to be eyeing the door to the box in rapt attention. Susan smiled at this and turned away. Her gaze lit upon her mother, in intimate conversation with Lord Fitzalbin and another middle-aged gentleman who had entered the box. The latter gentleman was a stranger, but he looked sophisticated and foreign and quite besotted with Lady Delafort.

Susan frowned in concern. How could she possibly ask Mama about these men? She couldn't believe that her mother was playing her father false, yet she hardly knew what to make of the fact that a new courtier appeared at every turn. Perhaps it was only that the Delaforts had been separated for fifteen years, and Mama was such a social creature that she had filled her lonely hours with the company of handsome and complimentary gentlemen. What attractive woman would not? Susan asked herself defensively.

But was there any more to it? And how could a daughter who was nearly a stranger find out something of such an intimate nature?

Susan knew that she wasn't even supposed to know of such things. There it was, though: she had been corrupted insofar as she knew that infidelity existed. The mere perusal of the London papers with their crim. con. stories had done her that favor. She had no idea, though, how such encounters were organized—Mama's social calendar was so very full already!— nor how a third party might detect a liaison.

The foreign man, apparently overcome, dared to press a kiss upon Lady Delafort's alabaster brow. Susan heard him style her mother's forehead thus and thought the expression would have been trite had it not been uttered in an attractive accent. Then the foreigner left the box, and Susan was mightily relieved.

Other men came and went, some of them as bold as the foreigner, others much more formal in their admiration. Still, there were so many! Susan cast ever-more-worried glances at Lady Delafort as the evening wore on. She even forgot to notice the ever-more-speculative glances which that sophisticated rake Lord Fitzalbin was casting at her inexperienced self.

7

"I have solved our problems, brother," Drusilla Camberley said on a note of triumph. "Your man of business may dawdle all he wants now, for I've beat him to it and found us a house."

Captain Camberley looked up from the *Morning Post*. "Have you, my dear?" he asked in a vague voice. "I wasn't aware we had problems. As to a house—"

"We will save no end of money," Drusilla went on, as though her brother had not spoken. "And though a hotel is most comfortable, it isn't quite the thing."

Vincent's eyes opened wide. "Since when do you care what 'the thing' is or is not?" He looked around their sitting room, the best Grillon's provided. "You can't persuade me that this isn't a most comfortable situation. I haven't thought it important to pester poor McCall about the house you wanted."

"I simply wish to entertain," Drusilla explained. "I have encountered some most congenial people at the lectures on ancient Rome, and I can hardly ask them to a soirée at a glorified inn."

This did make some sense. Vincent nodded soberly, wondering if he had been unfair to his sister by not hurrying the project of getting into proper lodgings.

"Tell me about this house," he said, striving for an air of avid interest.

"It is in Mount Street and most compact. There are only a couple of bedrooms, a drawing room and dining room downstairs which can be opened into one room for parties, and a small study"—here she gave him a steely look which he interpreted to mean that she would not easily give up the study for herself, and that he might keep a desk in his bedroom—"and of course the servants' quarters and the offices."

"And you've seen it? It's ready for our occupation?"

"I haven't seen it, but it is quite ready. I heard of the house through Mrs. Jones, whose sister was going to rent it to bring out her daughter this Season. As it happens, some children's illnesses will keep the family in the country, and so the place will be empty. They're letting it for a modest figure."

"I see. Well, it sounds most suitable. And I perceive from your determined looks that we'll be moving there in any case. Do you not think it better to see over the house before doing so, though?"

Drusilla tossed her head. "The details of domestic arrangements don't interest either one of us. Why should we pretend they do? I, for one, shall pack my things this morning and go to the house when my trunks do. I have no interest in running back and forth along the streets unless I have some practical reason."

"Very well." Vincent shrugged and went back to his paper. He did not care where he lived in London. Drusilla had made a habit of staying with her bluestocking friend Mrs. Jones during her visit to the metropolis, with Vincent putting up at a hotel and taking his dinners at the United Service Club in Albemarle Street. But for this sojourn they had both made Grillon's their headquarters, since Drusilla disliked to trespass upon her friend's good nature for an extended stay.

Drusilla had her theories about Vincent's purposes in town. She wasn't fool enough to believe that her brother was remaining for her sake, and fully expected Vincent to stay in London as long as the Season lasted—or as long as Miss Danvers remained in town. Drusilla meant to keep an eye on her twin and, not incidentally, to do so from an address at which Miss Danvers might call.

She said nothing of this to her brother, of course. Without further ado, they settled to move house later that day. Vincent's man would pack his traps for him, Drusilla said, waving her brother away on his morning ride.

"And that dog will be much more comfortable in lodgings of our own," she said, pointing to Neptune. The large beast eyed her with the worshipful longing of unrequited affection. He was nearly full-grown, and Drusilla secretly thought he was a monster.

"True, sister. Very true." And Vincent, accompanied by his loyal pet, left for his customary ride in the park.

Susan met Viscount Buxford in front of her mother's house. The large young man stood pacing back and forth while a groom held two horses, one a massive black gelding so many hands high that Susan assumed it must be Buxford's. This horse was snorting and leaping as though it had not been easily reconciled to the monastic life. The other was a gentle-looking mare that did not appear ruffled even in such ill-mannered company.

Susan was attired in the riding habit which had just come home from the modiste's. A bottle-green velvet, the ensemble was trimmed in black braid and accented by a small black hat. Susan's curly hair had been tamed into coils done up at the back of her head, her usual style for riding, but with an extra fashionable flair since her new abigail had done it, rather than Susan herself struggling with it.

Mama had easily given permission for the ride with Buxford. "How sweet! The boy was smitten on first sight," had been her estimation of the situation. "You may go riding wherever and whenever you wish, my dear, upon condition that you don't wake me up to see you off. People ride at such impossible hours."

And so Susan was assured that riding with Lord Buxford would be most proper and of all things unexceptionable, though she hoped that Mama was wrong and that Buxford wasn't smitten, but only friendly, as his manner seemed to indicate.

"Happy to see you, Miss Danvers, and looking so fit," Buxford said. His huge hands reached out, and before Susan knew it, he was throwing her up into the mare's saddle.

Left winded by this precipitate greeting, Susan caught her breath while Buxford mounted the testy gelding. "Your horse seems very spirited," she said.

"The devil's much gentler than he used to be," Buxford replied in a confidential tone. "Lucifer is his name. Yours is Lady."

Susan found her mare to be aptly styled. The small horse didn't put a hoof wrong during the long trek from Portland Place to the gates of Hyde Park. Lucifer, on the other hand, was spooked by everything from a piece of paper blowing across the cobbles to a lavender-woman crying out her wares. Luckily, the hour was early, and the beast did not have to contend with crowds, Buxford informed his fair companion.

The riders entered the park with a sigh of relief from both Buxford and his steed. "Let's let 'em out, what do you say, Miss Danvers?" he called. He was obliged to raise his voice, for he had sprung Lucifer before finishing the sentence, and the massive black was already across a stretch of turf.

Susan exchanged glances with Buxford's groom and ambled after. She couldn't seem to coax Lady to more than a walk.

After Lucifer had made a few mad dashes into the distance and back, Buxford considered his horse tame enough for social riding and sidled in next to Susan. "Well, now, Miss Danvers," he said with an admiring look at a certain portion of her anatomy, "you've quite a seat. Could be I was gulled into thinking you wouldn't be a bruising rider. Can't say it was my fault; you look like you'd scare easy. What do you say, though? Would you wish to try a nag with more spirit than that one next time we come out?"

"With more spirit than Lady?" Susan cast a rueful look at her placid mare. "I hate to be disloyal to such a good horse, but I wouldn't mind at all. That is . . . Will we be coming out again?" She suddenly wished she had not put the question that way, for she didn't know if she indeed wanted to have any further dealings with Lord Buxford. She was ignorant of society as yet, but surely letting him monopolize her time would expose them both to wild speculations that Susan already knew she had no intention of fulfilling.

Her confusion seemed to please the viscount and, indeed, to fasten Susan with the duty of another ride with him.

"Don't be so modest, m'dear," Buxford answered with a wide smile. "I'd be charmed. I'll find you the best horse in my stables. Famous that you're a spirited girl after all. And I'm dashed glad to see that fellow Semerton ain't got his hooks into you."

Susan chose to ignore part of the last comment, but welcomed the chance to talk about another man. "You and the earl are friends, I believe?"

"Since schooldays. Can't say I've any use for the fellow now he's set on making tongues wag. Had a lot of us down to his abbey, he did, and was all for making us think it was a dashed orgy. The clunch."

Susan was sure that her eyes must be filling her face. "But it was no orgy?" she asked, trying for a matter-of-fact tone. She supposed that this was a sophisticated conversation and that she ought to try to hold up her end. Besides, she was curious as anything.

"Not a bit of it," the viscount replied cheerfully. "Dug up a pair of old skulls somewhere to drink out of, and had bats fly through the place—nothing new. Byron thought of it all first, and what is more, the women Semerton had hired for the event . . . Deuce take it! Your pardon, madam." Buxford suddenly turned brick-red and clamped his mouth shut.

Susan felt herself blushing too. She could think of nothing to respond and believed it was better that way.

"The thing is, Miss Danvers, I feel a sort of freedom in talking to you that makes me come out with things better left unsaid," Buxford said after a lengthy pause. "You're a deuced comfortable sort of girl."

"Thank you." Susan spoke pleasantly, but her alarm was mounting. This young man was of no interest to her, and she simply couldn't be as important to him as he pretended. Not on such short acquaintance.

The two walked their horses through an alley lined by trees newly in leaf, Lucifer held barely in check by the strong hands of his rider, Lady plodding along as calmly as a dray horse. Susan worried over the young man's opinion of her and wished she could think of a polite way to suggest an immediate return home. As she scanned the path ahead of her, searching for a conversational diversion, she saw a massive black animal cross her path.

Buxford laughed. "A piece of luck that wasn't a cat. A black dog crossing one's path must mean good luck. What, Miss Danvers?" He wiggled his carroty eyebrows at Susan in an annoyingly intimate fashion.

"That's a friend of mine," Susan said in heartfelt gratitude. "That is, the dog belongs to Captain Camberley, if I'm not much mistaken. He must be about if Neptune is. Oh, yes, there he is!'' she cried out in excitement.

When Buxford thought of her exclamation, Susan was never to know, but she hoped she hadn't sounded quite as desperate as she felt. "Captain Camberley!'' she called.

That very gentleman, on a good-looking roan, rode toward them. Buxford nodded pleasantly, and the captain smiled and touched his hat. "Miss Danvers! I didn't know you rode.''

"Oh, yes. Riding is quite a rustic pastime, you know,'' Susan answered, dimpling. "I always kept to my grandmother's land in the country, so naturally you wouldn't have seen me.''

"Just so. I'm very glad to see you now. Will you do me the honor to dismount for a moment? Neptune, as you see, is most eager to greet you properly.'' He gestured to the dog, who was indeed dancing around Susan's horse with the lolling tongue of a would-be lover.

Lady took no exception to Neptune's antics. Buxford's Lucifer, however, reared back mightily. The burly viscount kept his seat, but not without a great deal of effort. When he had calmed his horse, both the others congratulated him, and Camberley apologized for his dog's behavior.

"Ain't the cur's fault,'' Buxford panted, swinging down from Lucifer's broad back. "Demmed screw will spook at anything. Let me help you dismount, Miss Danvers.''

The viscount moved toward Susan, but Camberley was before him. The captain's horse was quite near Susan's, and he was on the ground in an instant and holding out his arms to the young lady.

Her heart began to beat at a quite unnecessary speed. She and the captain would embrace—in front of Buxford, and in an unobjectionable manner—but they would embrace all the same.

In an instant it was over. Susan barely had time to revel in the caress of Camberley's hands around her waist, the strong muscles of his arms when she placed her hands on his sleeves. When he set her on the ground she looked up helplessly, wishing she were more mistress of herself. As it was, she greatly feared he would be able to guess her feelings.

Camberley smiled at her and removed his hands in what Susan

fancied was a lingering way. She turned away in confusion and concentrated on Neptune, who was panting for his turn in her attentions. She caressed the dog while Buxford stood by making remarks about the beast's size and wondering if Camberley had had him weighed.

The captain allowed that he had not.

"Let's take him down to Jackson's, then, and set him on the scales if they will hold such a brute. Ought to, for they hold me. I'd like to get a few of my friends in on it. We'll have a wager on how many stone. Famous sport."

Camberley acquiesced politely, but Susan could see that he was not as excited by the idea as was Buxford. The two men made an appointment to meet in Bond Street later in the day.

"Do you often make wagers on such matters, sir?" Susan asked Buxford in innocent curiosity. "It seems an odd way to pass one's time."

"Does it, now? But then, you're a female," Buxford said, looking as curiously at Susan as she was regarding him.

Captain Camberley coughed; at least Susan thought he coughed, though, upon reflection, she could swear he had really been trying to smother a laugh.

Buxford seemed inclined to carry on the conversation forever, but a cry from his groom, who held the horses and had just narrowly averted being drawn under Lucifer's hooves, reminded him of his duty. "Mustn't leave the horses standing. We'll take our leave, Camberley."

Susan was immeasurably disappointed to be one of a pair with Buxford instead of Camberley. She feared her sadness would be apparent on her face and schooled herself into what she trusted was a bland expression.

To add to her discomfort, Buxford made sure that he was the one who threw her back onto her horse. She couldn't help a look of dismay as the large young viscount clasped her. Her eyes met Camberley's at that moment, and she turned away in confusion. She was much afraid that the captain knew whom she would have chosen to put her on her horse.

He bowed and mounted his own steed, whistling Neptune to him. "My sister sends her compliments and hopes you will wait on her soon in our new house in Mount Street," he said with a sudden smile before he went on his way.

"Oh! Tell her, sir, that I would be delighted," Susan exclaimed with too much enthusiasm; or so she thought an instant after the words were out of her mouth. She looked after the captain, exasperated at her own lack of sophistication.

"That chap don't play fair. He doubtless knows I've got no sisters," Buxford grumbled. "Well, Miss Danvers, I should get you home. The traffic will be heavy going back, and Lucifer—"

"Say no more, my lord," Susan said in easy agreement. "I believe we have stayed out quite long enough."

Captain Camberley and his attendant canine paused hesitantly at the door of Gentleman Jackson's rooms in Old Bond Street.

The proprietor was sparring, gloved, with a young fellow whose dogged determination and shining eyes proclaimed this bout to be one of the highlights of his introduction to town. A couple of other youthful gentlemen were watching the match in respectful silence.

But the real center of interest was the scale at one corner of the room. Buxford sat on it, surrounded by a loudly conversing crowd of men Camberley immediately characterized as sporting young blockheads. On catching the captain's eye, Buxford sprang to his feet, scattering weights.

"Captain Camberley! Daresay you know everyone here." The young viscount repeated about eight names, of which the only one Camberley recognized was Lord Semerton's.

A pause in the action ensued as one of Jackson's assistants, eyeing Neptune, went off to fetch more weights. The dog looked wary as the crowd of strange gentlemen speculated on his ability to sit on the scale and commenced to reckon his probable size. Wagers were made on both issues.

Camberley stood apart, soothing the dog in low tones. He happened to be near Buxford and Semerton. When a familiar name reached his ears, he realized that they, unlike their fellows, were not discussing the prospective wager—at least, if it was a wager they were talking of, it did not involve Neptune.

"You haven't a chance, Bux," Semerton said with a knowing smile. "I plan a series of poems on her charms. What female could resist that? Miss Danvers has been raised in the country. Rustic maidens are the very sort to be overwhelmed by such attention from me."

Buxford snorted. "Poetry! Poor stuff. The lady's been raised in the country, as you say. She'll be hungry for adventures. And those I can give her."

"Adventures." Semerton repeated the word thoughtfully. "A country miss, seen nothing of life—you might have something, friend Bux."

"Brighter than I look," Buxford acknowledged modestly.

Camberley cleared his throat. "You gentlemen are discussing Miss Danvers, I believe—forgive me, I couldn't help overhearing. She is my neighbor, you know, down in Surrey."

"Is that so?" Semerton asked. He stood, arms folded, in a consciously poetic attitude and surveyed the captain with appraising eyes.

"Say, that's right, you are her neighbor," Buxford said enthusiastically. "What do you think, Captain? Miss Danvers would like to see a bit of town life, wouldn't she, after being brought up in the country?"

"Why, my lord, she is in town for the Season. She sees life every day." The captain paused. "You weren't thinking of anything improper, I hope? Miss Danvers would never agree."

"Proper, is she?" Semerton said with a scowl. "Can't have learned it from her mother."

Camberley took a deep breath while he considered whether his one outing with Lady Delafort bound him to protect her from such comments. Deciding it did not, he confined himself to saying, "Lady Delafort must command the respect of us all, Lord Semerton."

"I worship the lady," Semerton cried, flushing hotly. "Have for over a year."

"Quite," the captain said with a cold nod.

"We all of us worship Lady Delafort," Buxford put in. "She's the fashion."

"And her daughter?" Camberley let the question hang in the air while the young gentlemen puzzled over what to say.

"Miss Danvers is . . . is . . ." Buxford began.

"A goddess! A nymph, I'm calling her in my latest poem. She is the only creature who could have succeeded in making us bitter rivals," Semerton said, indicating his friend the viscount. "Known each other for years, haven't we, Bux?"

Buxford nodded soberly.

"Bitter rivals, are you?" Camberley asked, a smile breaking out on his sober face.

"We wagered on the matter not two minutes ago," Lord Buxford confirmed.

Camberley had been afraid of this. He hoped the matter of such a vulgar bet would not come to Miss Danvers' ears. "Don't trouble the young lady, my lords," he said, trying to make his words brotherly.

"Not a bit of it," Semerton said with his self-styled wicked grin. He turned to Buxford. "And I must thank you for that idea about adventure, man. You may be correct. Miss Danvers strikes me as a spirited creature. I'll soon think of the very way to amuse her."

"I say!" Buxford's face reddened, and an argument was narrowly averted by the arrival of Jackson's man with the weights.

Attention turned to Camberley and the canine of the hour. The captain's manner was pensive as he brought Neptune forward. The young rivals' words promised a certain amount of annoyance for Miss Danvers. He must hope she would be above any clever tricks to win her attention.

Remembering the gleam of intelligence in her fine eyes, Camberley would have been ready to place his money on Susan in any wager on that matter.

Later in the day, Vincent and his furry companion ran up the steps of a certain number in Mount Street. Buxford had won the wager on Neptune's size, and the captain feared that the large and talkative viscount was now his friend for life.

Lifting the knocker of the new abode, Camberley observed the house front with a critical eye. Everything was as it should be. The bricks were a little blackened, perhaps, but one could expect no more from let lodgings. The door and window frames were painted a gleaming white. The paint looked quite new.

Too new. Vincent put a finger to the door. It came away wet.

Childhood memories assailed him. He was surprised to feel a certain nostalgia at the memory of his father chasing him from the drawing room, which had been liberally decorated with the prints of a child's chubby hands when the pinafore-clad Vincent found a new-painted hall at his disposal.

Fond memories or no, Vincent hoped that the freshly painted door was an aberration. He had never liked living in confusion.

A butler answered his knock.

The captain had already considered that removing to their own house would entail hiring a staff and had assumed Drusilla had the task in hand. He hadn't expected this servant to be familiar to him, and thus it took a second look for him to recognize the man.

"Charles! What are you doing here?" He smiled at the butler employed at Royce Park. He had been so pleased with the man's work that he planned to employ him at the Yorkshire estate once the repairs were complete and he went to take up residence.

"Miss Camberley sent for a skeleton staff, as she pleased to call it, sir. We all came at once."

"And when did you receive her message?"

"Not above three days ago, sir."

And she had seen fit to tell her brother about the move only on the morning it would take place! With a word or two of pleasure and welcome, and an amused shake of the head at Drusilla's absentmindedness, Vincent proceeded into the entry and nearly tripped over a ladder and dropcloth.

"Only the ceiling, sir," Charles said in distress, seeing his master's exasperated look.

"The ceiling? Who has been hired, Michelangelo? One does not simply put a coat of white over *that.*" And Vincent made a gesture of disdain in the direction of the baroque design of cupids and pasture which decorated the entryway ceiling.

"A poor young artist, I believe, sir, whom Miss Camberley wished to patronize. She sent for him as soon as she got into the house this morning. The gentleman had to step away after examining the job to purchase the right paint."

Vincent could see that the cupids indeed had chips missing

from their rounded limbs, but he called that no excuse. Who looked at a ceiling? "Which way is the drawing room or the library or any room where I can be by myself?" he asked in a dangerously calm voice.

"There is no library, Captain, and Miss Camberley has moved into the study, but the dining parlor and the drawing room are both to be reached through that set of doors." Charles spoke quickly, and Vincent was reminded that the repair of the entryway ceiling was no more his butler's fault than his own.

"It's only one ceiling," he said, nodding pleasantly to Charles. He strode into the drawing room.

Holland covers! And at work in one corner of the room was a carpenter.

The man rose, rubbing his hands on his apron and touching his cap. "Beg pardon, sir, but the lady says to get right on with putting in these moldings. Says her brother can't stand an unfinished house, and no one had never put floor moldings in here when it was built. Cheap work, I calls it."

"I am the lady's brother," Vincent said in a tight voice. "You may continue."

He walked through an interior set of doors into what he supposed was the dining room. Here he found Drusilla at the table. With pen and paper before her, she was engaged in taking an inventory of the Wedgwood-ware in the cabinet and ranged along the sideboard.

She met Vincent's gaze unflinchingly.

"Now, brother, I know how you dislike being on the spot when work is being done, but these minor little repairs simply couldn't wait."

Vincent looked as though steam might issue forth from his ears at any moment, Drusilla noted in dismay. She hadn't thought the projects would bother him that much.

He stared at her for a long, uncomfortable moment. Then he let out a hearty laugh.

"Oh, Vincent, I'm so glad you're not angry. Everything ought to be shipshape, as you would say, within the week," Drusilla said in relieved tones.

Vincent nodded. "Which room upstairs am I to make my own, or will I know it by the laborers sawing the bed apart?"

Drusilla was about to answer when she suddenly stared past her brother in horror.

Vincent glanced behind him, then burst out into loud peals of laughter that brought Charles running in from the hall.

All three looked at Neptune, who had followed Vincent into the drawing room. Behind the door huge nile-green foot-tracks marked his passage.

"Oh, heavens, can he have been upstairs already?" Drusilla moaned. "I'm having the trim in my bedroom redone."

Vincent's hilarity was winding down. "Perhaps," he said through chuckles, "we are meant to confront our childhood bogies after all. Laughter, they say, can cure many old resentments."

"I have none of those," Drusilla claimed, putting up her chin. "I liked our old house, and I know I'll be disappointed when I go back to Yorkshire and see it quite finished off. Paint and sawdust and holland covers mean home to me."

"Dear sister, I wish it were so with me," Vincent said, shaking his head. "One of the great pleasures of shipboard life was the nice, finished state of my cabin."

"Perhaps you've simply never realized how you love construction," Drusilla said. "Look how happy you are now. Isn't he, Charles?"

"To be sure, madam. Shall I take up the carpets now and set the maids to scrubbing the floor?"

"If you please."

Drusilla and Vincent exchanged glances and erupted into chuckles together while Charles left the room in his best family-retainer style.

"I hope he can get out of our earshot before he starts laughing," Drusilla said. "It would embarrass him so to be caught out."

Vincent gave his sister a stern look. "Tell me you didn't arrange this disaster to cheer me."

"What? It was your dog—"

"Never mind," Vincent said with a sigh. "If you're determined that I shall be happier living in confusion, so be it.

What with the carpets and the scrubbing, I should be in a fever of ecstasy by nightfall.''

"Dear brother," Drusilla said with a pleased smile. "I knew you would look on the bright side."

8

Susan had seen Monsieur Beauclair before.

She was called to the drawing room one morning, there to find that the carpets had been rolled back and the furniture shifted to leave a large open space in the middle of the floor.

The arrangement of the room was the first thing Susan noticed. The second was that her mama and a gentleman were standing in close conversation near the hearth.

"There you are, my dear." Lady Delafort beamed. She was clad in the finest morning costume Susan had ever seen or imagined, a drift of white cambric and precious lace and a whisper of cap that did not in any way age its wearer. "Monsieur Beauclair, this is my sweet daughter, Miss Danvers."

Susan had no more than curtsied to the dancing master before she recognized him as the foreign gentleman who had been so intimately polite to her mother that night at the opera. He was a swarthy individual, robustly built and with a bold eye. Or perhaps it was only a critical eye, Susan thought, noticing that the Frenchman's gaze was trained on her curtsy.

"Tolerably graceful, madame." Monsieur Beauclair turned to Lady Delafort.

"I am most relieved to hear it, sir. We have years of work to make up, you know, for my poor daughter has been left unknowing of all the little airs and graces that distinguish a lady. She has already come on famously under my tutelage, but I cannot do everything, can I?" Her ladyship's laugh trilled forth, and Susan squirmed in discomfort.

"Madame, I am here to be at your service, as I would be in more than this," Beauclair declared with a sweeping bow. "And now, mademoiselle"—he turned to Susan—"shall we begin with that reverence you but now were so charming as to give me? Repeat, if you please."

Susan spent the morning in curtsying and walking across the room, making her muslin skirts drift and swirl about under the dancing master's instructions. Lady Delafort soon went away, leaving Susan's abigail, Hortense, as chaperon.

Susan had thought it quite exciting when her mother hired a Frenchwoman to be her personal maid. Though Lady Delafort and Angleton were devoted to each other, her ladyship had for some time wished for an infusion of continental taste in her domestic arrangements, and her daughter's need for a dresser gave her an excellent excuse. The two abigails had been caring for the ladies of the house interchangeably and in a brittle harmony based on Angleton's superiority and the younger Hortense's obsequiousness.

Though Hortense was quiet and not inclined to be friendly, she did not rebuff Susan's hesitant attempts to practice French with her, though she answered only with critical nods. Susan was as comfortable with the dark, sharp-eyed young woman as she would have been with any maid—for she was used to doing for herself. Grandmama Palmer's notions of simplicity and natural savagery did not run to waiting women.

Susan expected that the two French people would converse in their native tongue in front of her. She knew that they were connected somehow, for Hortense had come to the house on Beauclair's recommendation. But the *émigrés* remained silent during Susan's lessons. Perhaps, Susan considered, they were too courteous to speak in French before one who could not follow the conversation.

Monsieur Beauclair came to the house each morning for a couple of weeks, and Susan soon graduated from curtsying and walking to dancing. The dancing master produced a wiry, long-haired young assistant who played the pianoforte for Miss Danvers' efforts. She conquered country dances, waltzes, and even the minuet, though her mother told her privately that there was little chance she would be called upon to display that old-fashioned dance.

"If you were coming out with your own ball, it would be a vastly different thing, my dear," Mama said one morning after the lessons, with a wise nod. "Sometimes it passes for a custom for the young lady of the house to dance a minuet with her partner while all the other ball guests look on."

"Heavens," Susan cried, truly alarmed at such a prospect.

"Sweet girl. I know you're shy," Lady Delafort said with an affectionate smile. "That is why I think I'm doing my best for you by simply taking you round to all the parties this Season. Delafort House has no ballroom, and I couldn't face asking Papa's old uncle to open his mausoleum in Hanover Square."

"Certainly not." Susan had never met the great-uncle in question and quailed at the idea of asking a stranger to provide so much.

"I will give a dress party for you here, naturally, in a month or so, when London is full of company and I can count on a press of people. I can't endure to give a party that is not a squeeze." Lady Delafort rattled on, expanding upon her favorite subject.

"Mama," Susan said into the middle of this, "are you and Monsieur Beauclair very good friends?"

"What? Why, child"—and Lady Delafort began to fan herself violently with the copy of *La Belle Assemblée* that she held in one hand—"how should I be friends with a dancing master? He is most congenial, to be sure, but one knows where to draw the line."

"Good."

Lady Delafort's head lifted at the sincere note in her daughter's voice. "Why should this be any of your concern?" she asked in a cold voice.

Susan was mortified and hastened to beg her mother's pardon. She could not put her discomfort into words. Perhaps she was only imagining that Monsieur Beauclair had designs upon her mother. What sorts of designs, she could not imagine, for Mama was a safely married lady; but there was something in the Frenchman's gallantries as intimate as anything Mama ever accepted from her better-born gentlemen friends, and Susan could not like it.

Her mama was regarding her in suspicion from eyes which still startled Susan, it was so like looking in a mirror to see them.

"You see more than you appear to, Susan," Lady Delafort

said. Her gaze was now appraising. "I wonder if you will really be surprised at Fitzalbin's suit."

Susan felt herself sinking into a mire of sophistication. "Good heavens, Mama! Lord Fitzalbin? But you are a married lady!"

Lady Delafort shook her head in weary amusement. "Dear child, he has asked me for you."

Susan was stunned into silence. Try though she did, she could remember no instance of particularity in the bald and aging lord's attentions to herself. He was her mother's evident admirer. Surely the one or two raking stares with which Susan had noticed Fitzalbin favor her figure did not count as a courtship.

"You *are* surprised." Lady Delafort gave her daughter's hand a pat.

Susan found her voice. "You didn't . . . you could not have agreed, Mama."

"I said that I would put the matter to you, and also that nothing could be done without Lord Delafort's consent. Fitz is one of those interminable bachelors who has finally taken it into his head to procreate. He wishes a young and conformable wife who will be happy in the country while he is in town. Someone with a large dowry. You, my Susan, fit all his qualifications." Lady Delafort paused, frowning. "And I have sharp eyes. I have reason to believe he finds your person pleasing."

Those leers had not gone unnoticed, then. Susan shivered in revulsion. To be so suddenly confronted with what the London Season was really about quite appalled her. Such men as Lord Fitzalbin shopped the balls and parties looking for dowries and for innocent and undemanding personalities. Trying to be objective about the matter, Susan had to admit that on the surface she was suitable on all counts. And it was impossible for her to tell, from her mother's description of this particular situation, whether Lady Delafort was pleased or no. Apparently Fitzalbin had put the proposition in such a way as not to rouse her jealousy. Could it be that she approved?

Susan spoke hesitantly. "And does his lordship mean to speak to me?"

"Oh, no. He sees no occasion for that, and I assuredly do

not. If I were you, dear, I would choose Semerton or Buxford. Both are richer than Fitz; and he is only a baron, the lowest title of the three. And there is something more." Lady Delafort sighed and looked at Susan quite kindly. "Your papa and I were near in age, you know, and how very happy we were."

Susan was silent, first to calculate the difference in age between herself and Captain Camberley and to decide that it was a trifling matter, then to think over her mother's revelation.

Would she be embarrassed to see Fitzalbin again? She expected so, though she realized that she should suffer no such agonies. According to Mama, Fitzalbin had made a pragmatic decision that had little, if anything, to do with the young woman involved.

As the thoughtful silence lengthened, Lady Delafort briskly turned the subject. "Now, let's ring for a nuncheon and think over what you'll wear to your first ball. Monsieur Beauclair says you're ready."

"Does he?" No matter what she might think of the Frenchman's motives, Susan had come to respect him as a teacher and an arbiter of taste. He was a Parisian, after all, and she had been discovering that anything or anyone from Paris had the last word in matters of fashion. She brightened at knowledge of his approval.

"Not only that," Lady Delafort said with a knowing smile, "but Lord Semerton and Lord Buxford have both begged me to intercede with you to give them the first dance. There! Does that not flatter you?"

"No, it doesn't," Susan said. "I don't like either one, Mama."

"You don't?" Lady Delafort clearly couldn't believe this. "Lord Buxford may be a little rough-edged, dearest, but he has a great fortune and will have an earldom someday. As for Semerton, he is an earl already, and so devastatingly handsome."

"I don't like them," Susan repeated.

"Then you are willing to consider Fitz?" Lady Delafort's eyes opened wide in evident surprise.

"Oh, no." Susan's instant response had enough of loathing

in it to assure her mother that she had no intention of setting up as a rival for Lord Fitzalbin's attention.

"Ah, me," Lady Delafort said with a wave of one hand. "Your young heart will know itself in time, mark my words. Now, what do you say to the shell-pink underskirt with the gold-spotted gauze?"

"Why not?" Susan said, sighing. Her heart, she feared, had already been deposited in the keeping of someone who did not figure on Mama's list of eligibles.

"Because we must select something to complement my new *grande toilette,* silly child, and I'm not persuaded that is the choice," Lady Delafort said. A touch of impatience could be remarked in her voice. "Fashion is hard work, Susan. Never forget that."

"I don't expect I shall," Susan murmured, thinking, not of clothes, but of the one man she would wish to lead her down her first dance. Would she even see Captain Camberley at the Farnsworths' ball? She hadn't glimpsed him in days, for he had been busily settling into his house, so she supposed, and Mama had made Susan stay in to practice dancing and hadn't been receiving her usual callers.

Perhaps, Susan thought in sudden inspiration, that was why Mama had seemed to favor Monsieur Beauclair. She hadn't had anyone else to take her mind off her loneliness.

The idea made Susan feel better than had any other disclosures of the morning.

"Lady Delafort. Miss Danvers," boomed the liveried retainer at the head of a sweeping marble staircase. A richly carpeted path led down into a crowded ballroom.

Lady Delafort nodded to her daughter and gave her a slight surreptitious wink.

Susan was heartened. She lifted her chin, smiled, and concentrated on following her mother's gorgeous figure down the daunting flight of steps while praying that she would not disgrace herself by tripping.

At the bottom of the staircase a mob of men immediately surrounded Lady Delafort, and, by extension, Susan. The

younger lady cast one frightened look at her newly declared
middle-aged lover, Fitzalbin; but he, as usual, had eyes for no
one but her mother.

Susan's concentration on this new and difficult aspect of her
life was broken as Buxford and Semerton both headed for her.
Buxford was the winner. Semerton's fatal pause to greet Lady
Delafort meant that his large friend was the lucky man to dance
first with Susan.

She had been well-schooled in the proprieties of the assembly
and understood that if she refused a gentleman for any other
reason than a previous engagement, she would be condemned
to sit out the rest of the evening on the sidelines. In other words,
she was not allowed to say no to all the men in the room simply
because they were not Captain Camberley.

She tried to hide her lack of enthusiasm as she accepted
Buxford's arm for the country dance that was just striking up.

Monsieur Beauclair's suave voice counting out the beats, his
hands leading her, and his critical dark eyes watching every
movement of her feet and torso: all these were before Susan
as she curtsied to Lord Buxford. She tried her best to banish
the Frenchman's image and concentrate on the company of the
red-haired viscount, who looked exceptionally debonair in a
well-fitted suit of evening clothes.

Buxford had no conversation during the dance. Beauclair had
assured Susan that polite exchanges of pleasantries about the
weather, the ball, and such banal subjects were the common
course. But Susan soon came to understand that Buxford was
unable to converse simply because he was beset by a complete
lack of rhythm and had to compensate by watching his feet and
the other dancers at all times.

Even this was not an infallible system. "Oh!" Susan let out
a surprised yelp of pain when Buxford's large pump connected
with her satin slipper.

"Your pardon, ma'am," Buxford panted, wiping his forehead
with a handkerchief as they separated again—thank goodness,
thought Susan—to turn with the adjacent couple.

By the time the dance was over, Susan's feet had been targeted
at least three times, quite a record considering how seldom
partners actually met in that particular set of figures. She

managed to smile brilliantly when Buxford delivered her to her mother's chair. Mama had been dancing too, but her partner had already brought her to a comfortable place on the sidelines.

"So you were the winner, Lord Buxford," Lady Delafort said with a tinkling laugh and a look of gentle raillery. "Lord Semerton must be quite put out."

"I hope so, ma'am," Buxford said, bowing. "I say, Miss Danvers, as you can see, I'm not worth much on the floor. What do you say to a drive in my phaeton tomorrow? It's high-perch, the latest thing, and I've a proper pair of springers to pull it. You'll have a fine time, a spirited girl like you. It will be an adventure."

Susan wondered where he had gotten the idea that she was spirited. "I . . ." She hesitated, not wishing to accept the invitation, yet not certain how to turn it down.

"You have my permission," Lady Delafort said graciously. "I trust you mean the fashionable hour, Buxford. My daughter won't be rising much before that tomorrow, for I believe all this unaccustomed dancing will fatigue her."

"Whatever time you say, my lady," Buxford declared.

The two settled between them that he would collect Susan at the hour of five. Susan sat by during this conversation feeling quite left out.

"Mama," she murmured into her mother's ear once Buxford had taken his leave, "I really don't like him. I don't wish to drive with him."

"Oh, nonsense, my dear, nothing could be more proper or more flattering to you. Lord Buxford is quite the catch."

"But . . ." Susan's words trailed away, for evidently her mother didn't understand any more than Grandmama had that Susan's desires would not always coincide with the proper thing.

Semerton appeared before her, devastating and darkly handsome, smiling with a wicked glint in his eye. "A waltz, Lady Delafort." He addressed Susan's mother. "May I dare? Miss Danvers will be the talk of the town."

"She certainly would. Do go away, dear Semerton, until another country dance is played. I can't have Susan waltzing before she appears at Almack's, and well you know it."

Semerton flashed another grin, claimed the dance following,

and went off. Susan watched him away and eventually saw him lead another young lady onto the floor.

She wished she had more acquaintance in London. Although she enjoyed watching the dancers perform the heady waltz, she would have found the pastime much more amusing had she known some of the performers. From afar she glimpsed Lady Emily whirling about the room in the arms of a tall man in regimentals. But she recognized no one else.

Then a familiar and most welcome face was before her. Captain Camberley bowed quite properly to Lady Delafort, then turned to Susan. "I know better than to ask you to waltz, ma'am, but would you grant me the dance after this?"

"Oh." Susan was absolutely crestfallen and did not have to look to her mother for the proper response. "I regret I am engaged, sir. I . . . Oh, dear, I knew how it would be," she added in vexation.

Camberley didn't seem to mind this honest disappointment. "The dance following that, then?"

"That is the supper dance, sir, and I believe my daughter is already promised to Lord Buxford for supper," Lady Delafort put in.

"You are mistaken, Mama. His lordship said nothing about supper," Susan said. "I shall be pleased to dance with you, Captain Camberley."

"Capital." With another bow, the captain went on his way.

Susan watched his tall figure disappear into the crowd and looked after him wistfully.

"Really, my dear," her mother said in a low voice accompanied by the whisper of plumes. "You need not be quite so obvious. The captain is not an eligible, you know. You must get over this ridiculous infatuation."

"What ridiculous infatuation?" Susan said with dignity. She avoided her mother's eyes. "I merely like him. He is my friend."

"At your age, Susan, you need more than friends. You must have suitors. Set your mind on that, if you please. And while we wait out this dance—absurd that Fitz shouldn't have been here to claim his promise, but perhaps he thought I must sit by you—simply enjoy the pretty picture we make. Every eye is on us.''

Susan chanced a little shudder at this and noticed that she and her mother were indeed the targets of more than a casual interest. They were dressed to complement each other, Lady Delafort in rose sarcenet of a daring cut, worn with her diamonds, and Susan in a pretty silk mull of soft, soft blue with some subtle trimmings of rose embroidery. A small sapphire pendant adorned Susan's neck. She had never felt more attractive; at least she had felt so at home in front of the glass, before she had seen the many finely dressed women at this ball.

Captain Camberley had evidently approved, she thought. She couldn't have mistaken the look in his fine brown eyes for anything but admiration.

When the waltz ended, Susan was shocked to see Lady Emily Forbes, in forthright yellow, whirl to a stop near Susan's chair and come forward with a quick step, dismissing her military partner without a second glance.

''How do you do, Lady Delafort, Miss Danvers?'' Lady Emily said pleasantly. ''Is this chair by you vacant? Famous. I hate to return to Grandmama at present, for she's sitting with the greatest lot of old cats, and I'm sure they would rather talk about me when I'm not present.''

Susan laughed. ''You're quite welcome, Lady Emily. I'm sorry I wasn't able to fulfill our engagement to go to the bookshops.''

''I have made her dance every day like some poor enchanted princess in a fairy tale,'' Lady Delafort put in with a smile. ''You will forgive my daughter, Lady Emily, for you know she had to study her steps in order to make her appearance tonight.''

''You hadn't had dance at the seminary or with your governess?'' Lady Emily asked in surprise.

''I never went to school or had a governess.''

''Well, you missed nothing but a few dance steps,'' Lady Emily said, fluttering her fan. ''I vow my governess never taught me a thing, and as for my years at Miss Towers' in Kensington! I got nothing out of them but a headache from reading so many novels in a bad light.'' She leaned forward confidentially. ''We had to hide our lamps under the bedclothes. It's a wonder we weren't all burned in our beds, leaving a Season's worth of singed young ladies.'' She laughed merrily.

"Only fancy.'' Susan was round-eyed at the thought of both such literary richness and such daring.

"What do you say to tomorrow for the bookshop visit?'' Lady Emily asked briskly.

"She is going driving with Lord Buxford,'' Lady Delafort said.

"With Buxy! Imagine that. Do you like him, Miss Danvers?'' Susan was modestly silent.

Lady Emily took this to mean what it in fact did mean. "Well, no one could,'' she said, ignoring Lady Delafort's desperate signals. "He is all very well as a companion, but I can't feature falling in love with a man whose hair is that impossible color. Or who trips one up quite so many times in the dance. Sweet young man, for all of that. We are neighbors in the country, you know. Childhood friends. Buxy and my brother and I did everything together as children.''

"How delightful.'' Susan's words were sincere, for she had much missed the companionship of others during her own childhood.

Lady Delafort's attention was drawn off at this moment by the arrival of her partner for the next dance. "As my daughter is also spoken for, I am safe in saying yes,'' she said serenely to a handsome gentleman Susan had never seen before. "Look for me back here, dear girl.''

"Now that your mother is gone,'' Lady Emily said, leaning close, "do tell me what I must do to capture the attention of your friend Camberley. He is the most vexing man. I've smiled and winked like anything this evening, but he hasn't asked me for a dance.''

"I happen to know he's free for the next—at least I think so,'' Susan said. "What a pity women can't ask men.''

"Oh, can't they?'' And Lady Emily, with a martial light in her eyes, rose from the chair.

"Lady Emily! You can't mean you will seek him out and ask him,'' Susan said, her eyes wide.

"It can't hurt. I am done being subtle with that man. Oh,

good, here is my brother, so I won't be leaving you alone. If you see Sir Edwin Post, my next partner, do tell him I'm off somewhere repairing my hem, there's a dear.''

As she watched Lady Emily sail away, Susan was serene in the knowledge that she wouldn't know Sir Edwin Post if she tripped over him, and would thus not be obliged to lie to any gentleman concerning Lady Emily's present occupation. Lady Emily disappeared behind a pillar, to Susan's disappointment. She would have been extremely interested to see whether the bold young lady would actually have the courage to approach Captain Camberley.

"Shall we be away to the floor, dearest Miss Danvers?" Lord Semerton said in Susan's ear, reminding her that she had vexations and obligations aplenty and had no need to concern herself with Lady Emily's. "You look lovely as a rare flower this evening. A rose, perhaps, or an orchid. I shall write a sonnet to your gown tomorrow."

Susan would have compared her blue gown to a hyacinth, if anything, but she accepted the compliment without cavil and allowed herself to be led onto the floor.

"Dear Captain Camberley," Lady Emily said in a breathless voice, catching her quarry by the sleeve, "you may do me the greatest favor if you only will."

"Anything, ma'am," the captain said politely. "Miss . . ."

Lady Emily looked quite put out that he hadn't even remembered her name from their introduction at the opera. She had seen him quite often since, but never to speak to. "Emily Forbes," she said shortly.

"Ah, yes. Lady Emily. Lord Semerton's sister. Do forgive me," Camberley said with every appearance of contrition. "You were saying I might aid you in some way?"

"Yes, you may save me from dancing with the greatest beast in nature. I have refused him, I have run away from him, but still he believes that I must dance with him. The only solution is for me to partner some other gentleman, and at once. I saw you and knew you would be so kind. You navy men are such true gentlemen, such saints compared to the vulgar persons who pass for quality at such a wretched gathering as this."

As the ball was one of the acknowledged social highlights of the opening Season, Camberley didn't know quite what to make of such a statement, nor of such an odd young lady, but he did the gentlemanly thing. He offered his arm.

"Miss Danvers suggested I ask you to help me," Lady Emily confided as they went to the floor. "She is a good friend of yours, I know."

"She told you that?" Camberley asked with a spark of interest.

"Heavens, no, the dear creature is too modest to say any such thing. But I know you are neighbors and all that. There's something about bumping around together on adjacent acres that creates a bond. I'm quite close to my own neighbors at my brother's abbey."

Camberley found himself laughing. Lady Emily Forbes was an odd young lady, but she did have a way with words. Now, if only she would make the time fly until his dance with Susan Danvers, he would call himself a lucky man.

Susan's eventual dance with Camberley was all she had dreamed. She shivered when their hands touched, fancying that she could feel a tension of a delightful sort even through gloves. She smiled at him with confidence and had the satisfaction of seeing him smile back. How different this from her painful experience with Buxford—her right small toe still pained her slightly—or her other dance with Semerton. The young earl wasn't clumsy in the least; the discomfort she had felt had been of another sort, as his lordship tried to impress her with his wicked ways by telling many a naughty anecdote.

But the dance with Vincent Camberley made up for a multitude of former vexations. And to cap her happiness, it seemed to be the convention for partners in the dance before supper to remain so through the meal. Susan gladly accepted the captain's arm, and they went off to look for her mother.

In the center of a knot of men they found her. Lady Delafort waved gaily, though she did look askance at Captain Camberley, and Susan and her escort ended up at one small corner of a table crowded with Lady Delafort's admirers.

"Is your sister here tonight?" Susan asked, picking at the

plate of delicacies the captain had procured for her and keeping her eyes on them. Lord Fitzalbin, at Lady Delafort's side, had just given Susan a meaningful glance which she meant to ignore.

"No. Drusilla doesn't care for dancing."

"Oh. Well, I look forward to calling upon Miss Camberley soon. Have you settled into your new house—in Mount Street, isn't it?"

"We have," Camberley said. He proceeded to regale Susan with the story of the dog Neptune's introduction to the house— and a certain bucket of paint.

Susan laughed until the tears came, and forgot all about Lord Fitzalbin. "I do hope the floor was easy to clean," she said with a final chuckle.

"I believe so. I know nothing of floors. My sister and I have been laughing together over the resemblance of this experience to our childhood. Our father, you know, was fixing up our family estate from the day of our birth to the day of his death. We weren't rich, worse luck. He simply had to take what measures he could, as he could, for I'm afraid he tore up the place before realizing his income wouldn't serve to put it back together. Our childhood was unusual, to say the least. We must have been seven before we realized that holland covers weren't the typical decorations for a drawing room."

"I never thought before that your childhood was anything but comfortable and normal." She had thought the same about everyone of her class, she realized, never considering that everyone might have his or her little dissatisfactions, little abnormalities that had made childhood less than a perfect dream. She grew serious as she considered this new idea.

"Your experiences and mine were probably much alike," Camberley was saying. "We were both raised simply, in the country."

"But you no doubt had teachers," Susan said with a sigh. "I was brought up to be ignorant. I didn't like it much, for naturally children pick up many things, and I knew that I wasn't being allowed the standard amount of knowledge."

"Did this frustrate you, my dear?" Camberley asked. For the first time it occurred to him that perhaps Drusilla's efforts at educating Miss Danvers hadn't been totally unwelcome. He knew Drusilla was a confirmed meddler, but Miss Danvers might possibly have wished someone would meddle.

"Yes," Susan said with a shrug. "But I've gotten over it. Mama has had someone teach me to dance, and my new friend Lady Emily is going to take me to a bookshop." Her eyes sparkled. "Fancy that! A whole shop where they sell nothing but books. And Mama has given me a generous allowance; I'll be able to buy."

"Your friend Lady Emily," he said thoughtfully. "She is a most lively young lady. Do you know her well?"

"We met very recently," Susan answered. "And her brother is . . . that is, he used to like Mama, but he has switched to me. I must suppose I have a very large dowry."

"Do you mean to suggest, Miss Danvers, that a young man could be interested in you for reasons other than your own charming self?" Captain Camberley asked in a teasing tone.

"Well . . . yes." Susan was surprised at the question; the answer seemed self-evident to her, knowing what she was coming to know of London and the matches made here.

Camberley laughed. "I assure you it cannot be. Can you seriously lack confidence in your powers of attraction?"

"Yes."

The statement was so blunt, so matter-of-fact, that Camberley was somewhat taken aback. Well-dowered, was she? He wished she hadn't told him that particular tidbit. He hadn't given the matter a thought, but he would hate to have her think, someday, that his interest in her had anything to do with finances.

He looked at her, feeling tenderness well up in him at the mere sight of her pure profile, her straight shoulders and clear, honest gaze. Her eyes, which often looked greenish, were turned to blue by her lovely gown. She was an enchanting creature, but young and inexperienced, far too fine for a worn-out sea captain who carried about with him the baggage of the late war. She would find someone better—not Semerton, please God, but someone more suited to her sparkling youth. At thirty, though his physique could not be faulted and his mind was keen, though his prize money had given him economic strength and his bloodlines, if not noble, were at least ancient, Camberley thought himself a poor specimen, a glum older man.

It meant little to his confidence that Lady Emily Forbes had thrown herself at him. These young misses who were fascinated by the armed forces were not new in his experience, though Lady Emily's boldness was.

"Sir," Susan said hesitantly, "you're staring at me. Is something amiss?"

"No, my dear," he said with another sigh. "Your grandmother raised you to be a child of nature. I was simply sitting here thinking that nature will inevitably take its course this Season, and wishing the lucky man well."

"Oh." Susan looked worried, and for the second time in as many minutes her escort was seized by an inconvenient desire to have her in his arms. "Shall we talk of something else, sir?" she asked brightly. "Tell me about Neptune. Did his paws come clean?"

Camberley had to laugh at how well, but how originally, his dear Miss Danvers was mastering the art of conversation.

9

Susan's stomach lurched as the phaeton took a particularly sharp turn at breakneck speed. "I do believe, Lord Buxford, that I should return home. We've been driving for an hour." She shouted to be heard over the sound of the horses, and the wind, and the hammering of her own heart.

"Just a turn more, ma'am," Lord Buxford shouted back. A grin stretched across his ruddy face, he boomed, "You've a rare spirit, Miss Danvers. Knew you would. We'll go riding tomorrow, then. What do you say?"

Susan, keeping her voice raised, mentioned an engagement with Lady Emily.

"Oh, Em won't mind," Buxford said. "She'd break an appointment with you in a moment if there was a gentleman in the question."

Susan had no reason to doubt it, but she still wanted to keep her agreement with Lady Emily. She earnestly stated her wish to be true to her word.

"The day after, then," Buxford said.

Susan frowned. This young man simply wouldn't be put off. She hadn't been amused by his dancing, and she was even less enthralled by his driving. Somehow he had gotten into his brain the maggoty notion that she was an adventurous girl—perhaps because she had admitted that his plodding mare Lady was a little tame. And he evidently thought that the way to impress a girl of spirit was nearly to overturn her in the highest perched vehicle Susan had ever seen in her life—which had been somewhat sheltered, to be sure.

While they flew across the park, out of it, around Hyde Park Corner where stagecoaches and drays traveled only inches from Susan's skirts, and back into the park again on one wheel, Buxford kept up a running conversation about speed records he had broken, races he had run, and the talents of his various cattle.

The first thing Susan wished to do when she reached home was to kiss the ground, then search her head for gray hairs. For the future, she would tell Lord Buxford she was indisposed, or became sick in carriages, or something—anything. Unfortunate that he should be so set on having her ride with him.

She looked forward to this with a touch of pleasure despite the company she would be forced to endure. She would like to ride a horse more vigorous than Lady, and, as her mother kept no saddle horses in town, she must depend upon a gentleman's goodness for a mount. Buxford was the only man who had expressed the wish to ride with her.

Susan noticed that they were near the gate of the park. "Will you take me back now, Lord Buxford?" she shouted. "Please?"

"Whatever you say, Miss Danvers. Your wish is my command, you know," her companion cried out, and he obligingly wheeled the phaeton about and drove through the gate.

Once in Park Lane, he was forced to slow owing to a press of heavy traffic, and Susan was able to catch her breath. Hesitantly she touched a hand to her new bonnet. She had adored the little curling feathers on this particular confection. Were they still there?

They were, and Susan was wearing the same bonnet next day when she and Lady Emily set out at long last for their trip to the bookshop. Susan had never before imagined being able to buy a book of her own. There was a library in Delafort House, but the tomes were all dry and antiquated. Neither Papa nor Mama was a great reader, and the library hadn't been added to in their time. Susan longed to read something less improving than bound sets of sermons. She confided this wish to Lady Emily.

"Is that so?" the young lady said with a wicked grin. "That settles it. I was going to take you to Hatchard's in Piccadilly, but now no place but Leadenhall Street will do." She pulled the checkstring and put her head out the window to speak to the coachman.

Susan was mystified more than a little by this comment. "What is in Leadenhall Street, Lady Emily? Another bookshop?"

"More than a bookshop, my dear. An institution." And Lady Emily reclined in her seat in a blissful attitude. She brought out the little pocketbook which Susan had noticed before and opened it to a certain page. "Yes, these will do for a start." Susan could glimpse a list of some sort. Taking out a pencil, Lady Emily scribbled something on the page, frowned in thought, scribbled some more. "We cannot go in, of course," she said. "We'll go back to Hatchard's after this little jaunt so that you may purchase what you will. But you simply must see this place. Such fun."

"Where are we going?"

"Into the City, my dear. Into the City." Lady Emily looked up from her project to smile. "You must look about you, for we'll be passing through more of London than you've seen, I make no doubt."

Susan had indeed seen nothing more than the narrowest precincts of Mayfair since her arrival in town. Lady Emily was evidently determined to make their destination a mystery, but now and then she pointed out to Susan some sight or the name of a street, few of which were familiar to a girl from the country.

Much time passed, and Lady Emily, still puzzling over her pocketbook list, said casually, "There to our right, dear, you may be able to glimpse part of the Tower."

"The Tower of London?" Susan bounced to that side of the Semerton chaise in her excitement.

Her friend laughed good-naturedly. "But of course. I could hardly charge you to look out the window at the Tower of North America, if there is such a thing. And we are nearly to Leadenhall Street." She still seemed much amused that her companion did not grasp the significance of this.

Susan found out soon enough. The Semerton town chariot pulled up behind another magnificent carriage by the side of a large and busy shop. "A circulating library," she cried, seeing ladies and gentlemen of all classes walking in with stacks of books while others came out under similar loads. Lady Emily's coach was only one in a long line of smart vehicles. Liveried footmen carried books to the carriages and handed them in.

"And we may not go in? Why not?" Susan sighed in disappointment.

"Too mixed, my dear," Lady Emily replied with a twinkle in her eye. "We're quite out of the West End, you know. One might meet with anybody within those portals. For that, my dear Miss Danvers, is the lending library of the Minerva Press."

Her pronouncement didn't have the expected effect on Susan. She merely nodded.

"You don't know," Lady Emily said in awe. Her hazel eyes grew round. "You really don't know."

Susan admitted to her ignorance.

"Well, I shall explain it to you while we wait," Lady Emily promised, patting Susan's hand. Then she ripped out of her pocketbook the page she had been working on and called out the carriage window to her footman.

The retainer in the Semerton livery disappeared into the shop, jostling along with ladies' maids, young men in shabby or fashionable clothing, and other footmen. Susan watched in fascination.

"He is taking my list inside and will return with a supply of novels that will do us for weeks, I assure you," Lady Emily said. "The Minerva Press, my dear Miss Danvers, is the place to obtain all the most lurid productions of the moment. You will adore them."

"Lurid?" Susan asked with interest.

Lady Emily nodded. "I am especially fond of horrid novels, but I've written down some sentimental titles as well, not knowing which ones you will prefer, my dearest creature. Oh!" While she talked, her ladyship had been looking out the window of the chaise. "Isn't that Grandmama's maid? Famous! That way we will have even more titles to choose from. Grandmama is a great reader."

Susan again marveled at the difference between old Lady Semerton and her own rigid grandmother, whom she could not imagine opening a novel. And they had once been great friends! Well, people did change.

"And there is someone I didn't expect to see," Lady Emily murmured. Her bright eyes were still surveying the passersby.

"Who is that?" Susan was determined to show interest, though to say the truth, she hadn't yet been able to tell apart many of her London acquaintance.

Lady Emily's eyes twinkled. "Never you mind, sweet child. Look! Here comes Peter already. The livery does help, doesn't it, to get one quick service? There is the veriest crush inside."

The footman was indeed returning, his face nearly hidden behind the stack of volumes he held. At Lady Emily's request, Peter put all the books onto the squabs beside his mistress.

"Here's richness." Lady Emily handed some marble-backed books to Susan. "I wrote down several of my old favorites for you to try. We have *The Idiot Heiress,* and *Manfroné, or the One-Handed Monk* by Miss Radcliffe—the other Radcliffe— and all five volumes of *Santo Sebastiano* besides these new ones. Oh, my dear, you will be well entertained. Now, tell me, do you prefer horrid novels or sentimental ones?"

Susan did not know. "I believe I'd find them all entertaining," she said, opening a volume at random and finding, to her joy, a whole page of conversation. "I've read only three novels in my life." So abysmal was her ignorance that she had had no idea that there was one Radcliffe, let alone two.

Lady Emily's eyes nearly started out of her head. "Only three novels! My poor dear! Your grandmama was strict, I believe. Which ones were they?"

"*Robinson Crusoe . . .*"

"Fancy! They say that is a very old book indeed, and amazing horrid. It is all about some island, I believe. It has never come in my way. What else?"

"*Tristram Shandy,* which was very entertaining but somewhat strange. I had four volumes, but Mr. Sterne seemed to indicate he would be writing more. That was also a very old novel, of course."

"I have never heard of it," Lady Emily confessed. "What was the third one?" In her eagerness to know about the other girl's reading, she put Susan in mind of Miss Camberley.

From her long-ago conversation with Captain Camberley, Susan had gathered that the French novel she was still trying to finish was a little risqué. But Lady Emily, who had read a book called *The One-Handed Monk,* would surely not turn from her in disgust. "I believe the third novel is translated as *Lessons in Life,*" Susan said. "I haven't gotten far with it. I have but a little French."

"My heavens! *That* book. My dear, you must and shall have the new English translation. I bought it, but I lent my copy to Miss Anderson, the sweetest girl you would care to meet, but she does forget to return things. She also has my mama's *Udolpho.* In any case, that book—the lessons book—has been making the greatest sensation this Season. Only think, it came out before the revolution in France and was most popular there for years. Then some anonymous scholar put it into English. I am excessively grateful to the person, for I haven't been so diverted in simply ages. When Zephyrine marries the foreign prince and goes into the German mountains—oh, delicious!"

Susan hadn't gotten that far in her own labored progress, and she begged Lady Emily not to spoil it for her. Her good-natured friend readily agreed.

"It isn't the sort of book I would be embarrassed to buy, then?" Susan asked timidly.

"By no means. It is no worse than the newest thing by Lord Byron, and much more instructive, for the literary circles are full of it, or so I hear from my friend Lady Margaret Lewis, who is the veriest bluestocking, though she is so wealthy even her squint won't hinder her in the Marriage Mart."

Susan was fascinated by her new friend's long sentences. And the encapsulated portraits of Lady Emily's acquaintance were most amusing. Susan couldn't but wonder how she herself would be described by that volatile lady. "The sweetest thing, and has a good dowry, but incredibly naive," perhaps.

Lady Emily had given the coachman instructions to drive from Leadenhall Street to Piccadilly, and after a rather slow, jolting progress into the West End of London the two young ladies found themselves alighting in front of Hatchard's, the famous bookstore.

Susan was given leave to look around, which she did with the wide eyes and craning neck which marked her as a stranger in town, as Lady Emily teasingly informed her. Then Lady Emily said they were running short of time and briskly asked the clerk for a copy of *Lessons in Life*.

To Susan's secret relief, the man did not look askance or frown at the idea of two young ladies purchasing such a salacious volume. Susan drew forth her purse, but Lady Emily insisted upon making the book her gift to Susan.

"My dear, do allow me the pleasure. Your introduction to London society," Lady Emily said grandly. She told the man to put it on her family's account.

Susan thanked her friend profusely and left the shop clutching the famous novel, which was bound in limp brown calf and stamped with gold. There was only one volume, a startling and welcome contrast to the multivolume stories from the Minerva Library. Susan planned to read this one through before she slept that night.

"Now, my dear, I do hope you can come home to Berkeley Square with me and have a coze with me and Grandmother," Lady Emily said. "Before we do that, though, I would like to make one more stop."

"I'm quite at your disposal, Lady Emily. Mama doesn't expect me back before the dinner hour."

"Capital." Lady Emily was mounting into her coach at this point, and she leaned up and gave the driver instructions for Mount Street.

Susan settled herself opposite her friend, and the two young women perused novels while the carriage bowled through the elegant streets of Mayfair.

They stopped before a white-painted door in a row of pleasant-looking houses. "We will make only a brief call," Lady Emily said, winking at Susan as they descended. "I quite depend upon you to pave my way with this family, my dearest creature. My very happiness is at stake!"

"Who . . . ? What . . . ?" Susan, whose acquaintance in London was so limited, couldn't imagine what her friend was talking about.

"The Camberleys," Lady Emily said in a confidential whisper. Then she hooked her arm through Susan's and resolutely mounted the steps.

"The Camberleys," Susan repeated, astonished.

It was too late to back down, for Lady Emily had lifted the knocker and a servant was opening the door. Miss Camberley was indeed in, said this retainer. She would receive them in the drawing room.

Susan looked about her in avid interest at the place where Captain Camberley actually lived, however temporarily. A neat and compact house. The fittings would naturally have been let with the place, so she would be able to discover nothing special about the Camberleys' taste. Still, she examined every stick of furniture as though the captain had carved it himself.

"Lady Emily Forbes. Miss Danvers," the butler intoned after opening a set of double doors.

Lady Emily breezed through, and Susan followed.

Miss Camberley had been reading. She looked up, and her spectacles fell down her nose. "My word!" was all she said as she hastily put her book away. "You are most welcome, ladies. I am surprised to see you—do forgive my scattered surroundings." She gestured to the area around the sofa, which was indeed littered with needlework, what looked like scholarly tomes, and a desk with close-written notes on a sheet of foolscap. "I do not have many callers. Charles!" She raised her voice, and the butler peeked in. "Refreshments, if you please."

Susan felt a bit embarrassed to have so evidently interrupted Miss Camberley in the midst of her work. She and Lady Emily were seated with the minimum of fuss, though, and their hostess, once her initial shock was past, did seem genuinely glad to see them.

Lady Emily came right to the point. "Is your brother not at home with you, ma'am? Does he spend all his time at the clubs and such, as my own sad scapegrace of a brother is wont to do?"

"Vincent? He finds something to occupy him every day," Miss Camberley said with slightly narrowed eyes. "If not the clubs, then he is always bustling about on some project or other. This week he is finding work for a crippled man who once sailed under him. The man wouldn't take a position with us, you see, and so my brother is determined he shall be provided for in some other way." She spoke with evident pride.

Susan remembered the legless man outside the doors of the opera house and wondered if this was the same person.

"Fancy that," Lady Emily said without interest. "And how do you pass the time, Miss Camberley? We seem to have interrupted you in some important task." She gave her hostess a significant look which Susan wondered at a little.

Drusilla Camberley actually blushed. Susan, who had never thought she would see the collected Miss Camberley change color, was even more curious.

"You can trust us," Lady Emily continued with a wink. "We saw your servant at the library."

Miss Camberley's expression cleared. She smiled at her aristocratic guest. "Your ladyship has caught me out. You do not disapprove of novels, then?"

Susan blinked at this turn in the conversation.

From under the pillow which Miss Camberley had in her lap appeared a marble-backed book. "*Treachery, or the Grave of Antoinette,*" she said with a smile. "I cannot resist a good tale of terror."

"Oh." Susan had never supposed that the studious Miss Camberley looked into novels, whatever the provocation. In her eyes the captain's sister instantly became more human, more approachable.

Miss Camberley said, "Miss Danvers is no doubt shocked. She is used to know of me as a stern schoolmistress, the narrow-minded intellectual who lectured her on which improving books to read."

"Oh, never that, ma'am," Susan protested, only half in earnest.

Lady Emily's laugh rang out, and soon the conversation turned to tales of terror she and her hostess had both enjoyed.

The ladies were beginning on some wine and cakes, delivered by the efficient Charles, when the drawing room door opened to admit Captain Camberley and his canine friend Neptune.

A short pause ensued while Neptune, eyes boggling with joy, renewed his acquaintance with Miss Danvers. Then, after a general laugh, Camberley consented to sit down.

He chose the seat nearest Susan, but he was forced by circumstances to devote himself to Lady Emily, the circumstances being that the latter lady pelted him with questions and never let up except to toss in a line or two about her admiration for naval heroes and for him in particular—as a patriotic young woman, nothing more, to be sure.

"You will turn my brother's head, my lady," Miss Camberley protested, her light eyes very sharp behind her spectacles.

"Oh, no, your brother has evidently a strong understanding and would never let my poor compliments go to his head," Lady Emily said airily. "I express myself only as a grateful subject of his majesty's, you know."

The callers couldn't in politeness remain very much longer, but before they took their leave Lady Emily made it quite clear that she now considered Drusilla Camberley a bosom friend.

"Do say you will come to my grandmother's little party," she urged for the third time. Miss Camberley kept protesting that she never went out.

"I shall think it over," Drusilla finally promised without enthusiasm, exchanging a look with her brother.

Susan stood by during all this. Often her eyes were drawn to Captain Camberley, and she thought she surprised him looking at her a time or two, but all in all it was a most unsatisfying half-hour for her. She did discern a certain significance in the way Captain Camberley lifted her hand to his lips in parting—or she hoped she did.

"That was most successful," Lady Emily said when the young ladies were once more settled into the coach. "Thank you, my dear, for providing the excuse to call. As their neighbor in the country, you would be expected to come to see her, but I had never met the woman before."

"How did you know what their servant looked like? The one whom you saw in Leadenhall Street?" Susan asked curiously.

"I have my ways," Lady Emily returned with a wink. "It doesn't do to be behindhand in these matters, you know. I must marshal all my forces if I'm to have a chance at that man."

"You want him, then. You are sure."

"I will be mightily surprised if I don't get my way," Lady Emily answered with an enigmatic smile. "After all, what is he? A mere man, used to real-world battles. He has none of my expertise in these fields of Mayfair."

Susan couldn't help laughing. Lady Emily, whatever her status as a rival, was so good-natured that one couldn't be cross with her.

They drove to the Semerton house in Berkeley Square—only a step away, Lady Emily proclaimed with satisfaction—while her ladyship speculated over whether the Camberleys would get into Almack's. *He* must be welcome anywhere, of course, but his sister was not much on the social scene, and their birth—what was their birth, anyway?

"I believe they are of an old family in the north," Susan said. "And Miss Camberley is much to be seen in scholarly circles. She mightn't care for Almack's."

"We'll see," Lady Emily said, descending from the carriage before her family's opulent, columned front door.

Susan found herself staring like a country gapeseed at the rococo magnificence of Semerton House, which she sensed was the antithesis of her grandmother's Palladian home.

"When I had my come-out ball," Lady Emily said as they mounted one side of a magnificent double staircase of veined marble, its lacy gilded balustrades intricately designed to incorporate the Semerton crest, "these steps were crowded for hours. Three ladies fainted in the crush. I was thrilled."

They went down a picture-lined gallery ornamented with sculpture and plaster moldings and soon turned into a sitting room which was remarkable for the number of mirrors and the delicate gilded floral designs on walls and ceiling.

On a petit-point-covered sofa sat old Lady Semerton. She looked up from her own Minerva novel at the girls' entrance, and Susan couldn't help smiling as she thought of how similar the circumstances were to what they had found at the Camberleys' simpler dwelling. The marble-backed novels had certainly permeated society.

"You young things must sit down and tell me what you've been doing," her ladyship demanded.

Lady Emily plunged into an account of their morning's work.

"Introducing this fair innocent to the pleasures of the Minerva Press? For shame, Emily. One can see her grandmother ain't brought her up to read novels."

"You are joking, Grandmama," Lady Emily said. "I see a gleam in your eye."

"But Lady Semerton is correct," Susan said. "You'll

remember I told you, Lady Emily, that my grandmother indeed brought me up in that fashion.''

"I meant that Grandmama was joking that I might corrupt you," Lady Emily explained. "I'm certain it can't be done. You have too strong a character, my dear."

Susan was astonished and flattered to find herself so described by such a forceful young woman as Lady Emily.

"I must see Cassandra one day soon," Lady Semerton said, returning to the subject of Susan's grandmother. "Any chance she'll come to town, girl?"

Susan was shocked at the very notion of Grandmama in London and responded as though her ladyship had suggested that Mrs. Palmer might soon find herself on the primrose path.

"Changed, has Cassandra," the old lady said with a shrug. "She was a wild one in our young days, you know."

Susan couldn't but be intrigued. "Was she? Do tell me, ma'am. I know next to nothing of Grandmama's past. She was much in France, I believe?" The question was held out as a lure.

Lady Semerton took it. She settled back in her chair and began as though she were telling a fairy story to children. "Well, before the wars, the more socially inclined amongst us used to spend as much time in Paris as in London," she said with a reminiscent smile. "Delightful, it was. And the poor queen— when I think what happened to her, and she younger than myself! Well, it's a shame, I tell you. Your grandmother and I were among Marie Antoinette's intimates at court for a time. There was much dissipation in those days, an attitude of living for the moment—which turned out to be the truth, the devil take it! Well, we enjoyed it to the full while it lasted. Your grandmother, my dear, was always true to Mr. Palmer. Don't mistake me. The two were quite besotted with each other—the scandal of our set, it was.''

"My grandparents stayed fond of one another," Susan said, smiling in recollection of her dear grandfather.

"But Cassandra was ever a wild thing all the same. The most dangerous scrapes, the silliest jokes. Ah, I do remember the time she set the sheep from the Hameau loose in the Galérie des Glaces—the Hall of Mirrors, I ought to say for the benefit of you chits. She blamed it on the Vicomte de Something—forget his name, but he was an evil fellow with a penchant for practical jokes. And then, of course, there was the book.''

''The book?'' Susan asked.

Lady Semerton's sharp hazel eyes seemed to look back a great distance. ''She had as much French as a Frenchwoman, did Cassandra. She could write it as easily as you and I read the *Times*. She had an idea for a funny novel, a story about what might happen if the French government should fall into disarray. A novel in letters, it was, and very naughty. A courtesan was the main character. Yet it was quite eclipsed by that other thing, *The Dangerous Whatever*—''

''*Les Liaisons Dangéreuses*,'' Lady Emily said a little too quickly. She turned pink, and Susan surmised that this was another French book of doubtful propriety.

''Yes. That one.'' Lady Semerton didn't seem any too concerned over her granddaughter's reading matter.

Susan was all agog that her own Grandmama had written a novel. ''Fancy my grandmother writing anything! Was this novel published, Lady Semerton?''

''To be sure, and had quite a success in its time. Lessons. Something about lessons.'' Her ladyship furrowed an already crinkled brow as she tried to recall more.

''Good heavens,'' Susan said with a gasp.

''Can you really mean that Susan's own grandmother wrote *Lessons in Life*?'' Lady Emily shrieked. ''But how too marvelous.''

As Lady Semerton allowed that that would indeed be the name of the book in translation, Susan interjected quickly, ''Oh, I am sure my grandmother would not want such a thing known, Lady Emily.''

''Indeed not, and you will say nothing, girls, for it was a great secret at the time because of the political things involved. Nobody believed a woman could have written it, though it said so right on the cover. 'A lady of the court,' it said. Shows you what opinion men have of women's minds,'' Lady Semerton said with a snort. ''Now, of course, the politics of the thing are by the way, but Cassandra enjoyed her anonymity. Do keep that in mind, Emily. Dash it, I forgot you were here when I spoke to this girl. Why were you so quiet?"

"I was fascinated by the subject, Grandmother. That book was translated only recently. Didn't you know? Nobody is certain by whom, and it is causing a sensation again, quite as you say it did in your time, but now it is a historical curiosity."

"Historical curiosity indeed! Insulting your old grandmother at every turn. Your tongue runs at both ends, but on this subject it must remain silent. Or else, miss," Lady Semerton said with a stern eye.

Evidently she wielded some real power over her granddaughter, for Lady Emily promised secrecy with the greatest of sincerity and even swore an oath. So, of course, did Susan.

She was amazed. To think that Grandmama, the upright Mrs. Palmer who so disdained society and mistrusted urban ways, had once been "a lady of the court," a female of enough sophistication that a clever novel had been born from her thoughts on French political subjects.

That did explain what the book had been doing in the attic at Pilgrim Court, Susan thought. She had wondered mightily at the time she found it and had carefully spelled out enough of it to recognize it was shocking. She had spent some amused moments in wondering if her late grandfather had hidden it from his stern wife's sight.

"Do tell me more about Grandmama's escapades, my lady," Susan begged. "She will never tell me herself. And how did she turn to Rousseau and simplicity and all that dull business she brought me up on?"

Lady Semerton continued to reminisce. "We all of us admired the noble-savage business, of course. It is quite the thing still in some minds, yet it was nothing new in our time. Cassandra always was one to embrace an idea wholeheartedly once she got it into her head. Perhaps it's that and nothing more." She chuckled. "I simply must see her before we die. What fun to quiz her on her new hobbyhorse!"

Much though the conversation enthralled her, Susan soon reached for her reticule and stood to take her leave. A glance at the statuary clock over the mantelpiece had told her that she ought already to be dressing for dinner. Her new maid, Hortense, was a miracle worker, but even she needed a little time to cast her spells.

Lady Emily also rose, to see Susan down to the carriage. Then the door opened and Lord Semerton walked in.

"They told me downstairs that I was lucky enough to be entertaining the divine Miss Danvers," the young earl said, coming forward to kiss Susan's hand. He didn't seem to notice that she pulled back at his touch. "Do sit down again, my dear. I want to read you a new poem I've but this morning composed. I stopped by at Lady Delafort's, but you weren't in. I read it to your mother, naturally, and she was kind enough to wish me good fortune. I call it 'The Nymph of London.' "

"Oh, heavens, brother," Lady Emily said with a giggle. "Not another one. Is poor Susan to find herself immortalized in your next volume? He has them printed, my dear, by Mr. Murray, who is good enough to say that they sell very well. We have quite a large family, you know."

Semerton cast a baleful look at his sister in response to this hit, but unfurled a piece of paper from his coat pocket and cleared his throat.

Susan knew that there was no escape. She sank down onto a chair and obligingly listened to several stanzas documenting the arrival of a new star in the heavens' firmament, and all the usual things. She would have blushed at the intimacy of some of the lines had not Semerton's womenfolk been good enough to make a joke of the whole thing.

"You must write more," Lady Semerton said at the end of the recital. "This young woman is a special case. If I'm not mistaken, you've written one poem to every new beauty on the scene for two Seasons past, and a handful of the things to Lady Delafort. You must show Miss Danvers she stands out from the crowd by writing a whole volume on her."

Susan was immediately cheered to hear that Semerton hadn't singled her out—so far—for this vexing treatment. She had never thought that having poems dedicated to one would be such an uncomfortable business. But she did wish that Lady Semerton, as well as Lady Emily, was not quite so certain that in Miss Danvers she had finally found the earl's mate.

"We are sisters already," Lady Emily whispered, squeezing

Susan's waist in leave-taking and confirming her worst fears in the process. Lord Semerton insisted upon seeing the young lady to her carriage.

"I hear that rascal Buxford has been riding with you," Semerton said as they descended the noble staircase. "Never could trust the fellow, even at school. Well, I shall soon come even with him. What do you say to a night on the town, chaperoned by my grandmother, of course? Do you like adventure, Miss Danvers? I know you must, for you can't have seen any."

"Well . . ." Susan hardly knew what to say. Here again was that puzzling allusion to her appetite for adventure. Yet she supposed that any outing which included the elderly Lady Semerton would be sedate enough. "What do you mean, my lord?"

"There is something coming up a few nights from now," the earl confided. "Something special which I know you'll like. Say I may surprise you."

Intrigued, Susan assented, provided his grandmother was agreeable. "Will Lady Emily be coming too?"

"Em? Let me think. I believe she already has plans for the evening in question. She mentioned chasing after the Camberley fellow to a certain musical soirée. She's having the hostess ask him. Her plans are all laid."

"Oh." Susan was somewhat crestfallen. Whatever this mysterious event was, Camberley would not be there.

"Never mind," Semerton said, mistaking Susan's looks. "If things work out, you'll have as much of Emily's company as anyone can take."

Susan determinedly ignored his hints and the meaningful leer that went with them. Clutching her now doubly precious copy of *Lessons in Life*, she mounted into the Semerton carriage for the ride to Portland Place.

10

Susan made it her first task to read *Lessons in Life,* a project she accomplished before she put out her candle that night. Morning found her still marveling over the fact that her very own grandmother possessed a sense of humor so vivid, a wit so biting. She longed to write to Pilgrim Court at once, praising the book and its author . . . but of course such an action was impossible.

She was in the morning room, still looking over the little volume, when Bland threw open the doors. "Lord Fitzalbin," he announced.

"Wait, Bland," Susan thrust *Lessons in Life* under a sofa cushion and rose nervously. "My mother is not yet down."

Fitzalbin strode into the room and possessed himself of Susan's hand. "I come to see you, my dear," he said with a lascivious wink.

Susan drew away her hand, placing it for safety behind a fold of her skirt, and cast a dismayed look at the butler. Though properly impassive, Bland seemed to sympathize with her. "My lord, Mama told me that you saw no occasion for meeting with me," she said with her sweetest smile.

The baron's eyes widened slightly at this plain speaking from a green chit. "I assure you, I have her ladyship's permission." He looked significantly at the doors, which Bland was just closing with a snap.

"Oh." Susan's heart sank at what she considered the butler's betrayal—though, upon reflection, he must indeed have had Lady Delafort's permission to leave her daughter in a closed room with a gentleman.

"Miss Danvers, I will keep this simple and to the point," Fitzalbin said.

Susan noticed that he was indeed speaking in a peculiar tone and at a slower speed than usual. She had had this treatment before, chiefly from men, and recognized it as a tribute to her innocence and country-bred simplicity. If it had been possible, her opinion of Fitzalbin would have sunk at that moment.

"Shall we sit down?" he continued, still in that careful tone.

Susan acquiesced, wondering what her mother could be thinking.

Fitzalbin positioned himself close to Susan on the sofa. She gave a sideways glance to the cushion under which reposed *Lessons in Life* as her suitor sat upon it. Luckily the book was thin.

"Miss Danvers, I have asked your mother for your hand, and, provided your father agrees, she sees no impediment to our match."

Susan could not look the baron in the eye. She focused her attention on his high forehead. "Plain speaking indeed, my lord."

"Naturally, Lady Delafort is too delicate, too fine to force her daughter's inclinations," Fitzalbin went on. "I have told her I perfectly comprehend, and, should it come to some sort of vulgar contest between myself and a more favored gentleman, I will withdraw my suit."

"You are most generous, my lord."

He shot her a pleased look. "She has also told me that I am the favored suitor so far. As the first one to address you this Season, I must have some sort of edge on any others."

"Oh." Susan wondered what her mother would be at. Lady Delafort had been teasing her admirer—hadn't she?

"You are a most sensible young woman. I look forward to addressing you again when your father's consent arrives." Lord Fitzalbin committed the reasonable impropriety of patting Susan's knee. Then he rose.

Susan felt her heart swell in relief. This hadn't been an offer—or had it? In any case, it hadn't been nearly so bad as she had feared. "Good day, my lord," she said in a cheerful tone.

And that was all. Fitzalbin left, having mentioned his arrangements with Lady Delafort for the evening. If Susan perceived a more proprietary cast than usual to the lingering look he gave her figure, she thought herself well repaid by the lack of any unwelcome physical contact.

"Fancy Fitz coming to matrimony at last," Lady Delafort said with a shake of her head when Susan described the encounter to her later that morning.

"I'm glad he's so halfhearted about the project," Susan replied. She could not tell, from her mother's light and joking manner, whether this official defection of her ardent suitor was displeasing to her or not. "Why did you tell him he was the favored one so far?"

"Why, because he is the only one to ask for you, of course! Provoking man. Fancy declaring himself so early in the Season. I merely meant to tease him, you know. I don't believe you would take Fitz if others should come to the point."

Susan nodded, not knowing what to say without insulting her mother's taste in admirers.

"That reminds me," Lady Delafort went on. "Do you know, my love, Buxford has told me you've been engaged so often of late that you haven't been able to ride with him. I took the liberty of promising that you would go with him tomorrow."

"Yes, Mama," Susan said, sighing over the difficulties of a young lady's lot.

When she came down in her riding habit on the day of this meeting and saw the steed Buxford had provided for her, she was a little daunted. A chestnut twin to the viscount's restive Lucifer waited impatiently in the street. The beast was to all appearances the most spirited horse in the world aside from its doughty black companion. The massive chestnut reared up, causing several passersby in Portland Place to shrink back and flee. Susan hesitated on the front steps and wondered if she could make some excuse to stay at home.

"Nothing to fear, Miss Danvers. The fellow is simply glad to see you," Buxford said encouragingly. "Shall I toss you up?"

Susan, not liking to be exposed as a coward, allowed her escort to settle her on the horse's back.

Once mounted, she felt immeasurably better. She was a natural horsewoman and really did enjoy the unaccustomed challenge of a mount that was not a weary farm horse or a lady's gentle hack. Her own strength and confidence flowed through her to the beast, and they set out without incident. Susan found herself laughing along with Buxford, and by the time they entered the park she was feeling more in charity with him than she would have dreamed.

Lady Delafort and Buxford had arranged this engagement for the fashionable hour. Susan saw with a little twinge of disappointment the crowds that lined the alleys and roadways on such a fine spring afternoon. How she would have enjoyed a good gallop, but such a treat would be impossible.

She had no sooner formed the thought than her horse, Britannicus, showed himself to be a mind-reader. He took off at a tearing pace.

Susan kept her seat, surprised but still in command. She could hear Buxford behind her, urging her to hold on. She did, sensing that Britannicus must run himself out. She concentrated on dodging the many pedestrians who looked up in terror as her horse pounded by. Then there were the larger targets of carriages. Britannicus narrowly missed a tilbury and sprang past a barouche. Susan's teeth clenched in terror, but she kept her hands light on the reins as she used all her seductive arts to urge her mount to slow.

She could hear little but the gelding's hooves. Then she felt a hand on hers and the horse suddenly reared back, then came to a halt. Susan was nearly unseated. "Lord Buxford, how dare you?" she began angrily, enraged at the silly trick that might have injured them both—though whether she meant his grabbing the reins or providing such a horse in the first place, she did not know.

Then she saw that her rescuer was none other than Captain Camberley and clapped her mouth shut in surprise. She had never before seen such a blaze in the warm brown eyes.

"What the devil do you think you are doing on that monster?" Camberley's voice was harsh. "It is not the fashion to kill yourself, Miss Danvers, merely to impress the *ton* with your horsemanship. Are you quite mad?"

Susan couldn't believe what she was hearing. Did he accuse her of endangering herself merely to cut a dash? Surely nobody

was that stupid. "You . . . you . . . I can manage any horse,"
she snapped, then wondered that she had spoken to the captain
in such a tone.

"Can you indeed? Well, I see the beast is more manageable
now in the wake of his mad scramble to perdition, but I warn
you, Miss Danvers, if I ever see you on him again—"

"Sir," Susan interrupted in a tight voice. "You have no right
to judge my actions nor to direct them."

Camberley looked startled. He stared at her, and his face
changed, softened. "You are absolutely right, ma'am," he said,
touching his hat. "I can claim only the right of friendship."

"Oh." Susan knew a moment of vexation. How could he
always know which words would melt her in an instant? She
was immediately contrite. "I . . . I'm sorry I frightened you,
Captain Camberley."

"From your white cheeks and terror-struck eyes, I don't
believe that I had the worst of that particular scare." The
captain's voice had turned tender, and he reached out to touch
Susan's face.

Britannicus snorted like a chaperon.

"You aren't alone?" Camberley looked about him with
interest. Seeing that a groom in the Delafort livery, mounted
on a middling hack, was just approaching Miss Danvers, he
nodded in approval. "I see you're not. I'll leave you, ma'am,
with apologies for my boldness."

"I . . ." Susan didn't know how to urge him to stay by her.
She supposed that Lord Buxford would arrive at any moment
and explain that the horse she was riding belonged to him. She
both longed for that to happen and hoped it would not, for a
little part of her wished that Captain Camberley *would* think
her an intrepid young lady who had chosen her mount with no
thought of danger. White cheeks and terror-struck eyes, indeed!

"My dear young lady, I never meant to cause you discomfort," Camberley said. "I will hope to see you soon, under
more fortunate circumstances."

He rode away just as Buxford, with curses and mutterings,
arrived on the scene.

Susan listened tamely to her escort's explanation of having
been delayed from rushing to her side by a meeting with a couple

of the fellows with whom he was setting up a race to Richmond Hill. As the viscount's description of this coming delight wore on, Susan wondered what impression Camberley had of her now. Should she hope or fear that he would think her capable of choosing to ride on a questionable horse?

Despite all wiser feelings, she rather leaned toward the wish that he would think that some little sense of adventure lived in her otherwise placid, innocent, and unremarkable nature.

"Capital that Lady Delafort had somewhere else to go this evening," Lord Semerton said to Susan later, as they sat in his carriage. "You and I ought to spend more time alone together."

"Hardly alone," Susan returned with a polite smile, edging away. In the glow provided by the carriage lamps she met the amused eyes of old Lady Semerton, their chaperon for the evening. "Besides, my lord," Susan continued sweetly, "I thought you were an admirer of my mother's. Are you not cast down by her absence?"

"Of course—I will be her slave until I turn up my toes, and all of that." Semerton was visibly torn between his twin duties to compliment the daughter and prove his chivalric fidelity to the mother. "But you, my dear Miss Danvers, are a different matter." He favored her with an intimate smile.

"The boy talks a lot of nonsense, but at bottom he's a good lad," put in Lady Semerton with a wink at Susan.

Susan writhed in embarrassment and decided that silence was the best policy. She did not even speak to ask where they were headed this evening. Lord Semerton had made a show of keeping their destination a mystery, his grandmother was in on the plot, and Susan was mightily curious. She nurtured a hope that Vauxhall would be their goal. Semerton might well think the gardens a daring place to take a young lady. Company there was rather mixed, or so Mama had told Susan, to explain why Vauxhall was not on their list of places to visit.

If not Vauxhall, where? Susan let her imagination be her guide and thought of several places she would also like to go. Astley's Circus. The theater at Sadler's Wells.

Lady Semerton kept up a running conversation about this musicale and that rout, all of which were too dull to be attending anyway. This evening would be a fine change, she asserted.

Susan was about to break down and ask some questions when the chaise rattled to a halt.

"Ah! We're here," Lady Semerton said in satisfaction. She clapped a hand to her reticule. "Yes, I have my purse by me, and it's fat. Famous. Wish me luck, Alistair."

"To be sure, Grandmama." The young earl leapt from the coach to hand the ladies down with a flourish. Susan saw that they were standing before a stately mansion in a square.

"Oh, we *are* going to a party," she said, a little touch of disappointment not quite hidden in her voice.

"A party? No, not quite." Semerton offered her one of his elegantly clad arms, his grandmother the other. The old lady advanced so quickly up the steps of the house that the young people had to scurry to keep up with her.

"Then what is it? Are we visiting some friends of yours?" Susan pursued. Now that she had arrived on the scene, she thought it only prudent to discover what she could. She hoped that she wasn't about to sit down to sup with some relations of Semerton's. Surely he couldn't have gone that far in his blind assumption that they were to be closely connected.

As it happened, he had not. "It is time to make my confession, Miss Danvers," he said once they were in an elegantly appointed entrance hall, with liveried servants rushing forward to take their cloaks. "You have not seen much of life, and I knew you would like this adventure. This is a place where one plays, ma'am."

Susan looked her confusion.

Lady Semerton saw the dazed expression and elaborated, "What my grandson means to say, miss, is that he's brought you to the most notorious hell in St. James."

"Hell?" Susan repeated blankly.

"Gaming," Lady Semerton whispered, leaning close. "A passion of mine, as it happens. Glad to chaperon you anytime you wish to come here. You've no notion how difficult it is to get any of my antiquated friends to set foot in the place."

"Gaming?" Susan wished she was not parroting every word the lady said, but was quite unable to do anything else, so great was her shock. She looked about her, fascinated. Despite all better sentiments, she felt her excitement building. She had never thought to have courage to enter a gaming establishment.

Semerton saw her interest and was satisfied that he had hit upon the very thing to amuse Miss Danvers. Guiding her into one of the rooms, he pointed out the faro table, the E.O. wheel, and the hazard table, where people were throwing dice. Susan had never before seen dice, and Semerton had to whisper to her what they were, but she was more interested to note the rich decoration of the rooms, the thick velvet curtains, the classical paintings of scantily clad figures from mythology. The crowd around her she scarcely remarked for the moment except to note that the gentlemen were of the type one might encounter at any social event.

Lady Semerton deserted them for silver loo, and Semerton continued with Susan on his tour.

"I shall stake you, my dear," he stated grandly. "What do you care to set your hand to?"

"Is there something that requires no skill? I've never been taught to play cards," Susan confessed. "I know. I'll simply watch you, sir. I'm certain I can pick up a great many hints from observing such an expert as you must be."

Semerton was flattered by this, as Susan had hoped, and he did not insist that she play too. Instead he consented to have her stay by his shoulder while he sat down to piquet with a young officer of his acquaintance. Susan, Semerton, and Lieutenant Daniels settled at a small table in one corner of the vast velvet-hung room.

Susan soon grew bored with the progress of the game, for she understood it not at all and could see remarkably little use in a pastime that led to no accomplishment. At least, she considered, eyes glazing over, if one were spinning or doing laundry one would have a pile of progress at labor's end.

She did have to admit that there was a pile marking progress here too, but it was a pile of vouchers in front of the lieutenant. Apparently Lord Semerton's luck was out.

Disliking to scrutinize her escort while he lost, Susan let her gaze travel the room. Liveried waiters were running here and there with trays of drink. The company was mostly male, but aside from that one detail Susan could have fancied herself at any party. Then she looked more closely at the few ladies who graced the assembly. There were some richly dressed elderly females in the style of Lady Semerton, respectable old ladies out on a lark, but the younger ones, without exception, appeared to be very dashing.

Susan began to shift uncomfortably in her chair and to be glad that it was in an out-of-way corner.

She studied the surrounding people with even more discrimination and found much to amuse, but also much to distress her in the gathering. Men were whooping or cursing alternately with each spin of the wheel at the E.O. table; many of the females were allowing their escorts such liberties that Susan was sure the women must be courtesans; everyone was drinking heavily, including her own protector, Semerton. Waiters appeared every five minutes at the young earl's elbow with trays of champagne. Susan made sure the one glass she had accepted stayed full and refused all other offers, though she hadn't been able to resist trying the unfamiliar beverage. She found it charming, no doubt the more so for knowing it to be a drink unsuitable for young ladies in their first Season.

Susan was having her first thoughts of going to Lady Semerton's side and demanding to be taken home when Semerton suddenly looked up from a losing hand, blinked, and seemed to see Susan for the first time in a long while. "We must go," he said in a rush, rising to his feet. "You understand, don't you, Daniels? Mustn't disappoint the lady, and we're late to our next engagement."

The lieutenant looked disgruntled. Susan gathered from the ensuing conversation, communicated in rough undertones in deference to her presence, that Daniels must have been on the point of winning even more from the earl than he had already. But Semerton escaped unscathed, and, taking Susan by the hand—a liberty she excused since it betokened his haste to leave the place—he crossed the room to the loo table.

"Grandmama," he said, pausing behind Lady Semerton's chair, "we must move on."

The old lady turned and looked up incredulously. "Move on? Are you mad, boy? Look at the pile before me! I'm on a winning streak, and here I stay."

Semerton cleared his throat. "But Miss Danvers depends upon you to lend her countenance," he whispered, though he did not need to bother lowering his voice. The other loo players would not have noticed if he had announced a fire.

"Here's my stake," Lady Semerton shouted.

Semerton looked at Susan and moved his shoulders in apology.

"Grandson, you can escort Miss Danvers with the utmost of propriety to her mother's house. It's dark out, for the Lord's sake. Nobody will see you," Lady Semerton said, making shooing motions with her hands.

"Don't you remember the other place we were to go?" Semerton asked with a mysterious glance at Susan.

"Oh, that. See you don't take her there alone, boy. It would be most improper."

"Not improper, surely. No one will know who she is."

"Do as you please, then, lad, but leave me out of it," Lady Semerton said in exasperation. She took another swallow from a glass by her side, and Susan surmised that she, in common with her grandson, had been pleased enough with the quality of the house champagne to take more than one draft.

Susan hardly liked to beg a lady in a disguised condition to see her safely home. She looked out the corner of her eye at Semerton. He was a solid young man at bottom, that she truly believed, and he seemed nowhere near as well-to-go as his grandmother. He would let no harm come to her, and most important, he would take her out of this notorious house.

"Shall we be going, Lord Semerton?" she asked.

"Capital, my dear. Knew you weren't a missish creature," Semerton said in approval. His hand on her back—an attention Susan normally would have been alarmed at, but which made her feel somehow easier in the raucous crowd—they made their way through the opulent rooms and to the entryway, where a footman magically appeared with Susan's light evening cloak.

Someone else jumped to call his lordship's carriage. Before long Susan found herself being shepherded down the steps. A footman walked before her, carrying a torch to light her to the Semerton carriage, and Semerton himself walked protectively behind her.

Susan settled herself gratefully into the chaise, trusting that she would be at home before long. She knew, at any rate, that she was safe and that she would never again let herself be tricked into visiting a gaming hell.

She sighed, looking across to the other seat where Semerton lounged. How very much there was to this business of becoming sophisticated. Would the longed-for day ever come when she would wake up knowing all the signals, all the secrets of this difficult labyrinth called society?

Captain Vincent Camberley happened to be walking through St. James's Square in his way from Pall Mall to Jermyn Street, where he was expected at a supper party. He hoped the gathering would be more entertaining than the musical soirée he had just escaped. He stood back to wait as a party emerged from one of the large mansions, the most notorious gaming establishment in town.

His eyes nearly started out of his head when he recognized the lady being ushered down the steps: a lady with golden-brown hair and a sweet face, a lady who had been figuring in his dreams of late. He blinked, doubting the evidence of his eyes. But it was she.

Lord Semerton was with her. Camberley saw Miss Danvers and the earl mount into the crested Semerton coach.

Though he looked long at the door of the house, no third figure emerged. He must suppose—must hope—that Miss Danvers' chaperon had already been waiting in the coach when she and Semerton came out of the house.

Had her expression been distressed? Camberley had thought it so, in the uneven flaring of the torch, but had not wanted to embarrass her by recognizing her in such a location. A girl's lark, no doubt. The lady had been starved for adventure all her life, as those scapegrace young suitors of hers had once discussed. Who was to blame her if her love of life, of learning about people, led her into some questionable situations?

These arguments were logical and showed sense. Yet Camberley couldn't let the matter stand. Looking around, he spotted a hackney. "If you can keep up with that chaise and go where it goes, my good fellow, it's worth twice your usual rate.'' He climbed into the shabby vehicle.

The coachman protested that he was waiting for somebody within the house.

"Thrice your usual rate," responded Camberley, and was satisfied when the coach moved briskly off into the night.

11

By the time the Semerton coach stopped again, Susan had worked herself up into a nervous state. How could she have been so foolish as to let the earl take her away from her chaperon? Yet how could she have stayed with Lady Semerton in that St. James gaming house? That lady was no doubt in the right of it; Susan would come to no harm, and her reputation would not be stained in the least merely because Semerton escorted her home alone. It was the dark of night. Who would see them or care?

Still, she could not be easy, and she passed the entire drive in silence while Lord Semerton, opposite her, looked off into the distance and smiled as if in expectation of a famous joke.

Susan descended in a distracted manner and didn't even notice until she was standing on the paving stones that they were not in Portland Place. Torchlight blazed, and people were passing by on every side. "Why, this is Covent Garden," she said in astonishment. "The opera house."

Semerton stepped up to her side. "That it is, my dear, and I've something for us to put on."

"What?" His statement was such a *non sequitur* that Susan looked at him as if he had run mad.

The earl signaled to a footman who stood at the door of his coach, and the fellow instantly approached. The man was carrying something. Lengths of cloth; cloaks, Susan guessed. Why should they put on cloaks, though? She already had one on.

"May I?" Semerton took one of the cloaks from the footman and placed it about Susan's shoulders. He pulled a hood up over her head.

Susan examined the garment and realized that it was made of the finest satin. In the light of the streetlamps she could see the color: a vivid peacock blue which she could sense would suit her perfectly. Semerton did have taste, whatever his other, more questionable qualities.

Semerton's footman was placing a black garment of the same type as Susan's over the earl's dark evening coat. When the man finished this task, he made a sign to the other footman on the coach, who jumped down and withdrew some small objects from a pocket of his livery. These were passed to the first footman, who handed them with great ceremony to Semerton.

"The wicked earl attends an opera-house masquerade," Semerton said with a laugh. He took one of the objects and tied it around his head; it proved to be a black mask which covered his eyes. He held out an identical mask to Susan.

What had been a mere suspicion in Susan's mind flowered into anger. "You've brought me to a masquerade at the opera house?" She waved away the proffered mask and touched the fabric of the satin cloak in curiosity. "This must be a domino. Indeed, Lord Semerton"—and she gave the masked earl a severe look—"I may not be up to snuff in many matters, but even I know that proper young ladies don't attend events such as this. The company is altogether too mixed, my mama says."

"I admit it, ma'am, you're correct on all points. And when, I ask you, will you ever have the opportunity again to do something so improper, yet which will do you so little harm? I will be at your side every moment to protect you, and you may see what few young ladies see: all of London society laughing and dancing together. And you'll be incognita, I might add." Semerton's smile bespoke his satisfaction with himself and his brilliant plan. "Admit it, now. Haven't I hit upon the very thing to amuse you and give you something to talk over with the other females? Dozens of whom," he added on a reflective note, "would give their very souls to be standing in your slippers right now."

"My lord, I cannot accustom myself to your conceit," Susan said frankly, turning away. "Take me home now, if you please."

"But the carriage has driven away already, sweet lady," Semerton said in his most persuasive tones. The comment about his conceit he evidently preferred to ignore, but from his pleased tone of voice Susan gathered that he didn't mind being so styled.

Susan whirled about. There was no sign of the Semerton carriage in the confusion at curbside. "How could you, sir?" she cried. How was she to manage now?

"Won't you come in with me for but a look—a masque night is a most intriguing spectacle, I assure you. And you can be safely home within the half-hour, if that is what you desire."

Susan shook her head. "You will forgive me if I don't trust you, my lord." She turned from him, not quite sure what her next move ought to be.

At that moment a large, jostling group of revelers in fantastic garb pressed forward, intent upon entering the opera house at once and not caring if a young lady was arguing with a gentleman on its steps. Susan was most efficiently separated from Semerton. Unfortunately, she was also borne forward with the crowd through the doors of the building.

Somehow she fought her way to a corner and stood there trembling. She had never been in such a press before. She closed her eyes and fought for control. All massed together, all moving in the same direction, the crowd didn't seem to be made up of people, but to be some odd, separate creature.

"Well, Miss Danvers?" Semerton was suddenly beside her again. "You're in; it would seem the fates wish it. Will you allow me to tie on your mask? You really must not be recognized here."

Susan was still weak from the brief contact with the menacing crowd. She stood passive while Semerton tied the mask around her eyes. "Take me away, my lord," she said. "At once."

"But a short walk around. I insist upon that, dear lady," Semerton replied in his suavest tones. "That little upset was most regrettable. You will be better for a look about you. Not at all alarming, is it? A charming sight, in fact." He grasped her elbow.

Susan did look about her, timidly at first, then with more confidence as she saw that the strange beast of her panic was really only a host of odd-looking people. Milling masqueraders crowded lobby and staircase. Susan stared, unable to believe her eyes at some of the characters. Here were Romans, Egyptians, medieval people of every sort, including knights in armor. Modern characters were represented too: men were dressed as counselors, as doctors, as laborers, each of these outfits exaggerated a little when compared to the real thing. The judge's wig, for instance, was humorously oversize.

The ladies in particular drew Susan's attention as the earl led her through the rooms. They made the females at the gaming establishment look modest. Though the characters ranged from country lass to nun to queen, Susan had never seen such low necks, such abandoned behavior, such wild and shrill voices as woman after woman shrieked: with laughter, with surprise at an assault by a forward male, or—less frequently—with outrage at some liberty. Some of them had to be women of the town, Susan thought with a little shiver.

She was dazzled beyond any comment and all resistance as Semerton led her into the stalls. There she could see that the stage had been given over to the dancing.

"Please dance with me, Miss Danvers. A waltz, I beg of you," Semerton said, speaking low. "There are no dragonesses of Almack's here to see you."

Susan came to herself all at once and looked into his eyes. Mistrustful as she was, she couldn't help knowing that she had nothing more than her own irritation to fear from this young man.

"They may not play a waltz," she said.

"Here?" Semerton laughed, a raucous laugh in a more consciously wicked tone than usual. "They play scarcely anything else."

He was right. The lively Highland reel that had been in progress stopped, and the musicians began another tune, this one in a dreamy three-quarter time. The dancers on the stage regrouped, milled about, and then they waltzed.

Susan let Semerton lead her forward to the stage. She was already here, she told herself, no matter how she had come. And she did so long to dance the waltz, though not with Semerton and not in this company.

Despite all better feelings, she looked around in dawning interest. Semerton was right. She was seeing something few young misses had a chance to view. They mounted the steps.

When the earl clasped her much tighter in his arms than Monsieur Beauclair had ever done, Susan had her first inkling that perhaps she had been wrong to trust him. But a glance around at the oddly dressed ballgoers made her consider that perhaps Semerton was merely following the form of this assembly. She began to enjoy the whirling movement of her first real waltz. She closed her eyes and shamelessly imagined that it was Captain Camberley who held her so close. Considering that Semerton was slighter and not so tall as Susan's secret favorite, this fantasy was no simple task, but she did do her best.

The waltz ended, and the musicians almost immediately began another.

"May we dance another, my dear?" Semerton murmured.

She hesitated, then nodded. She determined to keep dancing, then, when she tired, to demand to go home. Surely her escort would oblige her since she had fulfilled his wishes and come in with him. She had noticed that the other major activity at this masquerade, besides milling about and quizzing the company, appeared to take place in some private boxes, where people were enjoying refreshments and what might kindly be described as flirtation. She had no wish for Semerton to take her into a box.

Susan had to admit that she welcomed the opportunity for another waltz. This time she let daydreaming go by the way as they twirled about the floor. Instead she observed the crowd around her as intently as she could, storing up memories, trying to see behind masks and perhaps recognize someone she knew.

"My dearest Miss Danvers," Semerton said when the music stopped. "That is, I suppose in this company I should style you simply Miss D. D. for divinity, for delectable, for delicious!" He bent down and kissed her.

The touch was fleeting, featherlike. A sophisticated young lady might have tossed it off as of no consequence. But Susan felt her anger mount.

She took a step back. "I am going to forget that, my lord," she said, flushing hotly. Her first kiss, to be stolen by this . . . this lout! "Will you take me home now?"

"Not now, fair lady," Semerton exclaimed. "I beg a thousand pardons for my indiscretion. Your beauty has turned me into an animal. But I'll reform right now and buy your forgiveness with the supper I've ordered placed in one of the boxes. I know it would never do to take you in to eat supper with the common herd. Will you let me lead you to our hideaway?''

This was what Susan most feared, and she didn't hesitate. "No, sir," she said. "Good night. I can find my own way home." She turned and marched off across the stage, hoping that her bravado would lead her to discover a safe way back to Portland Place. Did she have any money in her reticule with which to hire a hackney? And how did one go about doing so? What did job carriages look like, exactly?

Susan felt an angry tear spring to her eye as she deplored her ignorance.

Semerton followed her. Susan was afraid that he would grab her and carry her off in true wicked-lord style, but he only pleaded with her to reconsider.

"No," she repeated, walking on with a new purpose. Her gaze had lighted upon someone. Semerton followed, promising her the world if she would but break bread with him in his box.

Susan stopped before a lady in an eye-catching outfit: in the character of a *belle sauvage,* this woman was decked in a beaded and fringed ensemble of white doeskin—authentic-looking if one discounted the low décolletage. A headdress of feathers and beads ornamented a fine head of raven hair. The female's escort, who had drawn more eyes than anyone else at the masquerade, was wearing nothing beyond a pair of deerskin boots and breeches, a black wig, and feathers. A muscular and hairy chest was exposed to the night air and had fixed the interest of many a female.

"Good evening, Mama," Susan said to the Red Indian lady. The escort she ignored. "I should like to go home now. Will you take me?"

"Heavens!" From behind a beaded doeskin mask, Lady Delafort's eyes dilated in alarm. "Susan! What are you doing here?"

"I might ask the same of you, Mama, but I know I have no right," Susan said with a demure half-curtsy in the direction of her mother's companion. She looked him over as well as she could, which was not very well, so embarrassed was she by his naked chest. She was almost certain it was Monsieur

Beauclair. "Will you take me home?" she repeated, turning back to her mother.

"Madame," put in the Indian brave. The heavy accent neatly confirmed Susan's guess as to his identity. "You cannot leave. The evening is but just begun."

"But I must," Lady Delafort said with a charming smile. "My daughter needs me." She reached out to clasp Susan's hand.

Semerton had been hovering around the group, and now he spoke up to say, "Is that Lady Delafort? Capital, my lady. Couldn't be better. Would you and your escort do me the honor to take supper in my box? Your daughter's reputation will be quite secure with you to guard her." He laughed on seeing Lady Delafort's astonished look, and leaned forward in a confidential manner. "It's Semerton. Miss Danvers has been safe with me the whole time."

"He took me to a gaming hell . . . house, and brought me here, all without my knowledge." Susan clarified the situation with a dark look at the earl. "He sent his carriage away . . ." Here her excuses trailed off, for she knew that although she had not entered the opera house of her own free will, her curiosity had made her stay and dance.

As Susan stood engrossed in self-recrimination, another voice spoke up. "I might have known, Miss Danvers, that you would never agree to such an outrageous scheme. He tricked you, did he? I am not surprised."

Susan whirled about and found herself facing Captain Camberley. He must have been listening to the conversation. Never had she welcomed the sight of anyone more, though mortification warred with relief in her mind. He was seeing her in such an odd situation! Yet he had heard her explain, and he seemed to believe the story.

"My lady," the captain continued, turning to Lady Delafort, "it would be best for all concerned if your party were to leave now."

"But, madame," protested the Indian who Susan suspected was Beauclair, "you must not. For so long we have planned this evening. The young lady may go home with either of these able gentlemen. Stay with me, I pray you."

"How strange in you to insist, monsieur," Lady Delafort said. "I have never known you to contradict a wish of mine before."

"Ah, milady." The Frenchman seized her hand and put it to his lips. "It is the night of masques which drives me to distraction. Take pity on a poor unfortunate and stay with me—I beg you."

"You ought all to stay," was the earl's contribution. "I've ordered plenty of supper. What do you say, Camberley?" Once again the masked young earl leaned forward and spoke in a lowered voice to disclose his identity. "I'm Semerton."

"I know who you are, sir." the captain said through gritted teeth, "and only your position as a peer keeps me from calling you out for endangering the honor of this dear young lady. You may have your friends wait upon me, if you will."

"Good heavens!" Susan cried. "You can't mean . . . That would be folly, Captain. Don't call him out, Lord Semerton," she pleaded, turning to the earl.

The self-styled wicked lord stood, arms folded, and seemed to consider the problem. Then he graciously allowed that he would not cut up Miss Danvers' peace in such a way.

"Thank you, sir," Susan sighed in relief.

"My word," Lady Delafort said, "men proposing to fight battles! Yes, my Susan, you are definitely coming on."

"May we go home?" Susan demanded.

Again Beauclair and Semerton filled the air with their objections.

The ball went on around them meanwhile, and luckily the place was in such a state of liveliness that no one was paying particular attention to the arguing group.

"Ladies," Captain Camberley said, "will you each take an arm? I have a carriage waiting outside, and I'll be pleased to escort you. Now."

Lady Delafort, with uncharacteristic meekness, laid her hand on the captain's coat sleeve. Susan followed suit.

"I cannot let you go, madame!" Beauclair declaimed, trying for a last bit of drama, Susan supposed. He caught at Lady Delafort's free arm and tried to detain her.

A long string of beaded fringe came away in his hand as she

whipped around. "Sir!" Her ladyship's scorn was evident; she plucked the fringe from his hand. "You forget yourself." With that, she swept out of the place, followed by Camberley and her daughter.

Susan noticed that Beauclair dashed away even faster than they did, but she didn't stop to wonder why, beyond a thought that his mortification at Lady Delafort's refusal must be great indeed.

As for Semerton, he had the sense not to go after the party. He remained on the opera house stage watching them depart.

Susan was glad that not many were at leisure to observe them. If she had recognized her mother, many others might have, and she had learned that Covent Garden on a masque night was no place for any lady.

In Portland Place, Captain Camberley assisted his two charges down from the hackney coach and shepherded them to their front door.

"Do come in, Captain, and refresh yourself after your labors in our behalf," Lady Delafort said in a gracious if cold voice. During the drive home she had seemed to warm to the captain slightly. He might have impossible hopes of Susan, but he had removed the two of them without fuss from a ticklish situation. Vexing though the necessity might be, such a gallant gentleman must be rewarded.

Susan was longing to ask her mother why she had been at the masquerade with Beauclair; why she had been there at all when she had cautioned Susan never to go near the place. The usual reasons had probably guided her, Susan thought romantically: love of adventure, curiosity, all those things which drove Mama's restless spirit.

The butler let them in, and Susan excused herself to go up to her room. She was turning the handle on the door when it opened and Hortense came out so fast that she bumped into her young mistress.

"Hortense!" Susan said with a nervous laugh. "How you startled me." Then she looked down at what Hortense was carrying in her arms. Mama's jewel case!

The abigail's eyes met Susan's for an instant; then she bolted.

"Captain Camberley! Help!" Susan cried, running after the maid.

Years of country living and running about in child-of-nature style had given Susan speed and grace superior to those of most young ladies. Hortense was certainly no match for Miss Danvers. Susan cut off her path to the back stairs, forcing the woman to head for the front of the house, where Susan managed to overtake her in the middle of the front staircase and to hold her, struggling. The jewel casket spilled out of the maid's arms and rained down the staircase: diamonds, the finest Indian rubies, all the treasures Lady Delafort had collected since the good turn in her husband's fortunes, plus the few baubles she had given Susan.

"Bloody addle-plot," Hortense burst out with a sneer, wrenching her arm from Susan's grasp. "Said 'e'd keep the family out until two." Folding her arms, she stepped a safe distance away from Miss Danvers and stood, chin lifted, the picture of defiance.

"What is this?" Captain Camberley and Lady Delafort were still standing at the foot of the staircase.

"I suspect, Mama, that Monsieur Beauclair and Hortense have been scheming to get us out of the house so that she might steal your jewels," Susan said, staring at Hortense. There had been no hint of Paris in her accent: the East End of London was nearer the fact.

"Impossible, child," Lady Delafort said. "Why, Angleton always sits up in my chamber to await me. She would never let anyone . . ." Her words trailed away in horror, and she glared at Hortense. "What have you done with Angleton?"

"The usual," said the maid with a shrug. "The old bird went off with just a drop of the stuff in her tea. Weak head. She's all right."

"My lady." From the head of the stairs came the voice of the butler. "We found this person sneaking in at the back door."

Susan looked up. Bland and a footman had each clamped a bare arm of a Red Indian she had seen before.

"Well, Artie, the game's up," Hortense said cheerily, with a wicked grin. "Mad for you, is she? Stay anywhere you tell 'er to? That's rich."

"Put a damper on it, Moll," Beauclair snarled. He also spoke in a new and decidedly un-French accent.

"Most interesting," Captain Camberley said.

"Heavens." Lady Delafort leaned upon Captain Camberley's arm in confusion. She had truly been taken in by the elegant *émigré*; this cockney savage was a new player in the game.

Susan, watching from her position midway down the stairs, was surprised by a jealous little flutter in her midsection: she wished that she might have been the one to ask the captain for support.

Then she noticed that he was looking up at her in what appeared to be admiration. "Good work, Miss Danvers," he said in evident approval. "You captured the miscreant all by yourself. How many young females would be so bold?"

She smiled, hoping that this was a compliment.

All was bedlam for a few minutes as Bland, in a raised voice, summoned other domestics to the task of taking Hortense and Beauclair away to the constabulary.

"Bow Street, I think, will do," Captain Camberley suggested. "There will no doubt be a need for testimony from some of your household later, Lady Delafort."

"I have been shamefully taken in," her ladyship said, glaring at Beauclair. "It was he," she said with a sneer, "who recommended Hortense as a most suitable abigail for my daughter. When I think . . . !"

"You must not blame yourself, my lady," Camberley said soothingly. "Do you not want to go into the drawing room now and rest? I'll take my leave and assist the criminals to justice."

"Oh, thank you, Captain," Susan said. "You are so good to us."

"Who would not delight in serving such charming ladies?" The captain had a special smile for Susan.

"Who, indeed?"

Susan turned round on hearing the unfamiliar voice. The front door had opened without anyone noticing it. On the threshold stood a light-haired, handsome older man whom she seemed to recognize but couldn't quite place.

The servants, Beauclair, and Hortense paused in their strugglings and arguments to stare.

Lady Delafort's feathers and beads rustled as she, too, turned to look at the gentleman.

"Oh, heavens." With a little gasp she toppled to the floor.

12

Susan ran down the stairs to her mother's side.

Bland also hurried forward. "A thousand apologies, my lord," he said, nearly stepping over his lady in his eagerness to bow before the strange gentleman. "What a homecoming this is!"

"A most amusing one, I assure you," the man said, drawing off his gloves. He spoke in a voice that teased at Susan's memory. She looked up and realized that the sun-bronzed face, even with hair lightened to a shade almost white, was indeed familiar to her. As for the voice, it had sung songs to her as she was tossed up into the air by those very hands, now so brown, but wearing the same signet ring.

"Papa?" she ventured.

"Can this be my little Susan?" the stranger answered with a smile that Susan saw reflected every day in her own mirror.

She longed to rise and throw herself into his arms, but not only were they surrounded by people, she was still holding her mother's limp hand. "My mother has never fainted before, to my knowledge," she said. "We really must send for the doctor."

"It's undoubtedly merely the shock. Allow me," Lord Delafort said, striding forward. When he reached Captain Camberley he extended his hand. "I'm Delafort. Do stay awhile, sir, and help explain what is going on."

Camberley shook the offered hand and expressed his willingness to help in any way he could.

Lord Delafort nodded briskly, then bent to pick up the still form of his wife. She opened her eyes. Susan sighed in relief.

"It *is* you," Lady Delafort whispered, staring into the tanned face.

"My dear Jenny." Delafort's voice was nearly as soft. Then he carried her most tenderly into the drawing room.

Once the door had shut behind them, Captain Camberley moved to action. Bystanders at the scene of family reunion included Hortense—or Moll—cowering against a wall halfway down the staircase, and the erstwhile Beauclair, who was still held in the grasp of the household's burliest footmen. The stairs were littered with Lady Delafort's jewels, and the casket had tumbled down into the hall, where it lay, lid down, on the carpet.

"Well," Camberley said pleasantly, "it is time we cleared up this carnage. Miss Danvers, if you would be so good as to pick up the jewelry? I wouldn't wish you to perform such a menial task, you understand, but I hardly think we can ask the maid."

"And we had better not involve any others if we can avoid it," Susan added. Glad of something to do now that she and Camberley were virtually alone, she sprang to her task, scooping all the baubles into the jewel case. She wasn't intimately acquainted with her mother's collection, but so far as she could tell, nothing was missing.

"This is an error, I tell you, a grave error," exclaimed Beauclair from the top of the stairs, once more in his heavy French accent. He stuck out his bare chest. "I regret to say anything of an intimate nature, especially before a *jeune fille*, but I was merely arriving by the discreet back door to keep an assignation with her ladyship. I have nothing to do with this *putain* and her thievery."

"An assignation with my mother! How dare you tell such lies?" Susan cried.

'Stifle it, Artie, the game's up,' Hortense said with another malicious grin.

The doubtful Frenchman smiled a thin wolfish smile. "You have seen, my good friends, that the lady was not at all enchanted to see her husband. It is because she will have some explaining to do, *non*?"

"Heavens, she hasn't seen him in fifteen years," Susan cried. "Naturally she was surprised."

"I think you've said quite enough," Camberley told

Beauclair. "Take him away, men. We will need another one of you to make sure this female doesn't slip away as you go to Bow Street." He indicated Hortense.

The butler hurried off to call another of his staff. Soon there appeared the stableboy, a rough-looking individual who carried a horsey smell into the room with him. Hortense seemed more than insulted to be placed into his custody and had some pithy comments to make. Susan was torn between wishing for a knowledge of slang and being glad that, since she didn't understand much of what was being said, she didn't have to blush.

The procession went on its way almost instantly, and soon Susan, Camberley, and Bland were the only ones left in the entryway. The three then recalled that a husband and wife were reuniting but a door away from the spot where they stood. They waited in a self-conscious cluster, trying not to hear anything. Nothing but a low murmur was audible in any case.

Sometime later, Lord Delafort came back out into the hall, closing the drawing-room door softly behind him. "She needs a moment or two to collect herself," he explained with a smile. "And now"—he held out his arms—"is the beautiful young lady I see before me too grown-up to give her old father a kiss?"

Susan ran into his arms and hugged him tightly. He kissed her forehead and stepped back to look at her. "Yes, you have grown to be a stunner. You are the image of my own mother. I must show you her portrait one day. It had the place of honor at the country house."

At this point Bland cleared his throat. "His lordship will undoubtedly wonder what was taking place in his home mere moments ago," he said in an expressionless voice.

"That's so," the viscount agreed. "Thank you, Bland, for reminding me. What was going on, please? There appeared to be quite a row, but I had every confidence in the combined efforts of this gentleman and my staff to take care of things."

Camberley spoke up. "We foiled a plot to steal your lady's jewels, my lord. It was the usual thing. One partner was to keep her away from home while the other, a trusted servant as it happens, made off with the goods. An old trick, but it often works. Her ladyship came home early."

"A household where no male is in residence is a prime target for such a scheme, I know," Delafort said with a nod. "I assume they were hauled off to justice?"

"Indeed, yes, my lord, and won't be troubling this house again," Bland put in importantly.

"All has indeed ended as it should," Camberley added. "And if I may say so, this has turned out to be a rare night of happiness for the ladies of the house."

The viscount inclined his head in acknowledgment of the compliment. He and Camberley still hadn't been introduced, but they took an opportunity to study each other. Susan looked at them both with pride. Her father had aged and grown weatherbeaten in the harsh tropic sun, but he was a fine figure of a man, most unusual and striking with his hair bleached so light. He couldn't be much above forty, if she remembered correctly, and he had an air of great strength and vigor.

As for the captain, she was long past making any rational judgments where he was concerned, but she was proud to have her father meet such a well-favored gentleman. Camberley too was sun-bronzed, and his stalwart figure showed particularly to advantage in evening clothes.

"Father, I'm so glad to see you. But we had no idea you were coming." Susan decided to break the silence when she remembered that she had indeed had no word of his arrival.

"Your grandmother's letter brought me home," Delafort told Susan. "She was bound and determined that I should forbid your stepping into the depravity of a London Season."

"But that was nearly a year ago! And you wrote me not to worry over what she said," Susan pointed out.

"Yes, I did. But I realized that I should come home. My daughter grown up enough for a Season, and I not there! I have always felt I knew you, my dear, from your letters. I had gotten used to having a daughter I never saw. But Mrs. Palmer's letter opened my eyes. I realized how much time had passed and how overdue my homecoming was. Time slips away out there, Susan my dear. One gets involved in making money, in giving all to business, and then of course the climate induces a queer lethargy. It's an odd sort of life."

Susan nodded, concerned to see the honest regret in her father's eyes, yet saddened on her own and her mother's account. He had simply forgotten them. She was beyond anything glad that Grandmama's letter had served to remind him of their existence.

She looked at Captain Camberley, who seemed a touch uncomfortable to be taking part in a family discussion. He still hadn't been introduced to Papa, she realized, and opened her mouth to perform that duty.

But Lord Delafort was looking about him. "This is hardly the spot for a coze, is it?" He moved across the hall. "Is the library still where it was formerly? What do you say we go in there? Sir, will you join us in a glass of wine?" he asked Camberley. "Bland," turning to the butler, "you will bring the proper thing, I'm sure. In the library."

"Very good, my lord." Susan noticed that Bland walked away about his business with a particularly light step. He was evidently more than happy to have his master back in the house after fifteen long years.

Susan and the two gentlemen walked into the library. There Susan finally performed the necessary social duties. "Father, may I present Captain Vincent Camberley? He escorted us home this evening."

"Yes." Lord Delafort shook Camberley's hand. "I am glad to meet you, sir. Even in my corner of the world we heard the news of the war. My thanks to you, Captain, on behalf of my country."

Camberley bowed. "Don't speak of it, sir. My naval career already seems like another life. I did my duty, I hope, but I haven't enjoyed being set up as a hero."

"Nevertheless, your exploits made exciting reading," Delafort said.

Susan was almost irrationally pleased that her father seemed to have taken a liking to Captain Camberley.

The viscount looked at both his daughter and Camberley and said, "My lady has been telling me about her little scrape and how you, Captain, helped her out of it."

"She has?" Susan said with a gasp.

"It didn't escape my notice, my dear, that you are wearing a domino and your mother was attired in character—Mr.

Chateaubriand's Atala, she confessed to me moments ago. And quite fetching she looked, too. You were both at the opera house, it seems.''

Susan nodded miserably.

Lord Delafort cast a rueful smile at his contrite-looking daughter. ''When I expressed my surprise that your mama would take you into such a situation, she admitted that she hadn't done so. She said you had met there by accident. As she tells it, she was lured there by that scantily dressed man who was in league with the thieving French maid, and theirs was evidently no last-minute engagement. But your mother tells me that you, my dear Susan, were there with another escort.''

''Yes.'' Susan made haste to explain. ''Lord Semerton, a young man who has paid me some little attention, took me out this evening with his grandmother. He . . . I'm afraid, Papa, that he had the idea that taking me into questionable situations would impress me. He likes to call himself a wicked lord and make much of his tendency to evil.''

Delafort chuckled. ''Yes, I know the sort of young man you mean.''

''And,'' Susan went on, alternating between uncomfortable glances at her father and at Camberley, ''first they took me to a gaming establishment in St. James's Square.''

''Good Lord! I'll have to have a word with the fellow,'' Delafort exclaimed. ''My daughter in a common gaming hell?''

''Oh, it was the finest place in London. They told me that,'' Susan assured him, not knowing what to make of his amused look at this tidbit. ''But Lady Semerton wished to stay there, and her grandson preferred to move on.''

''I remember Lady Semerton,'' Susan's father remarked in an aside to Camberley. ''She would be difficult to shift from a seat at a loo table.''

''You have it exactly, sir,'' Susan said. ''She was playing silver loo.''

''And so you left her there and went off with young Semerton,'' Papa said encouragingly.

''Yes.'' Susan shrugged. ''I told him to take me home, and Lady Semerton said there would be nothing compromising in that, as no one would know in the dark who was with us. But when I got down from the carriage, we were not at home, we were at the opera house." She hesitated, for the next bit was hard to confess. "I . . . He insisted I go in, Papa, and he provided this domino and a mask, and then"—for an instant she relived her fear and shuddered—"a lot of people were pushing, and I found myself inside. And the people in fancy dress looked so interesting. Once in, I felt I must see the spectacle."

Lord Delafort laughed. "My dear, you are allowed your curiosity. I see nothing to cavil at."

Susan stole a glance at Camberley and saw that he, too, looked indulgent. She breathed a great sigh of relief. "When we had been inside for a little," she continued, "Lord Semerton refused again to take me home. I had recognized Mama at some point, and so I went up to her and asked her to take me. Her escort didn't want her to return home either—I believe we now know why—and finally Captain Camberley appeared as if from nowhere, took charge of the situation, and brought us back."

At this point she looked gratefully at the captain.

"And you, sir," Delafort said, observing the byplay between his daughter and the gentleman. "I suppose you were at the masquerade for no particular reason. You have left off your domino."

"He didn't have a domino," Susan remembered in surprise.

"I wasn't a visitor to the masquerade in the ordinary sense," Camberley said. "As it happens, I had seen Miss Danvers leave the St. James establishment and followed her to make sure she was in no danger."

"And thank heaven you did," Susan said in heartfelt tones. "I shudder to think what your opinion must have been, sir. Did you think I was a gamester?"

Camberley laughed. "No. I assumed it was all some mischief of Semerton's. I had been wishing to see you anyway, Miss Danvers, to apologize for the incident in the park."

"Incident in the park?" So full had this evening been that Susan had already forgotten her morning's adventure on the spirited gelding Lord Buxford had provided her. Now the whole matter was recalled to her memory, and she felt again the pounding hooves, the captain forcibly stopping her, her momentary anger—and her half-wish that Camberley might think her intrepid, might believe that it had been her idea to ride the restive Britannicus.

"I'm afraid I thought you had chosen that dangerous horse for yourself, and berated you accordingly," Camberley said. "I later met Buxford, and he told me all about the incident, dwelling on your bravery and . . . er, your good seat."

"This sounds interesting," Lord Delafort said with a keen look. "I'm glad you are an intrepid rider, Susan. Do tell me all about it. Oh. Here is Bland with the tray."

The butler brought in an array of eatables and a bottle of wine with three glasses. When he had left, Susan served the wine and spoke of her adventure on Britannicus' back. Her father was appropriately impressed that he had given birth to such a fine horsewoman, and angry that Buxford had been daft enough to put Susan into any kind of danger.

"He didn't mean it," Susan said. "He is a very good sort of young man, really."

"How good?" Her father's gaze was penetrating.

"Not that good." Susan lowered her lashes and willed herself not to blush.

She was almost certain that she heard a sigh of relief from Captain Camberley, but perhaps that was only wishful thinking.

"I hope these young men who flock around you won't be too disappointed when we leave town," Delafort mused, looking up at his own portrait above the mantelpiece.

"Leave town? In the middle of the Season?" Susan cried, eyes wide. "What will Mama say to that? She hasn't been out of town in years except for flying visits to country houses."

Papa shrugged. "I don't know what she will think. But that young man"—and he gestured to his youthful figure represented in the heavy gold frame—"has a fancy to woo his wife again. I wish a country setting where I won't be interrupted by her droves of gentlemen admirers."

"You know about them?" Susan cried, then blushed quite as if she and her mother had been co-conspirators.

"I know your mother." Papa gave an understanding smile. "Shall you mind leaving town, little Susan, in the midst of your first triumphs?"

"Not at all," Susan said decidedly. In fact, it would be most restful not to have to worry about Lords Buxford and Semerton for a while, not to mention the casual yet irritating courtship of Lord Fitzalbin. But . . . She looked in sudden dismay at Camberley. Leaving town would mean leaving him.

His expression was most sober, and his eyes met hers in concern. Could it be . . . ? Susan was almost certain that he would miss her. She stared at him, fascinated by the idea of having any sort of power over this man.

"Do you mean to return to your estate in Derbyshire, Papa?" Susan asked politely.

"No." Lord Delafort leaned back in his chair and took a draft of wine. "I have no wish to uproot you from familiar places, my dear. Your grandmother has graciously given leave for me to bring the family to Pilgrim Court."

"Oh." Susan brightened and glanced at Camberley.

He left off looking sad and began to appear devious. Susan assumed he would be thinking up some excuse before long to go gack to Surrey himself. Would he really do so or was she merely indulging in more wishful thinking to fancy that there was such a bond between Camberley and herself?

"Are you certain you will be comfortable at Pilgrim Court, though, Papa?" Susan voiced her main concern over the project. "Mama is used to every luxury, and Grandmama's house is rather . . . simple."

"A little country simplicity will exactly suit us," her father assured her. "You forget I have visited your grandmother's place before."

"But that was long ago, and before Grandpapa's death," Susan said. "She has become ever more primitive, sir. She even got rid of the dining table so that we might always picnic in rustic style, but she had to give up that notion when her rheumatism pained her too much to allow for sitting on the floor. She did bring in a small hunt table. It should seat four."

"I see." Delafort frowned at this news and shook his head. "Even so, my dear, some instinct tells me that Pilgrim Court, your mama's childhood home, is the place for us all to become a family again.''

"Oh, Father," Susan said with tears shining in her eyes, "it is so good to have you home. Now I won't have to worry."

"About what?"

Susan didn't know what to say. About her mother, of course, but she could hardly disclose that to her father, however much he had guessed about his lady's social life during his absence.

"About anything," she said with a demure smile.

"What do you mean, we are leaving London?" Drusilla Camberley demanded the next day with an exasperated look at her brother. "I've planned my first soirée for this day week. And the paint is barely dry on the ceiling in the entry."

"You don't have to remind me, sister, that we have had that odd artist hanging on our sleeves forever," Camberley replied with an ironic look. "I'm leaving town for Royce Park. You may come or not as you please. Perhaps you'd like to go on with your soirée and then join me later. You might even invite some of your scholar friends for a little visit. You could give each other lectures out at the ruins."

"Oh. That does sound most interesting," Drusilla said, pushing her spectacles up her nose. "I'll make the invitation at my party. And why, Vincent, are you leaving town? Is the lionizing still too much for you?"

"No," her brother said reflectively, "it hasn't turned out to matter as I thought it would. I simply growl and turn the subject when someone tries to put a hero's halo above my head. The truth is, I wish to settle the sailors in at the cottages down in Surrey."

Drusilla nodded. Vincent had sought out some disabled ex-seamen and arranged for them to have temporary habitation near Royce Park until they could be moved nearer the sea. He had even arranged for some useful work for them, such as making sails. She knew this project assuaged his guilt for having come through the war whole. But the last she had heard, he was simply going to send the men down in the care of his man of business, McCall.

"You have some other reason," she said.

Vincent didn't answer her, but went on with his reading.

"And what about your literary work?" Drusilla asked. "Didn't the publisher wish for you to do another translation?"

Vincent shrugged. "I can do that as well in the country as in town. Besides, I don't know if I wish to. The project I've done was the one close to my heart. I don't need the money. It was merely a lark."

"A lark Mr. Murray wishes you to repeat. And he wants you to come out of anonymity as well."

"That is a bad idea that will come to naught. A translator feted as an author! The very thought is absurd."

"You are too modest," Drusilla said with a sigh.

With a laugh, her brother disappeared behind his newspaper. Drusilla went away to plan the practical aspects of having a party down to Royce Park.

Vincent stayed where he was, wondering if Lord Delafort would look kindly on an untitled suitor for his only daughter. Surely his following the family down to Surrey would betray his plans at once. Well, he would get there first.

As for Susan, Camberley had no choice but to put his fate to the test. Whether or not she would take him was a mystery. Sometimes he saw a light of understanding in her eyes and thought they shared a secret already. At other times she seemed so contented and happy in town, in the company of younger, livelier men, that he lost heart.

Then that light would appear again in her beautiful eyes. She would look at him across a room as though she were standing beside him and holding his hand.

Somehow Camberley believed that his dreams were grounded in reality. Despite the fact that he and Miss Danvers had done most of their courting in the company of others, despite the fact that her mother was not amenable to his attentions to Susan, he was peculiarly certain that a courtship was taking place, a courtship whose inevitable conclusion was fast approaching.

13

Susan was as hesitant about coming down to breakfast the morning after her father's return as she might have been to disturb honeymooners in their bedchamber. How had Lady Delafort borne the romantic reunion with her handsome husband?

In the breakfast room Lord Delafort sat quite alone, reading the papers. The instant Susan saw him, all vestiges of resentment left her. Though thrilled to see her father the night before, once alone in her chamber she had balked at his easy return to his family. After all, this cheerful-looking man had passed fifteen years without her and her mother and was back in England now only because it suited him.

Now forgiveness seemed as easy as the sunrise. Susan was delighted to be filled with a peace and contentment she had never before known in her mother's house. Everything was as it should be now. Naturally Mama hadn't come down to breakfast. She never did. But here at last sat Papa, like any other husband in London.

He looked up and smiled. "A pretty daughter. What a fine sight in the morning. You look remarkably fresh, my dear, considering your late night. Sit down and talk to me while you eat, and then your mother would like to see you in her boudoir. About making some arrangements for the trip to Surrey, I believe."

"You've told her?"

"Yes, and she takes it well," Lord Delafort said in satisfaction. "Naturally we are to make an appearance in town before we leave. Your mama would show me off before all her friends, she says."

"And no wonder, Papa. You will be the handsomest man to appear on the scene all Season."

He shrugged his shoulders in a self-deprecating manner, and Susan perceived a similarity between him and Mama: they were both vain. With good reason, of course, but vain all the same.

"And then, when my lady's social urgings are satisfied, we'll be off to the country," Lord Delafort continued.

Susan let a worried sigh escape her. To imagine her united parents dazzling all and sundry at the events of the Season was a most delightful prospect. Going home to the country also sounded like a good idea. Not so pleasant, though, was the idea of Lady Delafort transported from the luxuries of town to the rigors of Grandmama's house.

"Is something amiss, my dear?"

"Well . . . there aren't even enough pillows at Pilgrim Court, sir," Susan said in despair. "Mama will never be comfortable."

"Pillows?" her father repeated in puzzlement.

"You know, on the settees and beds and chairs. Grandmama thinks all such furbelows encourage sloth. Mama will have to spend all her time in the French drawing room there, which is the only normally decorated chamber in the house."

"We'll take some pillows with us," Lord Delafort suggested. "What do you say to that, my dear? You make up a list of the comforts lacking at your grandmother's, and we'll take provisions down quite as if we were making for a desert island."

Susan laughed, thoroughly charmed by her father's effortless solution to the problem. "That sounds like fun," she remarked.

"So it should be. I intend for us to make up for lost time."

"Oh, we can, sir! I know we can."

"Before you leave us to be married, we'll have at least a short holiday as a family."

Susan looked startled at this. "I have no plans to marry, Papa."

"You may not, my dear. But it takes more than one to make a marriage."

Susan was left to wonder if her father had actually received an application for her hand. It was early on his first day back in town. What might have happened?

Lord Semerton had told her he rarely arose before he dressed for dinner, but the athletic Lord Buxford always got up with the birds . . . and Lord Fitzalbin! She had forgotten him. He was bound to ask.

She gave her father a sidelong glance. "Do you mention my marriage for a particular reason, sir?" She was determined to be honest with her father from the outset of their relationship. "Has anyone . . . ? Have you . . . ?"

"No, it's merely idle speculation," Papa assured her with a smile as he settled back down to his paper. "When one has a daughter as sweet and lovely as you, it's a good bet that someone in town is considering matrimony."

Susan decided not to warn her father beforehand of any applications he might receive. He would surely not force her inclinations. Her heart was not light as she left the room, though; strange indeed was the fact that her father was present in her life and had the power to tell her whom she could or could not marry. A sire in far-off India, who must give or refuse consent through the slow passage of the mails, had been more convenient to one who had unwanted suitors.

She found Lady Delafort before the dressing table in her boudoir. Angleton hovered over her, and they were both busy as bees over some aspect of her ladyship's complexion. Angleton was rather pale, but otherwise looked remarkably fit for a woman who had been drugged the night before. Susan stood by diffidently, waiting for a break in the scene in progress.

"You may go, Angle," Lady Delafort said, noticing her daughter. The abigail left, carrying with her several garments for the afternoon's work.

When the door had closed upon Angleton, her ladyship held out her arms. "Come to me, sweet child. Oh, isn't this a lovely morning?"

Susan crossed the room to her mother and gave her a hug. "You were happy, then, to see Papa."

"How should I not be? Did you notice how handsome he is, how dashing? The dear man had clothes made by Weston and sent out to him. Can you imagine the delicacy, the sensitivity to my feelings? He told me he didn't want to disgust me with the untonnish garb he had lived in for years." She chuckled. "Can you imagine Papa in unfashionable clothing, dear? The mind revolts."

"I would imagine they don't wear the latest thing in India," Susan said, frowning. She had expected some sort of confidences about her father's kindness, even his romantic inclinations. But clothes? Well, Susan consoled herself, at least if Mama was rattling on about the frivolous attributes of some man, it was the right man.

"And though he is set on visiting your grandmother for some dreary reason having to do with country air, he agrees to let me show him off before we go." Lady Delafort continued the catalog of her husband's virtues. "I was quite disposed to be cross with him before he told me that, but since he conceded me a week or so to display him, I could not but say yes to whatever he wishes. He is my lord and master, you know. And holds the purse strings." Lady Delafort winked at her daughter.

"I'm so glad you're not unhappy about the country." Susan hesitated, then looked timidly at her mother. "Was Papa at all angry that you had gone to the masquerade with Monsieur Beauclair?"

"Heavens, my dear. Husbands and wives do not live in each other's pockets as an ordinary thing, and especially not when they are on separate continents. Your father quite comprehends my need for amusement with the gentlemen. My former need."

Such talk was heartening. Susan smiled sunnily. "Oh, Mama. I'm so thrilled that you like him as much as I do."

"Much more," her ladyship said with a sly note in her voice. Susan was more satisfied than ever.

Viscount Delafort and his family duly put in an appearance at Almack's, visited the opera, and attended a grand private ball in the next week. More than this Lord Delafort did not care to do. His time out of the social scene had given him a wariness about sinking back into it. And he certainly had no wish to stumble into his old gaming and drinking circles.

This schedule of frivolity, modest though it was, gave Lady Delafort the chance to wear the three new gowns which had just come home from Madame Hélenè. That, she confided to Susan, had been her major objection to leaving town at once.

Everywhere they went, numbers of the *beau monde* stared in astonishment, then pleasure, at the return of the viscount to their midst. Unlike other men who had simply fled their creditors, he had returned triumphant, having paid all his debts with interest. He was now richer than he had been before he'd wasted his fortune.

The ladies looked on him with indulgent pleasure. He might be a married man, but such were the numbers in society that any male, whatever his status, was most welcome.

His old friends and those who had once played with him viewed Delafort's homecoming with mixed feelings. He was no longer young and foolish and couldn't be counted upon to be fleeced out of these new riches—not that they wouldn't try.

The highest sticklers would have been pleased to set him down for daring to come into their midst when his hands had been soiled by trade, but so charming were the viscount's manners, and so noble his bloodlines, that this little detail had to be ignored in the face of his new opulence.

Susan was proud of her father, delighted to be seen with him at those gatherings of the rich and great which had intimidated her a little before. She sensed a real difference, too, in the treatment she was accorded. A woman who had a male protector was simply granted more respect. Deplorable this situation might be, but Susan was glad to be within this particular pale at long last.

As for Lady Delafort, she seemed to bloom. She had not only her regular admirers but also her handsome husband. Susan could see her mother's usual court fluttering round the warmth of the flame, but no one came into the foreground. Susan was most grateful to all the gentlemen for this delicacy.

It didn't damage his case that Lord Delafort had brought with him trunks of exotic presents for his two ladies. They spent a morning exclaiming over India shawls and finely worked foreign jewelry, embroidered muslins and gossamer silks shot with gold and silver threads.

Then they began to pack for the trip down into Surrey. Susan and her father joked often about how they were fitting themselves out for a trip abroad when they were to travel only twenty miles, but the family had fun collecting not only household comforts but also exotic foods to supplement the Spartan fare Grandmama Palmer called proper victuals.

"Do you know, Susan, I have been surprised by one thing," Lord Delafort said one morning from behind a stack of cushions he was punching down into a trunk. He and his family were seeing to the actual packing for their own amusement, though they did not doubt that a competent servant would do their work over again the moment their backs were turned.

"What is that, Papa?" Susan asked. She was at her writing desk, where she was looking over the list she had made and wishing she possessed the famous organizational talents of Lady Emily Forbes.

"I expected to see Captain Camberley visit us at least once before we went out of town."

"He is doubtless too busy, Papa." Susan's face reddened, and she was beyond anything glad that her father wasn't looking at her. She had spent some time wondering over this problem herself, and had come to the unflattering conclusion that Captain Camberley must think the less of her, after all, for going to the masquerade and the gaming house. She had not even seen him at any of the parties they had attended since Lord Delafort's return.

Stoutly she told herself that it was best she forget the captain. If he had been attracted only to her untouched innocence and had been disgusted to see that altering, he was not the man for her.

Lady Delafort spoke from her place on a sofa near the chimneypiece. "He was not an eligible *parti*, Delafort," she said, patting back a yawn. "No title."

"By his own choice, or so I hear. I wasn't suggesting that he might have been courting our Susan, my dear. A man of his stamp probably wouldn't be interested in a girl just out of the schoolroom. I merely—"

"Oh!" Susan's cheeks grew even hotter, in mortification. So the honest opinion of her own father was that naturally Captain Camberley wouldn't want her. He would demand sophistication or at least a little town bronze in the woman of his choice.

Lord Delafort turned to his daughter, his expression contrite. "I'm sorry, Susan. I ought not to have insulted such a fine young lady by calling her a schoolroom miss. Moreover, I know that you've never seen a schoolroom in your life." He smiled.

Susan had to forgive him and appreciate his effort to turn the situation into a joke. She let him go on thinking she had been insulted only by the reference to her youth; best if neither of her parents guessed that her real concern was Captain Camberley's opinion.

The doors opened while Susan was still trying to hide her vexation. Lady Emily Forbes walked in.

"My dearest creature." The young lady fluttered straight to Susan. "The greatest tragedy! Oh, my lady." She bowed to Lady Delafort. "I beg pardon. I didn't see you. And my lord! Heavens, I have disrupted a family party. The butler ought to have told me—but I did rather barge past him. Oh, dear."

Lord Delafort came forward to hand Lady Emily to a chair. "Think nothing of it, ma'am. You must not stand on ceremony with us. Now, you have piqued my interest. You were saying something about a tragedy? Or is that a story you wish to relate only to the sympathetic ears of another young miss?"

Lady Emily, who would never see one-and-twenty again, looked suitably flattered to hear herself termed a young miss. "Not at all, Lord Delafort," she said, taking off her bonnet as though to prove she did not stand upon ceremony at all.

Or perhaps, Susan considered as she watched her friend in fascination, that amazing high-crowned structure surmounted by fruit was simply too uncomfortable to wear for an extended period of time.

Lady Emily was continuing her story. "I have wondered why a certain gentleman of my acquaintance—Captain Camberley— has not been seen at any of the usual places for above a week now. Well, I have found out." She paused and looked darkly at her listeners.

"You are a mistress of suspence, my dear," Delafort said. "Do go on."

"He is gone out of town, the wretch!" Lady Emily burst out. "Now what am I to do?"

Out of town! Susan's spirits lifted perceptibly. The captain hadn't been avoiding her. He had simply had business elsewhere. Had he already returned to Royce Park, knowing that her family would soon be staying next door?

"And what can there be to do in Surrey in the middle of the Season? I can get nothing out of his sister but some dreary talk about a charity case or something," Lady Emily was continuing.

Susan had to wonder at her own good luck. She and the captain did, then, share something more than mere neighborly feelings. He wished to see her again. That had to be the reason for his trip.

"You must know, Delafort, that dear Lady Emily makes no secret of her admiration for the captain," Lady Delafort said with the wise smile of an older woman.

"Naturally I do not," Lady Emily agreed, acknowledging the viscountess's words with a nod of her head. "What use would that be? It is my experience that young men are thickheaded enough as it is. Subtlety is wasted on them."

"Thank you very much," Lord Delafort said with a delighted laugh.

"But you're not a—" Lady Emily cut off her words abruptly.

"Worse and worse." Delafort shook his head. "I'm not a young man, you would say? True enough. I plan to enjoy my middle age, ma'am, and I hope that when you come to that distant time in your life you will enjoy yours too. And I am much impressed by your attitude toward the opposite sex."

"Oh, sir, you are the veriest tease! I do beg pardon if I have given offense."

"How could you, my dear? You are much too charming. Now, do go on with your tale," Lord Delafort said pleasantly.

Lady Emily leaned forward, pleased to have an attentive audience. "My situation is quite shocking. No matter what I've done, Captain Camberley simply won't be brought round to my way of thinking. I believe he would make a most suitable match for me, and I have no parents to rage at an earl's daughter making a dead set at a commoner."

"Plain speaking, my lady," Delafort said.

Susan had by this time grown used to Lady Emily's flights. She had also observed several assaults by that determined young woman upon the peace of Captain Camberley, assaults which had been firmly repulsed. Yet Lady Emily had not lost heart. Perhaps persistence was everything in matters of the heart.

"The three of you will have no difficulty in encountering the captain,'' Lady Emily said on a plaintive note. ''You are going down into Surrey in the next day or so, aren't you? And he lives right next door to your house.''

Susan immediately saw where her ladyship was leading. She looked to her parents and noticed a certain determined gleam come into her father's eye as well as her mother's.

''We would be delighted to invite you to stay, Lady Emily,'' Lady Delafort said in a soothing voice, ''if we were going down to a house of our own. We do but visit my mother, you know. And we can hardly—''

''Of course you can't,'' Lady Emily said briskly. ''You mustn't think I was hinting for any such thing. I merely wish you to remember me to the wretched man when you see him. You'll surely see him, all being down in the country togther.''

''I don't suppose we'll be going much out into society,'' Lord Delafort said, ''but rest assured we'll do our best. Don't worry, though, my dear young woman. No man could forget you.''

Her ladyship preened. ''Do you think so? I don't see how one could. Heaven knows I bring myself forward sufficiently. But it is all in a good cause, in this case Camberley's happiness.'' She rose to go.

''That was a strange visit,'' Lady Delafort remarked when the young lady, bonnet swinging from one arm, had gone on her way. ''She has set her cap at that Camberley fellow. I wonder why.''

Susan could have told her mother at least ten reasons for Lady Emily's infatuation, but she kept silent and brooded over whether the brash young female would win the day with the captain. Perhaps he would simply give in to her to stop her badgering him. Did men ever marry for that reason?

Susan was nearly put out of countenance when she noticed her father winking at her. Flustered, she thought of some task that would take her out of the room.

Lord Buxford answered the summons as soon as he received it. He presented himself in Berkeley Square within three hours of opening an urgent message from Lady Emily.

Shown into one of the minor reception rooms of Semerton House, the burly young viscount found his childhood friend pacing up and down the vast, richly decorated place, in an obvious frenzy. "So you're here," she snapped. "It's about time."

Buxford had an excellent excuse which involved, as his excuses usually did, horses and some of the fellows, but he wasn't allowed more than two words of it before Lady Emily interrupted.

"Oh, I know very well you can't help your infernal tardiness," she said with a glare. "Do sit down, Buxy." This in a softened tone. "I need your help."

"The note said so," Buxford continued, settling into a wing chair. He immediately tipped it back on its two rear legs. "What will it be, Em?"

"It's simple." Emily came forward and laid her hand on Buxford's knee. "You are my closest friend. I can trust no one else."

"Closest friend?" True, Buxford and the Forbes brats had played together in childhood, but it was news to him that Lady Emily considered him in the light of anything but a nuisance. Immediately his suspicions mounted.

Lady Emily gave him an exasperated look. "You idiot! I simply need you to drive me somewhere. That ought to be easy enough even for you."

"Even for me! I say, Em, there's no need to be insulting," Buxford cried, rising abruptly. The chair crashed to the floor and he righted it with the ease of one to whom that sort of accident often happened. "You know I drive to an inch."

"Indeed I do." Lady Emily's voice was changing sentence by sentence, sure sign of an emotional upset of some kind. Now her tone was cooing, and she looked at Buxford as though he were indeed her dearest friend. "And I would like you to drive me down into Surrey someday soon, in your curricle."

He nodded soberly. "Why?"

She opened her eyes wide. "Why not? We are two friends who wish to enjoy a country excursion. I've always wished to see Box Hill. It's a local beauty spot in Surrey," she explained when she saw his blank look. "We'll take a picnic, and in an open carriage our jaunt will be most proper."

"Why take such a jaunt with me? Why not one of the fellows you're trying to land as a husband?"

"Heavens, you make me sound like a fisherwoman. I have never tried anything of the sort. If I had, I would have succeeded. Besides, can't you understand"—and here Lady Emily brought forth her finest skill, a tear in the corner of one luminous hazel eye—"I wish to take a restful drive in the country with a true friend, someone who won't try to take liberties. Someone who won't think that because I ask him to drive I'm asking something else altogether."

"Take your brother," was Buxford's advice.

"Semerton is cow-handed," Lady Emily said simply.

Buxford could understand such an objection, and he agreed with the opinion wholeheartedly, though never in front of Semerton, who, like Buxford, prided himself mightily on his driving. "When do you want to go?" he asked, conceding defeat. Lady Em always had a way of getting what she wanted. Best simply to give it her and save all the dramatics. She would explain the true reason for her odd start in her own good time. Meanwhile, it wouldn't hurt the chestnuts to be driven out into the country some fine day.

"In a few days. It will depend on the weather, of course." Lady Emily was all sunny smiles at her friend's capitulation. "We'll take a grand picnic. I'll have Cook make up all your favorites."

Buxford nodded. "Do you have your pocketbook? Best write them down."

Since Lady Emily always did have her pocketbook by her—she found it useful in so many instances—she obligingly jotted down some pet dishes of her dear childhood friend. She had been thinking of throwing a bundle of bread and cheese, if that, into the back of the curricle. Silly of her to mention Cook and food. Buxford had ever been devoted to the pleasures of the table.

Lady Emily smiled to herself. This plan would be a sure way for her to work her wiles upon Captain Camberley. And even if it didn't turn out, it would be great fun.

14

Mrs. Palmer was at the door of Pilgrim Court when the Delafort carriage pulled into the sweep. She welcomed her family with a decided air of triumph. "So," she greeted her son-in-law as the party walked indoors, followed by servants carrying baggage, "you heeded my warning about Susan's appearance in town and came straight back to England for her. Unfortunate the trip took so long that she was left to languish for weeks in the capital."

Through long habit Susan squirmed at her grandmother's disapproval, though she was resolved not to let herself be intimidated. During her time in town she had learned that other points of view than Grandmama's existed, and, more important, that these might be valid. Now she paused to wonder at her grandmother's brusque manner. Not one word of proper greeting to the son-in-law she hadn't seen in fifteen years!

"Look at her," Mrs. Palmer continued. "The picture of fashionable silliness in that dreadful hat. Ah, we'll soon cure that, won't we, Delafort?"

"I think my daughter is charming. I wouldn't change a thing." Lord Delafort smiled at Susan.

She cast him a grateful look. She was proud of her appearance in a fashionable high-crowned bonnet of cream-colored straw lined in a rare shade of blue that just matched her eyes.

The experience of the perfect hat is rare in a woman's life, and Susan was new to the feeling and reveling in it. She was absolutely certain that nothing had ever become her half so well.

Quite understandable too was Grandmama's point of view: the old lady must think the confection downright frightening and certainly frivolous, so different was it from the close bonnet her granddaughter used to wear. Grandmama would have a like opinion, no doubt, about the matching carriage dress Susan was wearing. Simply made, it yet carried with it the aura of a London modiste's salon, besides being in a dreaded color rather than the white Mrs. Palmer decreed for young girls.

Susan's only quarrel with her looks was that Captain Camberley couldn't see her in her lovely new bonnet. But though she had been taking surreptitious looks out the carriage window ever since they had arrived in the district, and had actually craned her neck when they passed the gates of Royce Park, no Camberley had appeared to view her in her glory.

"Susan is dressed in perfect taste," Lady Delafort was saying, fluffing out the collarette of her own spencer. "I taught her how. The poor dear child was quite ignorant of such matters. But then, you would know that, Mother. You're the one who kept her that way. If she'd only been allowed to read some of the fashion magazines I sent down to her—"

"You did?" Susan was surprised. She had never heard of this before and felt a little thrill that her mother had tried to communicate in some way, even though she had scarcely ever answered letters.

"I confiscated them, of course, Jeanne-Jacqueline, as unsuitable reading matter for a young female," Mrs. Palmer declared with a glare at her daughter. She turned to her son-in-law. "Well, Delafort, I hope you've some strategy for keeping my daughter and me from coming to blows during this visit."

"Of course," the viscount said with a laugh. "I intend to guard Jenny from your sight as much as possible by keeping her all to myself."

Lady Delafort couldn't but preen a little at this; and Grandmama Palmer looked more satisfied, if still grim. She directed Susan to show the Delaforts to their chamber and swept out of the room. "My bees are waiting," she offered by way of explanation.

"Do excuse Grandmama, Papa," Susan said with a little shrug. "I probably should have changed into my country clothes to come down, but I simply didn't want to be dishonest. I have changed, and Grandmama might as well know it."

The viscount shook his head and looked very thoughtful. "I hadn't realized . . . You told me in your letters, Susan, how your grandmother had become quite a fanatic for simplicity,

but I didn't realize she had altered this severely.'' He gestured
at their surroundings. On their arrival Mrs. Palmer had led them
into the library, not the French drawing room. Rows of built-
in bookshelves held only one or two tracts, a Bible, and a couple
of volumes of Rousseau, and the room boasted only two straight
chairs. There was also a standing desk, but no other furniture.

The library had served one useful purpose, Susan thought as
she glanced about. Its barren state had induced in her a love
of reading—elsewhere. Her favorite place was in the garden,
a cabbage leaf filled with strawberries by her side as she perused
some delicious forbidden book which had been forgotten when
the library was sold.

"Wait until you see your rooms," Susan said with a grin.
"I hope the footmen will be quick in taking up the trunks."

Despite the impediment posed by Grandmama's way of life,
Susan and the servants accomplished the task of settling her
parents into Mama's childhood bedroom and a dressing room
adjoining with the minimum of fuss and much help from the
trunks of necessities the family had brought down. Then Susan
retired to her own chamber to put off her outdoor things and
change back into a simple country girl.

She surveyed the wardrobe, which was gaping open and
showed only the few threadbare white dresses she hadn't thought
worth bringing to London. Angleton was busily unpacking a
trunk of varicolored garments. Since the routing of Hortense,
Mama's dresser had insisted she could serve both ladies and
would prefer that to training another shifty-eyed trollop. Lady
Delafort, who was somewhat under Angleton's thumb when all
was said and done, had not quibbled.

Susan didn't even think she required a maid of her own, and
was glad that a new dresser had not been hired. "You needn't
bother with all of this, Angleton," she said now. "Mama will
be wanting you. I'd be glad to do my own unpacking. Or I can
call the housemaid," she added, remembering that Angleton
did not approve of a lady handling her own garments.

The abigail's long arms flew about as she folded a shawl.
She smiled a thin smile at Susan and said, "Thank you, ma'am,
I'll be finishing up this one trunk, and then I'll go."

"Very well." Susan went to the window and looked out. She

had formerly spent many an hour gazing out over the gardens toward the estate next door; now she instantly fell back into her old habits. Shaking her head at her own folly in thinking that Captain Camberley could be glimpsed from here, she wandered back across the room.

She halted before the only looking glass in her chamber, a minuscule one above the washstand. The bonnet was so lovely.

"Angleton, I believe on second thought that my mother and father will wish to be alone for a while before you unpack for her ladyship. Might you accompany me to pay a call on a neighbor?"

The dresser agreed, though her sharp eyebrows flew up at this odd request.

"We shall walk," Susan said. "It won't take us above twenty minutes, but better be sure you have the proper shoes. I'll change into my half-boots."

This was soon accomplished. Angleton, to whom sun and air were less than refined elements, saw herself shawled and bonneted against the bright day and shod against the rough country ground, then followed her young lady back up the drive of Pilgrim Court, along a leafy lane, and through the gates of a certain nearby estate.

Susan's mood was defiant. Grandmama had always forbidden her to visit in the neighborhood, but surely neither of her parents would do so. And she was under their guardianship now. She was longing to see Miss Camberley again, she told herself firmly. Miss Camberley had been so kind that she deserved every courtesy.

Please let him be there, she had enough honesty to beg of the heavens as she and Angleton strolled along the avenue of beeches which made the approach to the pleasant Jacobean manor of Royce Park.

As they walked up to the front door, Susan noticed that a familiar figure was heading off across the side lawn carrying a shovel. "Miss Camberley!" she called.

The figure turned, waved, and began to walk back in Susan's direction.

Susan rushed to meet her. "I do hope you forgive me for calling upon you without notice, ma'am," she said earnestly.

"I can see that you're busy, and we won't keep you." She blushed. "I ought not to have disturbed you, but simply have left my card. Manners are such complicated things."

"Please don't stand on ceremony here," Drusilla Camberley said. She propped her shovel against a convenient garden statue and held out her hand. "I'm glad to see you. Why don't we go into the house for some refreshment? I'm certain my brother would be glad to join us."

This last was spoken with a knowing look, or so it seemed to Susan. She felt her cheeks burn hotter. "Is the captain at home? Oh, but I really must let you go on with your work. You were heading out to the ruins, were you not?"

"Yes, but I wasn't going to do much digging," Miss Camberley replied. "I was only about to do some scouting. I've invited some friends down for a sort of ancient Roman party, and now that I've sent out my cards, I was concerned over whether there was anything worth seeing in the meadow."

"I'm certain there is a whole Roman villa with tiles and . . . and aqueducts and everything," Susan said. "I always thought so, and so the villagers' stories say, though my grandmother maintains that nothing much is there."

"Are there really such tales? Country people often know the truth. You sound like an enthusiast. You must come and join us when we go out to see the ruins."

"Oh, thank you," Susan said with a fervency that couldn't be attributed to her excitement about ruins, Roman or otherwise.

Drusilla led the way into an airy parlor which looked out upon a terrace. There she rang for refreshments. Angleton looked grateful to be sent to the housekeeper's room for restoratives of her own.

"Do ask Captain Camberley to join us if he has the time, Charles," Drusilla added. "He should be in the library."

Susan smiled brightly at this and began to answer Miss Camberley's questions about what she was doing down in the country in the middle of the Season.

"Dash it all, Em, what the devil do you mean by bringing us this way?" Viscount Buxford was exclaiming at that moment in a country lane not far away. "Box Hill is nowhere near here, according to that farmer we just passed."

"What does he know?" Lady Emily, who was consulting a map, negligently waved a kid-gloved hand to express her opinion of a mere native of the region. "I am certain, Buxy, that if we turn right at this crossing we shall be at Box Hill in no time."

"And why go there now? We ate the lunch," Buxford grumbled.

It was true. Buxford had proved so intractable during the winding journey into Surrey that Lady Emily had been forced to tempt him with Cook's pigeon pie, beef-and-pickle sandwiches, and macaroons, to say nothing of a bottle of the finest French wine and an entire seedcake. They had partaken of these delicacies perched upon a high bank several miles back.

Lady Emily took a deep breath. This was the time for her confession, and, now she was come to the point, she didn't know if her dear childhood friend would think her devious plan a good one or no. She was counting on his famous sense of humor to see her through the rest of the day.

"If you must know," she said in a confidential manner, after a short and pithy argument which had resulted, as all Lady Emily's arguments did, in her winning—in this case, in the necessary turn in the right at the crossroad—"I have a particular reason for wishing to come into Surrey today."

"I ain't a flat. Knew that all the time. Are you ready to come out with it?" Buxford demanded.

Lady Emily took a deep breath. "It's rather personal, but I know I can trust you. Indeed, that's why I wished for you to be the one to escort me."

"Stop batting your lashes, Em, and come clean," Buxford said with a cynical lift of a carroty brow.

"Well . . . " Lady Emily hesitated, then plunged in. "You must know I cherish a certain *tendresse* for Captain Camberley. He has been slippery and come down to the country without giving me a proper chance at him. I wish you and me to have an accident outside the gates of his estate. Then we'll be forced to take shelter there, and I'll soon be able to bring him round my thumb."

"What?" Buxford's face grew ruddy. "You're asking me to help you get compromised, that's it. Want to trick the fellow into marriage, do you? Well, I won't play such a trick on Camberley, Em. He's a fine chap. One of my best friends, in fact. His dog helped me win a famous wager."

Lady Emily was mystified by the reference to a dog, but she was determined to carry her point. "But, Buxy," she said sweetly, "the captain is in love with me. He is simply too shy to come to the point. If I can but be installed in his house, he will realize how much I mean to him."

"In love? He ain't paid you a scrap of attention all Season, you clunch. If you ask me, it's Miss Danvers who's on his mind."

Frowning awfully at this unwelcome news, Lady Emily said, still in a sweet, controlled voice, "I know you are fond of Miss Danvers yourself, Buxford. If you help me, you will clear your way to her side. If"—and she sniffed expressively—"you are correct that the captain is taken by that little blond nobody. I happen to think he needs a bit more sophistication, more town bronze in the woman he marries, and that she simply has one of those hero-worshiping infatuations that schoolgirls often fall victim to."

Buxford sat frowning in thought, his hands light as ever on the ribbons. "You know, Em, this sort of thing don't serve. What happens will happen, with or without our meddling."

"Nonsense," Lady Emily said. "My schemes always succeed."

"You have me there," Buxford had to admit from the vantage point of a lifelong experience of his friend's plots. "What do you say to a little wager on the matter?" His eyes lit up.

Lady Emily did not possess a wagering sort of temperament, but she saw that the prospect of betting would put Buxford in her way of thinking. "What do you mean?"

Buxford was one of those young men who, when deep in thought, are visibly so. Lady Emily watched the wheels turn for at least two minutes before her companion said, "It ain't proper, I suppose, to wager for the ready with a female. What do you say to your Millicent to my Britannicus?"

"Millicent is my very favorite mare," Lady Emily shrieked.

"And why should anyone even want that dreadful Britannicus? Isn't he the one who nearly dashed Miss Danvers to pieces in Hyde Park?"

Buxford was ready with a spirited defense of the gelding in question. Lady Emily was resolute in refusing to part with the mare she had raised from a filly. Finally, after making a detailed inventory of each other's stables, they decided on two horses that would be fit stakes.

"What are the terms?" Lady Emily asked next, having assured herself that Holly, the mare she had finally agreed to put up, was heavy in the hocks anyway—not that she would lose, by any means.

"Simple," Buxford said. "You wangle a proposal from Captain Camberley and you win my Lady. You don't, and I claim your mare."

"Done." Lady Emily held out her hand, and Buxford transferred the ribbons to his left and shook with her. "Now," she continued, scrutinizing her map again, "we are almost to the gates of Royce Park, according to this. Do let's stop the carriage now, and you can saw through your wheel."

"Saw through my wheel?" Buxford said with a yelp. "Are you mad, Em? This is my newest rig."

"But, Buxy," Lady Emily replied in a wheedling tone, "I packed the saw on purpose. And I'll gladly reimburse you for the wheel, of course."

Buxford glared. "So that's why the luncheon basket was such an odd size."

"Please?" Lady Emily made her eyes go wide and sad.

The viscount ran his gloved hand through his riot of red hair, dislodging his hat. "Never. You may pretend you're ill, and I'll back you on that, but saw through my wheel I will not."

"You're impossible! What could be more suspicious than my being taken ill right outside his gates? They'll never believe it."

"Take it or leave it," was Buxford's dark reply.

The two drove on in irritated silence until they came to a set of iron gates. Within, a straight line of beeches marched up an avenue to a manor house in the distance.

"Royce Park?" Buxford shouted to the gatekeeper.

Upon being assured that it was, Buxford identified himself as a friend of the Camberleys. The gates swung open.

"Remember, now," Buxford muttered to a fuming Lady Emily, "the wager is forfeit if you don't get him to offer. You'd best start looking ill."

"You are detestable!" Lady Emily hissed. She turned over in her mind whether it would be preferable merely to claim to the Camberleys that she and Buxford had lost their way to Box Hill and had happened upon Royce Park. Oh, dear. Nothing sounded believable at all.

"You'll never pull it off, you know," Buxford remarked as he pulled the curricle up at the front door of the manor.

Lady Emily, her eyes now sparkling with decision, mutely let Buxford assist her down.

When a butler opened the door, Lady Emily said in a voice of great urgency, "Where is your mistress? Quickly, man."

The retainer made an inarticulate motion of his hand toward the back of the house, and Lady Emily marched off.

"Let me conduct you, madam," the butler said, hurrying after her.

"You'd best leave her be," Buxford remarked, strolling in the lady's wake. "She won't let herself be crossed when she's in this mood. Silly wench," he added under his breath.

Lady Emily heard this aside and fancied that steam must soon issue from her ears.

The butler flung open a set of doors. "Visitors, madam."

Miss Camberley and Susan looked up from the glasses of lemonade they had but a moment before taken from a tray.

"Miss Camberley," Lady Emily cried, running across the room. "You must save me."

"Heavens, my dear girl. Whatever is amiss?" Drusilla had barely time to rise and set her glass down on a table before Lady Emily Forbes was upon her, casting herself into her arms with a sob.

Susan looked on in mystification.

Lord Buxford appeared at the door. "Forgive us the intrusion, ma'am," he said, addressing Miss Camberley. His eyes lit on Susan. "What? You here, Miss Danvers? Famous." He walked in and seated himself near the young lady, pausing to pour himself a glass of lemonade and take several biscuits from the loaded tray.

"This beast," Lady Emily said, indicating Buxford with a flourish, "this fiend, has . . . has . . . oh, I cannot bear to speak of it!" Covering her eyes, she burst into tears.

Susan and Drusilla both looked at Buxford with feminine suspicion.

He shrugged. "She hasn't thought it up yet," he explained, swallowing a biscuit. "Perhaps she's ill."

Lady Emily made an incoherent sound of fury.

At this point Captain Camberley, looking eager, came into the room. He smiled at Susan. "Miss Danvers! Charles told me you were here. I am very glad to see you."

"Vincent," Drusilla said from her awkward position in the embrace of Lady Emily, "we have other guests as well."

"I can see that. How d'ye do, Buxford?" Camberley came forward to shake the viscount's hand. "And this young lady, I presume, is . . ." He looked in indecision at the bonnet and gown draped across his sister. The young female's back was to him; she might be anyone.

Lady Emily plainly took it as an insult that the captain had not managed to recognize her from the back. "Sir," she said, turning to show him wet and sparkling eyes and an unfortunately reddened nose, "I have come to cast myself on your mercy."

Drusilla gently set the girl a little distance away from her. "My dear, do you think you could manage to tell us what brings you here?"

Lady Emily nodded. "Well, Lord Buxford invited me to take a drive into the country—to Box Hill. As he is an old and trusted friend of the family, I saw no harm in it. We brought a picnic, and we have gone on excursions together before, and I thought everything would be most proper." She hesitated, with a sidelong look at Buxford. "Then he—the beast—he tried to take l-liberties!" Once again she burst into tears which struck more than one of her listeners as artful.

All looked in astonishment at Buxford.

"I say," that young man burst out, "have your wits gone begging, Em? I take liberties with you, indeed! I'd as soon—"

He cut himself off, evidently unwilling to make an ungentlemanly remark.

"Naturally he denies it," Lady Emily cried. "He is a fiend!"

Buxford said to Camberley in a man-to-man tone, "She's taken ill, that's all."

"Do give me your sanctuary, dear Miss Camberley," Lady Emily sobbed. "Don't make me drive back to town with that libertine."

"Libertine? I?" Buxford was clearly astounded by this remark.

"It would seem to me," Captain Camberley said in a careful voice, "that poor Lady Emily needs rest and quiet. She should not upon any account drive back to town today. Drusilla, you might show her up to a guest bedroom."

"Of course. At once," Miss Camberley agreed. "Come, Lady Emily, you'll feel more the thing after a lie-down and perhaps a cold compress."

"Shall I come too?" Susan asked diffidently.

"Oh, yes," Lady Emily said with a glance at the captain.

"By no means, my dear." Miss Camberley spoke. "Do stay here and entertain the gentlemen for a moment, if you would be so good. I'll return in a nonce." And without even ringing for the butler, Drusilla put a firm hand on Lady Emily's arm and led her from the room. Lady Emily drooped and sniffled quite as though she were on the very edge of a vaporish turn.

Her ladyship also looked quite put out, if Susan was not mistaken.

When the other ladies had left the room, Susan smiled helplessly at the gentlemen. "I do hope Lady Emily feels more the thing soon," she said. "Lord Buxford, I know she would never tell such stories if she were not . . . ill." Of the many things she had observed in the last five minutes, Susan felt most sanguine about Buxford's honesty. He had been thoroughly shocked to be so accused by Lady Emily.

Buxford bowed. "Thank you, Miss Danvers. She's an odd creature, is her ladyship. Known her from the time we was both in leading-strings. She's mistaken. I wouldn't lay a finger on her, and well she knows."

Camberley came to sit beside Susan on the sofa she had earlier chosen with just that hope in mind. Buxford might be on her other side, but she consoled herself that her wish had come true. The captain was having full opportunity to scrutinize her in her new bonnet, though he had not mentioned it, and he had already said that he was glad to see her.

"I hear that you will be having a group down to investigate the Roman villa," she said.

Camberley laughed. "Drusilla's friends are indeed about to descend on us, Miss Danvers. Do I dare to hope that you might make one of the investigating team?"

"Well, I know next to nothing about ruins, but I did used to sneak over to the meadow, sit on the rocks there, and dream about the ancient Romans when I was a child," Susan told him. "I'm certain I could wield a shovel."

"You will hardly be required to do that, Miss Danvers, but we would be glad of your company," Camberley said with a look full of affection—or so Susan interpreted the intensity of the brown eyes.

Buxford, on Susan's other side, cleared his throat. "I say, that digging party sounds like sport. What do you say, Camberley? May I join you if I'm still down in these parts? Must ask you to direct me to the nearest inn, by the way. I shall stay in the neighborhood to escort Em back to town when she comes to her senses."

"What?" Captain Camberley, still staring into Susan's face, didn't appear to have heard.

Buxford, in an exasperated tone, repeated himself.

"You can't go to an inn, my lord," Camberley said with a smile. "You must stay with us as well."

"Wasn't hinting for an invitation," the viscount protested. "Besides, if Em is styling me a libertine, she won't much like sitting down to table with me."

"Don't give it a thought," was Camberley's advice. "You are my guest and she is my sister's. Besides, I'd wager her ladyship won't be feeling fit enough to come down to dinner, especially once she knows you're here."

Buxford, after a few more protests, was persuaded to stay at Royce Park.

"I'd better go out and give directions about the horses," he said, rising. "Miss Danvers? If you were going, I might drive you home."

"Your poor horses must be worn out already," Susan said. "But you're correct, sir, I've stayed far past the proper time for a morning call." She stood up as well.

"Dramatics take a deal of time, that's a fact," Buxford said cheerfully. "I won't take it as an insult to my cattle that you think they're worn down after a mere twenty miles, ma'am, if you come with me now."

Camberley rose. "Might I suggest that we both walk Miss Danvers home?"

"Oh. Well, there's no harm in that," Buxford said with an exasperated look at the captain.

Susan knew she should feel honored to walk back to her grandmother's under the escort of not one, but two gentlemen. At least she tried to convince herself that she didn't mind Buxford as well as Camberley getting the full benefit of her new bonnet—which had still not been noticed.

The trio spent the entire walk in making up ever-more-elaborate excuses for Lady Emily's strange behavior. Susan's feminine intuition—or her instinctive sense of rivalry—told her that her ladyship had forced her way into the Camberley's house for some devious purpose.

Glancing up at Captain Camberley's profile, Susan wondered if she were only fancying that he was as irked as was she that they couldn't take this walk in the company of only Angleton. Unlike the maid, who was walking most properly a few paces behind, Buxford was definitely underfoot.

"May I call on you soon, Miss Danvers?" Captain Camberley asked when they were standing at the door of Pilgrim Court. He took Susan's hand in both of his.

Angleton cleared her throat loudly.

"I say," Buxford put in, his unfriendly eye surveying the hands in question. "I should be glad to accompany the captain when he calls."

Camberley leaned close to Susan's bonnet to whisper, "Not the most romantic of situations, my dear. We must wait for better times."

Romantic! That was a fine and welcome word. Susan gazed at him, wishing for much more than she had heard.

"What was that?" Buxford asked with interest.

Susan smiled at the captain, then offered a lesser smile to Buxford. "Thank you, gentlemen, for seeing me home," she said demurely.

With Angleton beside her, she didn't care to stay on the steps to sigh over Captain Camberley's manly form as the two gentlemen walked away. She and the maid entered the front hall.

There, arms folded, stood Grandmama. "So, miss! You've been paying calls in the neighborhood, have you? You know my rules on that subject."

"Oh, Grandmama," Susan said with a little sigh, "I've grown up. I'm sorry if you don't like it."

Mrs. Palmer's face relaxed a very little. "You're right, my dear, I don't like it one bit. But I suppose that this is the way it must be. You've fribbles for parents, and you're under their care now."

Susan couldn't agree—exactly—with this estimation of Lord and Lady Delafort, but she thought it best not to argue. Giving Grandmama a quick peck on the cheek, she escaped to her bedchamber.

15

Dinner at Pilgrim Court was a subdued affair. Mrs. Palmer dwelt for much of the meal on the Delaforts' good sense in returning Susan to the country before it was too late.

"While I was sorry to cut short her Season, I think Susan made the most of it. She will hold her own in any society," Lord Delafort said with a pointed look.

Since Mrs. Palmer had brought her granddaughter up, she could hardly accuse her of weakness of character. She remained silent just long enough for the viscount to turn the conversation to his many adventures in India.

"And only think how sad it was for him to have to leave London when he had not told half his charming stories," Lady Delafort put in with an eloquent sigh when her husband paused at the end of an anecdote. "We must go back soon."

Mrs. Palmer sniffed. "If you young people wish my opinion, you will make for your place in Derbyshire and never leave it—except, to be sure, to visit me. And naturally Susan is welcome to stay here in the home she has known all her life."

"We will indeed visit my estate, and soon," Lord Delafort said with a smile for his mother-in-law. "As for Susan, she will choose where she wishes to live—she is at that age when several choices may be open to her." At this, he gave Susan a conspiratorial smile which she hoped did not refer to an offer he had already had for her hand. "But I've learned, ma'am, that my dear wife needs society. What but society has kept her in such blooming beauty all these years?"

"Ah." Lady Delafort sighed in gratitude. "Isn't he simply the most glorious man?"

Mrs. Palmer ignored this flight. "I believe that eel was to be removed with a plate of brains?" she said to the footman behind her chair. "Get to it, man."

At Pilgrim Court, the ordinary diet was nearly vegetarian. Susan and Mrs. Palmer lived largely off the produce of the estate. Grandmama must have ordered the extra dishes to honor her visitors, Susan thought with a shudder of revulsion. As she pretended to eat, she wondered if Grandmama would ever admit to that other life of hers, that continental, sophisticated existence which old Lady Semerton had related with such relish and which had expressed itself so perfectly in that scandalous French novel Grandmama had written.

"Young girls," Mrs. Palmer said with a severe stare, "should never look sly at the dinner table."

Susan nearly choked on her water, the only beverage Grandmama thought suitable for young ladies, as she returned an innocent, injured look to this wry comment.

The morrow brought changes for Susan, as Mrs. Palmer decided to return her granddaughter posthaste to the activities she had enjoyed prior to her descent into the sinks of London. "That gown will hardly serve for the day's work," Mrs. Palmer said, eyeing askance Susan's blue sprigged muslin as that young lady sat with her grandmother at an early breakfast table.

Susan swallowed the last of her milk and left her piece of bread and butter unfinished on the plate. "Grandmama, I . . ." She paused, not quite wishing to assert her independence yet again. Grandmama was already so disconcerted by Susan's emergence into fashion and disobedience that perhaps she didn't deserve another example of defiant behavior. "I'll go and change," Susan finished, slipping out of her chair.

Later, in an ancient white cambric gown, Susan sat staring into space as she churned butter in the model dairy. She was finding menial chores to be an excellent vehicle for daydreaming about Captain Camberley. How delightfully he had smiled at her yesterday when he was whispering in her ear as they said good-bye. What would happen next?

That question was answered when the door to the shed opened to admit Lady Emily, who looked rather wild in what must be an ensemble borrowed from Miss Camberley. The gown was much too short and tight across the bosom, and the bonnet was in a severe style Lady Emily would surely never have chosen for herself. "There you are, my dearest creature," she said, rushing forward. "What in heaven's name can you be doing? Ah, never mind, you can listen to me while you go on with it." Sitting down in the one chair the shed boasted, Lady Emily began her tale while Susan was still getting over the shock of seeing her.

"I must escape from Lord Buxford, dear girl. Do you know, he has actually talked round the Camberleys? I didn't think he had it in him, but there it is: they invited him to stay the night, quite as if he had been an ordinary traveler! You may imagine my dismay when I came down to breakfast today, to find Captain Camberley out upon some business having to do with dreary cottages, Miss Camberley inviting me to come poke about with her in a meadow, and Buxy—Lord Buxford—sitting at the table as calm as you please, shoveling ham and mustard into his silly face! I couldn't support the sight of that treacherous creature. I came instantly to you, and your butler told me where I might find you. Now"—and Lady Emily paused at long last for breath—"what shall we do about this sad tangle?"

"What do you wish to do?" Susan asked after a pause in which she tried to ascertain what, exactly, Lady Emily was trying to elicit from her.

Her ladyship was silent for a moment while she leaned her chin upon her hand and thought furiously. "My dear, I simply wish for your companionship," she said finally, as if inspired. "Miss Camberley, bless her, is no kind of chaperon. She is too busy with shovels and stones and things. You must stay with me today to ensure that Lord Buxford won't be able to get me alone and . . . and . . . You understand me."

"Did the viscount really try to take advantage of you?" Susan asked with wide eyes.

"You simply must help me," Lady Emily said, ignoring Susan's question. "Do let's go back to the Camberley's now, and you may spend the day with me while I decide what to do next."

"Don't you wish to return to London?" Susan asked. "That is, your clothes . . ."

"Oh, of course," Lady Emily said airily. "I shall wait to hear from my family, though. I sent off a message to my brother last night to tell him where I was, and he will surely come for me.''

''Thank goodness you sent to him,'' Susan remarked. ''Otherwise Lady Semerton would have been so worried.''

''How sweet! You are eager to see my brother.'' Lady Emily's eyes took on a sly expression.

Susan vehemently denied any such motive. ''I am simply glad that your grandmother didn't have to remain in suspense.''

Her assurances were lost on Lady Emily, who continued to plead her own cause. ''To be sure. Do say you'll come with me, dear. I took the liberty of telling your mama, whom I met in the garden, that I would be stealing you away, and she made no demur.''

Susan finished the churning and stood up, smoothing down a gown that was already the worse for some digging in the garden. Luckily the housemaid was due to arrive at any minute to wash the butter; Susan could leave her project with a conscience at least halfway clear.

''To spend the day with the Camberleys, I must change my things,'' she said.

''Oh, nonsense, I know you to be a creature above vulgar vanity. Here's a bonnet,'' and Lady Emily grabbed Susan's battered leghorn hat from a hook on the wall. ''You're quite fine enough to sit with me alone. The only other thing you might do at Royce Park today is help Miss Camberley in her meadow, and for that you're too fine.''

Susan laughed. ''Very well.'' She did wish to be a creature who was not ruled by vanity, and she need not stand on ceremony with neighbors.

A short walk through the garden brought the girls to the Grecian folly, scene of Susan's first meeting with Captain Camberley. She let a little sigh escape her at the memory. Then she briskly got down to business and showed Lady Emily the way through the paling into Royce Park land.

''How charming,'' Lady Emily said. ''I suppose you and your neighbors use this shortcut all the time?'' This with a sharp look.

''We have hardly had occasion to do so,'' Susan replied.

She and Lady Emily continued to stroll, now through the finely laid-out lawns of Royce Park, until they arrived at a

terrace. "There are French windows at the top of this," Lady
Emily said. "And I believe this is the very breakfast room I
left earlier. Buxy is probably still at his meal, for all I have
been gone half an hour."

"I thought you didn't want to encounter the viscount," were
Susan's last, softly uttered words before she and Lady Emily
entered the breakfast room.

Lord Buxford was not in evidence; only servants clearing
away the remnants of the meal. Lady Emily made a little noise
of frustration and led on.

In the drawing room they finally encountered the young man
they wished most to avoid.

"You see, Buxford, I've brought Miss Danvers to be my
protector," Lady Emily said grandly.

Viscount Buxford had been comfortably spread out in a deep
chair, his booted feet on a footstool and his nose in a newspaper. He started to his feet on hearing the lady's voice.

"Well, Em," he said with a cough, "you won't wish Miss
Danvers to continue in her mistake."

"What mistake?"' Lady Emily arranged herself on a graceful
sofa, motioning Susan to sit down too.

Buxford smiled sheepishly at Susan. "You must excuse me,
Miss Danvers, for speaking somewhat strongly to my old
friend," he said gently. Then, turning to Lady Emily, he
continued in quite a different tone, "Em, your wits have gone
begging if you believe Miss Danvers will be likely to form a
tendre for a libertine! And that's what you've made me out to
be. Ain't it your plan for me to draw her off?"

"Draw me off?" Susan asked curiously, beginning to see the
light.

Lady Emily scowled. "You, Buxy, are the stupidest man in
the world," she snapped. Then, to Susan, "Don't mind the poor
man. He is talking nonsense as usual. Perhaps"—and here she
smiled sweetly at Buxford—"he means to confess to you that
he merely made improper overtures to me because he was so
overwrought with unrequited love for you that he ran mad."

Susan laughed. "Oh, Lady Emily, I've read too many novels
lately to believe any such thing."

"Pity," Buxford said with a thoughtful look. "Seems like a pretty good story to me."

"I think the pair of you would do much better to admit that there were no improper advances," Susan said with a keen look first at Lady Emily, then at Lord Buxford.

"Deuce take it, ma'am, you may have my oath there were none," Buxford said earnestly.

Lady Emily looked insulted at this aspersion on her veracity. Before she could think of a scathing remark, the doors to the room opened and the impassive Camberley butler uttered, "Lady Semerton. Lord Semerton."

Susan stared as the elderly Lady Semerton bustled importantly into the room, leaning upon her stick. She was followed by the young earl.

He made straight for Susan while Lady Emily and her grandmother burst into a flow of simultaneous talk. "Miss Danvers," he said, having given Buxford an offhand greeting, "you look delightfully bucolic in that pretty white gown. Emily, now, looks a quiz. Don't know where she could have found such a get-up."

Susan shifted her hands in her lap to hide one of the worst smudges on her ensemble. "Thank you, sir. So you have come to take your sister home?" She couldn't forget that the last time she had seen this gentleman in any intimacy had been the uncomfortable night of the gaming house and masquerade, and she was determined to keep the conversation on the most innocuous of levels to avoid a renewal of his unwelcome attentions. She had still not forgiven him for that kiss—short though the salute had been.

"Actually," the earl confided, leaning close, "I've come to get her off my hands, Miss Danvers. Watch this." He winked, then stood up and clapped his hands for attention.

His two female relations stopped chattering. "Really, Alistair," Lady Semerton said with a dark frown. "Your manners—"

"Forgive me, Grandmother, but we must go on with our business," Semerton said with the air of one who is about to make an announcement of great importance.

"What business is that?" Captain Camberley now strolled

into the room. "How do you do, ladies. Semerton. Miss
Danvers! What an unexpected pleasure."

"I was about to announce a marriage," Semerton said with
a bow. "How d'ye do, Camberley?"

"Whose marriage?" the captain asked.

"Yours," the earl replied with a well-bred smile.

"What!" Camberley stared, while the other inmates of the
room held a collective breath.

Semerton drew himself up importantly. "This matter is quite
clear to me. Unsavory, but clear. Camberley, my sister has
passed a night under your roof. You must make an honest
woman of her without delay."

Lady Emily brightened at his speech. Lady Semerton thumped
her cane on the floor and shook her head in disgust. Buxford
barked out a laugh. And Susan felt herself suddenly near
tears.

"Come now," Captain Camberley said. "Her ladyship may
have spent a night under this roof, but so did my sister. I assure
you Lady Emily was under the strictest chaperonage at all
times." He looked at his other guest. "So, I might add, was
Lord Buxford."

"Now, there's a thought," Semerton said, grinning at his
friend. "Here's the fiend who made off with my sister. Why
shouldn't he marry her?"

"For a host of reasons," Lady Emily cried.

"I submit that my sister has been ruined, and someone must
marry her," Semerton said with finality. "You may decide
between you who's to be the lucky man."

"Boy, you go too far," Lady Semerton put in. "Neither of
these young men deserves . . . that is, what Camberley says
about Emily's situation makes sense. She's had a chaperon with
her at all times."

"I don't see Miss Camberley, this so-called chaperon," the
earl remarked.

"She's in the meadow," Susan said. "Lady Emily came
instantly to me this morning and asked me to sit with her here
rather than risk being alone with Lord Buxford, my lord. We've
been together every minute. She has been most strict about the
proprieties."

"Naturally her ladyship is the very soul of propriety," the captain added.

Lady Emily looked less than pleased at these tributes.

"Be that as it may," Semerton said, seemingly imperturbable in his zeal to have his sister settled, "Emily has spent the night out of town, and it's bound to get out. She must be married, I tell you. And immediately."

Drusilla Camberley had quietly entered the room in time to hear Lord Semerton's last speech.

"Nonsense," she offered, coming forward. "Lady Emily has merely arrived a few days early to join my Roman party."

"What?" Semerton's eyebrows lifted in what he was often told was a truly devilish manner.

"It's true," Camberley said. "My sister is expecting guests. Never mind that their aim is to discuss ancient Rome and that Lady Emily isn't widely known for preferring such an activity. It's almost respectable gathering that will probably be announced in the papers the same as any other." He smiled. "Thanks, that is, to my infernal celebrity. Otherwise I believe my sister would be allowed to hold her parties in private."

"Nobody would believe it of my sister. Ancient Rome, indeed," the frustrated young earl exclaimed. "Will you marry her like a man, or will you name your friends?"

"This is ridiculous," Susan burst out. "You, my lord, are a meddler. Perhaps your sister doesn't wish to be married."

Lady Emily, who might have been expected to add something to the discussion at this point, remained obstinately silent.

"Do you really wish to expose your sister to the unsavory publicity of a duel?" Camberley asked Semerton. His tone was incredulous. "I wouldn't have thought it of a loving brother, but if you insist—"

"Damnation," Lady Semerton said with another thump of her cane. "Miss Danvers is right. This passes all the boundaries of good sense. I'm leaving at once. You, Semerton, will escort me and your sister. Come, Emily, I have a call to pay in the neighborhood before I take you back to London and put you on short rations for this foolish start."

Lord Buxford and Miss Camberley burst into simultaneous laughter.

"Well, that's settled," the viscount said. He was sounding remarkably cheery. "I'll be in touch with you about that mare, Em. I say, ma'am"—this to Miss Camberley, while the others were puzzling over the reference to a horse—"why don't you let me come out and help you in those ruins you were talking of at breakfast? I've a strong back and a willing pair of hands."

Dazed, Miss Camberley left the room with the young viscount, sparing only one startled backward glance for her brother.

Susan busily began to think over the possibility of a match between those two. Miss Camberley might be a couple of years older, but stranger couples could be seen walking around London every day.

"Nothing is settled, no matter what Buxford says," Semerton protested. "My sister is to be married, I tell you." Again he scowled at Camberley.

Lady Semerton spoke up. "Camberley, do you care to ride on the box of my barouche? I shall take Miss Danvers home, and I have every reason to suppose you would wish to be with her."

Lady Emily made a little indignant sound. Susan looked away from Camberley's twinkling eyes.

"Lady Semerton," he said, "you are most kind."

"Let's be off, young ladies," Lady Semerton said. "Emily, do you really wish to wear that? You can't have arrived in it. With all respect to Miss Camberley, she is half a foot shorter than you and not so generously built."

Lady Emily exchanged a glance with Susan, who obligingly rose to help her ladyship change, but Lady Semerton held Miss Danvers back with, "I'm certain there's a maid about this house who can button my granddaughter into her gown. You stay by me, Miss Danvers. Tell me what you've been up to since you arrived in the country."

"Not a great deal," Susan said, watching Lady Emily out of the room. "My family only came yesterday. I'm afraid the major excitement in the neighborhood was Lady Emily's arrival with Lord Buxford."

"You can't mean it's known?"

"No, merely that I happened to be here when they showed

up yesterday," Susan said. "You need have no fear of scandal, my lady. This is a quiet neighborhood. And in any case, Lady Emily has indeed been well chaperoned every moment."

"Except during the drive," Semerton said thoughtfully. "We might make something of that."

"Buxford is your friend," Lady Semerton said, taking aim with her reticule as though she wished to teach her grandson a forceful lesson. "Let's have no more of that talk."

"Deuce take it, Grandmama, you've mentioned a time or two that Emily should get married."

"I don't expect my advice to be taken. And I certainly don't hold with forced marriages, no matter who the victim. Besides, Alistair, it's you whom I've been pestering to marry this Season."

"Ah, Grandmother," the earl said in his most worldly-wise manner, "let us not be precipitate in front of the very young lady whose hopes I mean to fulfill."

"Conceited, but he ain't a bad lad," Lady Semerton told Susan, who had reddened in embarrassment. "Conduct me to the carriage, Alistair. We can wait for Emily there. Miss Danvers, will you give an old woman the pleasure of your company? My relations are like to drive me into Bedlam."

Susan rose from her place. Captain Camberley was there to give his arm, and all at once she became aware of her shabby dress and shabbier hat.

"Do you know, Miss Danvers," Camberley said in a low tone, "I don't believe I've ever seen you look so pretty."

"I'm dressed in rags," Susan protested.

"Then we must give points to your grandmother's belief in nature's wisdom, for you rise above your clothing marvelously well," Camberley said, smiling.

Lord Semerton cast dark and poetic looks at this byplay, but Lady Semerton soon prodded him to her side.

The procession was about to leave the drawing room when Charles flung open the doors. "Mrs. Palmer," he said with a special flourish of his hand.

Susan stared as her grandmother moved into the room.

16

"Cassandra!" Lady Semerton dropped her grandson's arm to hurry to the doorway.

"Livvy!" was Mrs. Palmer's amazed gasp. The two ladies fell into each other's arms and embraced energetically, pulling back after the first moments of affection to gaze with avid curiosity on the ravages time had wrought upon each.

Susan, Semerton, and Captain Camberley looked on with interest, Susan's heightened by the fact that she had not known her grandmother to leave the boundaries of Pilgrim Court since the death of Grandpapa Palmer.

"Shall we sit down again?" Captain Camberley suggested with all the smoothness of the perfect host.

The two old ladies looked up at this and seemed to recall their surroundings.

"We are honored, deeply honored, Mrs. Palmer, by your visit," continued the captain. With polite firmness he saw to the seating arrangements. Mrs. Palmer and Lady Semerton somehow found themselves side by side on a sofa. Lord Semerton and Susan took chairs, and Camberley sat down last—near Susan, although he had to carry a chair there. Susan was filled with joy at this maneuver, but it seemed to disgust Lord Semerton.

Susan was unable to keep silent any longer. "Grandmama, why are you here? You never go out."

Mrs. Palmer turned from an exchange with Lady Semerton on the subject of aching bones and looked over her spectacles at her granddaughter. "My dear, can you even doubt it? I've come to put stop to your ridiculous gadding. When your mother told me you had flitted over here for the second day in a row, I knew I had to bestir myself to keep you from acting in a most improper manner. Things may be different in town, Susan, but you are under my roof now.''

"Oh." Susan was crestfallen and felt her color begin to rise on being talked to as though she were a naughty child. She willed herself to say no more and concentrated on the respect she owed her grandmother, not to mention gratitude for a lifetime of care, no matter how misguided that care might have been.

"Nonsense, Cassandra," the Countess of Semerton said in a tone of disgust.

"What? How dare you, Livvy?" Mrs. Pallmer glared at her old friend. "See if I give you that recipe for rheumatic tea if you insult me.''

"You're coming it much too strong. Fancy denying the girl the right to visit the neighbors! I've never heard of such a thing.''

"We do not go out," Mrs. Palmer stated firmly.

"Grandmama," Susan put in, "I was given Mama's permission to come here today, and Lady Emily most particularly needed my company.''

Her grandmother merely snorted at this.

Captain Camberley, who had been a fascinated bystander, chose this moment to play his card as host. "I daresay you ladies could do with a glass of lemonade. Or rather, wine," he corrected himself, intercepting Lady Semerton's disgusted glance. "And then, Mrs. Palmer, so long as you are here, you might like to see the gardens. They are nothing to Pilgrim Court, make no mistake, but there is a little Shakespeare corner that's pleasant, and a small maze that amuses me.''

"A maze." Mrs. Palmer lifted up her eyes. "A Shakespeare corner. My dear sir"—and she looked sharply at the captain—"you have lured my granddaughter onto your premises. I do not intend to lend countenance to your behavior by poking about your gardens.''

"I say," Semerton spoke up, "did you lure Miss Danvers here as well as my sister? That's double dealing for sure, Camberley.''

The captain surveyed the earl in exasperation. "My lord, we have already discussed your sister and her visit here. She arrived of her own volition, and with a male companion. Your grandmother wishes to take her home, but I still believe that all of you would do better to remain here.''

A thoughtful silence greeted this pronouncement.

''There's plenty of room,'' Camberley continued, speaking into the void. ''You may send to town for your things and all join my sister's party, which will be assembling in a couple of days. This would be an excellent way to divert all the *ton*'s suspicions that there was something out of the way about Lady Emily's drive into Surrey. And your ladyships,'' he said, bowing to Lady Semerton, ''might spend more time with Mrs. Palmer.''

''Camberley,'' Lady Semerton said, ''I believe you have something there. But I wouldn't inflict myself and my sad scamps of grandchildren on you for the world.''

The last sentence was spoken on that half-note of query which begs to be talked round. The captain proceeded to assure Lady Semerton that she and her young relations were more than welcome.

As he was finishing this invitation, watched in admiration by Lady Semerton and Susan, and glared at by Mrs. Palmer, Lady Emily came into the room. She was attired in her ordinary clothes, the ones she had worn the day before, and one gloved hand was clutched to her middle.

''Grandmama,'' she said in a faint voice, ''it took all my strength to dress. I fear I'm not feeling quite the thing.''

''You may save all that, Emily. Captain Camberley has chosen to be gallant and ignore your tricks. He has talked me into staying here for a few days,'' Lady Semerton said dryly.

''Oh!'' Suddenly more radiant than wan, Lady Emily beamed at the captain.

He nodded at her in a brisk naval manner clearly meant to dash her hopes, and moved to pull the bell. Charles, who had evidently been hovering quite near the interesting group in the drawing room, was dispatched for refreshments.

''And now,'' Mrs. Palmer said as soon as the servant was gone, ''it is time for me to take my leave. Susan, you will come with me. Livvy,'' she addressed Lady Semerton—''we might have our differences, but glad I would be to meet again and fight them out. I would be delighted to receive you at Pilgrim Court. We have years of talking to do.'' She rose, and Susan, not knowing what else to do, rose with her.

"Not so fast," Lady Semerton objected. To Susan's astonishment she actually pulled at her old friend's gown, causing Mrs. Palmer to descend back onto the couch with a plop. Susan quietly sat back down also.

"Have you run mad?" Susan's grandmother spoke in irritation. "Is this what years of town life does, Livvy? You have let the last vestige of conduct go by the board."

"Rubbish," Lady Semerton stated with a thump of her cane. "What is old age for, if not to speak one's mind and do as one pleases? And you, my dear old friend, are not escaping from this room until you tell me what I wish to know."

"Do you dare to take with me, your schoolfellow, that arrogant tone of worldly rank?" Mrs. Palmer's voice was hard and cold, and her eyes radiated scorn. "Remember, Livvy, I was by when you married Semerton. I was your bridesmaid, you absurd female. You never expected to catch a title. You were the humblest of the humble, and now you've become autocratic as any aristo of the old regime."

Lady Emily let a strangled half-whoop escape her at this tidbit. The others in the room could well imagine that her ladyship had never been noted for meekness in Lady Emily's time.

"You ain't yourself, Cass," Lady Semerton stated with a disgusted look. "That remark was not worthy of you. You've forgotten all you knew of society. Now I needn't ask you why you're so set on staying in the country, for it's clear enough that you're a fool. Probably always were, literary leanings notwithstanding."

"Literary leanings, Mrs. Palmer?" put in Lord Semerton at this point. As a poet, he was much interested in the work of others, especially such an unlikely authoress as Miss Danvers' choleric grandmother. "I would be fascinated to hear your stories of the literary salons of your day. You were a poetess, no doubt?" Little light verses, nothing like his own strong and manly rantings, would have been this lady's pleasure in the past. Judicious praise of these might work to his advantage in his pursuit of her granddaughter.

Lady Emily's eyes had lit up, and she whispered something into her brother's ear while the two grandmothers continued grumbling at each other, completely ignoring the young people.

"You don't say!" Semerton cried. "And you tell me Miss Danvers knows of it?"

Lady Emily nodded with a mischievous grin. "It is a family secret, of course," she murmured.

Susan, sitting near them, heard all this and grew alarmed. Her grandmother would be mortified if—

Before Susan could think of any course of action, short of bundling the brother and sister into the large Sheraton cabinet near their chairs, Lord Semerton burst out with, "Mrs. Palmer, you must allow me to congratulate you. I cannot believe it! Miss Danvers' grandmother the author of *Lessons in Life*. You may be sure the secret will never pass my lips, for my sister tells me that our family alone is privy to it, but I am enchanted, madam—enchanted."

The earl rushed forward to clasp the hands of an astonished Mrs. Palmer, who looked at him as though he were a wild beast and shook him off. Semerton retired, abashed.

"Livvy," Mrs. Palmer said on a warning note, turning furious spectacled eyes to her friend, "you gave me your word of honor."

Lady Semerton had the grace to look a little ashamed. "Well, Cass, I may have done so, but it was forty-odd years ago."

Mrs. Palmer drew herself up. "To think that you would spout that old tale to these gibble-gabbling children! I am appalled, Livvy. Truly appalled." Her gaze moved from Lady Emily and Lord Semerton and lit on Susan. "Good Lord!" She passed a hand over her face.

"Don't worry, Grandmama," Susan said, rushing across the room to place a comforting hand on her grandmother's shoulder. "I've known of this for a long while. I think you're splendid, truly splendid. I've read it, and—"

"You've read it?" Mrs. Palmer said with a gasp.

Susan nodded.

"How did you even get the French?"

"An old grammar in the attic," Susan said, determined to give up her deceptive ways for all time. "That is also where

I found the book. You kept a copy for sentiment, I daresay.''

"Livvy, this is all your doing,'' Mrs. Palmer said, turning on her friend once more. "You told her, did you not?''

"She had every right to know what shaped her own grand-mother,'' Lady Semerton said, sounding furious. "You have been false, Cass, to hide what you once were. And that was never like you.''

Susan turned from the threatening exchange of hostilities and saw Captain Camberley. He looked most interested in the revelation; his expression was almost one of glee. Susan's distress mounted. She wouldn't have thought the captain one of those vulgar people who delighted in gossip. Frantic, she motioned him to go out of the room before her grandmother realized he was present and that her secret had passed to yet another pair of ears.

To Susan's dismay, he ignored her warnings and moved to stand before Mrs. Palmer. That lady looked up from her snapping exchange with Lady Semerton and glared at the captain.

"So! You mean to taunt me with my former sins, sir?''

"But no means, ma'am,'' Camberley said with an earnest expression. "Like his lordship, I find I must compliment you on your work. When I think how I've longed to know the writer of that charming novel—when I remember how many wrong guesses I've made, how many eminent statesmen and grand ladies I've suspected of writing it—Mrs. Palmer, words fail me.''

"I wish they would,'' Mrs. Palmer said with a toss of her head which put her heavy widow's bonnet slightly askew.

"All the while I was translating it, I admired your fine mind, your incisive grasp of the French society of your young days,'' Camberley continued, a true light of admiration in his fine brown eyes.

"Well, naturally. Cass always had a head on her shoulders, and she knew the French court like her own garden,'' Lady Semerton said with an approving nod at Mrs. Palmer.

Susan, now standing behind her grandmother's sofa, had paid close attention to Camberley's words. "What do you mean, sir,'' she asked, "when you say you translated the book? Didn't you know that it's now been published in English? Why, you must. It was you who first told me about the English version.''

Camberley's smile was wry as he turned his eyes to Susan. "You and your grandmother have every right to know. I am the anonymous person who translated *Des Leçons dans la Vie* into English. I did it as a sort of lark, once while I was convalescing from my wounds in a place far from home, and the book was the only thing to hand. I captured it from a French privateer, in fact." He looked around at the astonished faces. "You are surprised that a plain sailor could do it?"

"I hope, sir, that your translation of Grandmama's novel rings more true than your characterization of yourself as a plain sailor," Susan said with a smile.

Mrs. Palmer was very quiet, as were Lord Semerton and his sister. Lady Semerton was the next to speak.

"I call it a famous thing you've done, lad. Cassandra's story deserves to be well-known in English. And heaven knows the generation coming up can't read French as we could."

"Well, Grandmother, we are hardly to be blamed that we couldn't hop over to Paris as easily as you could in your day," Lady Emily said with a touch of resentment. "And you refused to take me only last year, when it became possible again."

"Didn't wish to see it. I want to remember the Paris of my youth," Lady Semerton said to Mrs. Palmer, who nodded in understanding.

"There was nothing like the Paris of our youth," she said with a wistfulness Susan had never heard in her voice before.

"Do tell me something, ma'am." Camberley addressed Mrs. Palmer. "Why did you change so greatly from the sophisticated court lady you were in your young days? Did you truly rebel against the excesses of society that caused the revolution? Is that it?"

"It is," Mrs. Palmer said, but her eyes were not on the captain's. Susan had moved again to her former chair, and she could see Grandmama's gaze shifting to one side.

Susan had always wondered why this understandable rebellion against the worldly ways of youth had affected her grandmother so strongly as to make her scorn all society and forswear every household comfort. Once again, she didn't believe she had heard the full story, but now she did think that she could hazard a guess. While she had been away from Pilgrim Court, free of its atmosphere, she had been able to find new insights about Grandmama's way of life.

"Now, Susan, now that I've been humiliated past all bearing, will you give me your company back to Pilgrim Court?" Mrs. Palmer said into the silence. "The Semertons will forgive us, I know." She looked once more at her childhood friend. "Do come to see me, Livvy, since you will be in the neighborhood."

"Let me attend you to your carriage, ladies," Semerton said, springing from his chair.

"We don't have one," Susan said. "Grandmama, I didn't think of it before, but you must have walked this whole way. I do hope you didn't tire yourself."

"Not at all, child," Mrs. Palmer said in a tone that bespoke mental, not physical weariness. "I took your father's carriage. And you, young man, may attend us there and no further," she added to Semerton. Then she looked at Captain Camberley. "Well, sir? I wouldn't expect you to be behindhand in this little courtesy to your neighbors."

"But of course, ma'am," Camberley said in surprise.

Susan, too, was shocked that Grandmama was actually seeking the captain's company in however small a way. Perhaps Mrs. Palmer merely sought to keep Susan from Semerton's particular attentions.

The procession soon left the room. Lady Semerton and her granddaughter were alone.

"Emily," the older lady said, "you can't do it. The little Danvers girl has him fast in her net."

"Fudge, Grandmama. She is only a little country chit, after all. And we've but this instant found out that Captain Camberley is the one who's responsible for *Lessons in Life*! How could such a man of the world possibly be wishful of an alliance with that simple little thing? She is much more in Buxford's style, and if we can only see to it that he stays here with us as long as possible, they will come together, you may be sure."

"I don't know whether you overestimate the girl's simplicity or are merely blind, my dear," Lady Semerton responded.

"How can you talk so, ma'am? The captain doesn't single her out."

"The eyes, my child. One simply has to look at the eyes."

"Whose eyes?" Emily asked sharply.

"Oh, anybody's eyes," Lady Semerton said with a wave of her hand. "You cannot expect me to do everything for you, dear."

Lady Emily sighed deeply. "I suppose, Grandmama, that I merely wish to play the game for as long as possible. Naturally I know I might fail, but I always find it amusing to try."

"That you do. I can think of a dozen like infatuations of yours this year alone."

"I am hardly that shallow," Lady Emily objected. "And I do know that Susan's mama will never approve a match between her and Camberley. Lord Delafort is bound to follow his wife's wishes. I might comfort the captain in his disappointment."

"Of all the caper-witted things to wish! A granddaughter of mine must want to be the first in the affections of the man she takes as husband."

"Piffle, Grandmama. There is no such thing as being first in anyone's affections. Now, shall we draw up a list to send back to town? I'm suffering for clothes, and if we act quickly, a messenger can be there and back with at least a pair of evening gowns before the dinner hour. My new one, I think." Lady Emily's eyes took on a shrewd gleam as she drew forth her ever-present pocketbook. "That low-necked pomona-green satin. And the straw-colored silk. And why not the cherry? A blonde like Susan Danvers can't wear cherry."

Lady Semerton, while deploring the extent of her grand-daughter's cynicism, had to agree that clothes must be the first order of business if they were really to stay for a few days at Royce Park. She had soon taken off her bonnet and gloves and was busily barking additions and emendations to Emily's efficient list.

17

The next day Captain Camberley, mounted on his favorite hunter, rode down the avenue of Pilgrim Court. He was in his best and newest riding clothes. The dog Neptune, frisking about in lumbering fashion, had been washed and brushed. A grim expression adorned the captain's face as he passed through sun and shadow.

He had not yet reached the carriage sweep of the house when he spotted, coming toward him, the very person he had ridden out to seek.

Viscount Delafort reined in a showy chestnut hack to call out, "Captain Camberley! Good day to you. I suppose you are going to sit with the ladies."

The captain shook his head. "If you wish the truth, my lord, I was coming to see you. On a matter of great importance."

"I see." Delafort's tanned face took on a thoughtful look. "Let me try to divine the import of your call. As the parent of an excessively pretty daughter, I daresay I won't have to venture many guesses."

Camberley found himself less than pleased by this comment, though it did augur a good outcome for his petition. "Sir, your daughter has many fine qualities besides her looks. I hope you don't think that a man would be drawn to her from mere admiration of her beauty?"

"Ah!" The viscount cast his companion a shrewd glance. "Serious, indeed. Well, Captain, since we find ourselves both on horseback, what do you say to a short ride around the neighborhood while we talk? I'm still reaccustoming myself to the gentle green of Surrey."

"Different from India, I expect, sir," the captain said, cursing himself in the next instant for saying something so banal.

"I could talk for hours about it, but I don't wish to turn the very interesting subject we began. The matter of my daughter.''

Despite this opening, silence reigned all the way back up the avenue. Before much time had passed they were riding along a leafy lane in the direction of Royce Park.

Camberley was not best pleased to have to shout out his feelings from the back of a horse, but he supposed that in compensation there was a certain ease that could not have been obtained in the interview he had imagined: Lord Delafort behind a massive desk, he perched in nervous anticipation on an uncomfortable chair before it.

"I want to marry your daughter," he therefore said in a raised voice suitable to the circumstances. "I've come to you to beg permission to pay her my addresses." The ordinary words, the proper form: why, then, did he feel that his life was hanging in the balance? That any discouraging words this careless peer might utter would finish the famous Captain Camberley more thoroughly than the heaviest cannon fire had done for many of his unfortunate men?

"Have you indeed?" Delafort flashed a youthful grin that reminded the captain of Susan's smile.

"Do you give permission, then?" Camberley's throat was dry; once again he deplored the fact that this important conversation must take place over the clopping of hooves.

"Lady Delafort tells me that you have several rivals. Men of fortune and title. What do you say to that?" Delafort asked with a knowing look.

"The only thing that a man in my position can say, sir," the captain returned. "That no one can love her better than I do."

"Lady Delafort goes so far as to style you a social climber and a fortune hunter," the viscount went on in that same strange, half-serious tone.

"My family is old enough to need no apologies, though I admit the Camberleys lack nobility, and a title has never come nearer than the one I was offered and turned down after the war," Camberley said. "As to the financial side of things, I can care for your daughter quite well. We won't require a dowry, though you may settle something on her children if you wish to be bountiful."

The words were stiff and uncomfortable; evidently the captain didn't make a practice of asking for young ladies' hands. Delafort looked sharply at his companion. "Shall I let you try your fate with Susan, then?"

"If it's quite convenient, sir," Camberley said, lips tightening.

The riders were now in the road that fronted Royce Park. The viscount's horse started, and both Delafort and Camberley turned their mounts aside just in time.

A pair of curricles thundered by them, one after the other—there was no room to drive abreast in the narrow road. Camberley noted in shock that one of the vehicles was his own prized turn-out, though the cattle pulling it did not belong to his stables.

The driver of this carriage noticed Camberley. "A famous wager, what, Captain?" Semerton called out. "Do you want to put something on it? A pony says I beat his shabby rig to the village."

"Shabby rig?" Buxford called back over the noise of hoof-beats and wheels. "You'll pay for that remark, man."

"Absolute folly, to race in a country lane," Delafort exclaimed, waving his hand to disperse the dust the two pairs had kicked up. "I never went in for that sort of thing, even in my most foolish moments. I much preferred wagering on which of two raindrops would make it first down a windowpane. Neater."

"My curricle," Camberley said in amazement. "He took my curricle without a by-your-leave."

Delafort, sounding more middle-aged and surly than Camberley would have thought he could, had several more pithy comments to make on the folly of the two young men.

The captain cleared his throat. "I suppose you know that both these young men are your daughter's suitors. I feel it necessary, my lord, to tell you that I didn't pay them to do this to make myself look better. They said at breakfast that they were bored senseless, but I failed to take them literally."

"There was no need for that display to tell me that you're the best man in terms of sense and maturity, I assure you, Camberley," Lord Delafort said with a wry look. "And you would laugh could you see the letter I got this morning from

Fitzalbin. Quite calmly informing me that he had set his sights on my daughter and inquiring as to the exact amount of her settlement.''

"Lord Fitzalbin!" Camberley was shocked that the dissolute peer who was Lady Delafort's *cicisbeo* should be lusting after her daughter.

"Don't worry," Susan's father said. "I anticipate a deal of pleasure in composing an answer to Fitz. He's older than I, devil take it. And Susan has told me she finds him unbearable."

"Unbearable." The captain perked up at this.

Delafort wheeled his chestnut about. "What do you say, Captain? Would you like to accompany me home and try your luck with Susan before I receive a letter from a royal duke? And make sure you bring that cur into the house. She sings its praises almost as much as yours.''

Camberley was much gratified by this comment; and not because of the viscount's kind inclusion of Neptune!

In the French drawing room of Pilgrim Court the two men found only Mrs. Palmer, who was busy at her knitting. She frowned at the both of them equally, Camberley thought; at least he could read no extra malice in her glare when it lit upon him.

"Let me go to find my daughter," Delafort said with a wink. "I won't trust the message to any servant."

"Sir, don't give me away, I pray you," Camberley returned.

The viscount assured him that every discretion would be followed.

"Well!" Mrs. Palmer said once she had been left alone with the captain. "I infer from those cryptic words that you've designs upon my granddaughter."

"I won't lie to you, ma'am," said Camberley. "I have."

"She is too young, too naive, and has seen too little of the world. What say you to that?"

"That she is old enough, not at all as naive as people think her, and that any lack of knowledge of the world has been by your express orders, ma'am," Camberley replied in a smooth voice. "I think this a matter I had best take up with the young lady herself. But since we are alone together, you and I, would you allow me to tell the author of *Lessons in Life* how much

I admire her? That you have hidden your identity for all these years is the world's loss, but rest assured that I respect your privacy.'' He paused. ''I will also undertake to see that the Semerton family says nothing to distress you. Your secret is safe.''

''Don't expect me to thank you for that condescension, young man,'' Mrs. Palmer replied in a flat tone. ''So you think you know the workings of my mind, do you, since you translated that worthless book into English so that the ignorant might tittle and tattle over the bawdy parts?''

''You don't think much of your work, do you?'' Camberley shrugged. ''I must disagree with you, ma'am. Your novel shows a brilliance far beyond your years when you wrote it. Your shrewd reading of French society was never surpassed, in my humble opinion. Your words deserved a reading by your countrymen, even if you won't come forward and reap the benefits.''

''The benefits?'' Mrs. Palmer gave an indelicate snort, though her eyes had appeared to soften at his praise. ''The notoriety, you mean. I have no patience with those who seek to lionize themselves, sir.''

''Nor do I. I have made my part in this anonymous,'' Camberley said. ''Even in the case of my naval exploits, I've always found notoriety a tiresome thing. By benefits I meant monetary ones. I have had my publisher hold back a share of the profits of the translation, on the chance you could be found. It's quite a tidy sum, for you know that little volume has swept through society high and low, and it was not cheaply priced in the first place, since we considered it would become only a collectors' oddity.''

''Money?'' Despite her best efforts, Mrs. Palmer let her interest show.

''Am I correct in guessing that your well-earned profits would ease your circumstances?'' the captain said gently. He feared to insult the lady, yet his researches into her means had come up with some illuminating answers.

Mrs. Palmer made no reply, merely glared at him.

Susan, accompanied by her father, now appeared at the French windows. ''Captain Camberley! And dear Neptune.

What a delightful surprise.'' She came forward to caress the dog.

Camberley watched her closely, wondering if that sweet affection would shortly be turned to him.

Out of the corner of his eye he noticed Lord Delafort whisper something to Mrs. Palmer and lead her away. The good lady seemed still in shock at Camberley's revelations, but she paused before going out into the garden and regarded her granddaughter in a regretful manner.

''Susan,'' she said in a compelling tone.

The girl turned from her ministrations to the dog.

''You must of course do as you like,'' Mrs. Palmer said. She left the room followed by Delafort, who cast his daughter a reassuring look before he shut the French windows behind them.

Susan stood upright, smiling at Camberley. ''How very odd of Grandmama to speak so. I believe I've spent all my life in wondering if she ever would believe I could do as I liked without making a complete mull of things.''

''Isn't that the essence of Rousseauistic training?'' Camberley asked. ''Doing as one likes, I mean. Running wild, developing as nature would have it.''

''Well, in this household the philosophy was tempered by the view that too much of anything was somehow not virtuous,'' Susan said. Then, declining to prose on about her grandmother's beliefs, she took courage and added, ''My father said you wished to see me, Captain Camberley.''

''I did indeed. Do you think you could manage to call me Vincent?''

''Vincent is a fine name,'' Susan said, gazing at him. Remembering her manners, she added with a blush, ''You may call me Susan if you wish.''

He stepped forward. ''Susan . . . I am a man of few words. This would be the time to fling myself on one knee and beg for your hand. Will you excuse my not following through with that particular tradition?''

She waited, saying nothing.

''You are so sweet, so gentle and good.'' Vincent took her hands in a warm clasp. ''I know you wouldn't play with me. Will you marry me, my dear?''

Susan made a little grimace at this catalog of her virtues and kept looking at him. "Oh, sir—Vincent, my very dear Vincent. How can I marry you if you will talk so?"

This statement was so at odds with her affectionate expression that Vincent drew back a pace to stare at her. "Is there someone else, then, or do you find you can't care for me? Forgive me, Miss Danvers. I won't trouble you again."

"Please, Vincent, don't call me Miss Danvers in that cold way," Susan exclaimed, pulling at his hand as he tried to draw it gently from hers. "You can't know how much I've wished for your good opinion. It seems impossible that you should care for me. It *is* impossible. You've as much as said so."

"What?" Totally confused, Vincent looked into the lovely face, dismayed at the anguish clearly to be read upon it. She seemed to care for him. Her father had given permission. What the devil could be wrong?

"You called me sweet and gentle and good. I heard you with my own ears," Susan said in a tone which mingled accusation and regret.

"Wouldn't that tend to prove my affection rather than the reverse?"

She sought to find another example and hit upon an issue that had been troubling her greatly. "There's the matter of the bonnet."

"Bonnet?" Her would-be lover's face betrayed complete astonishment.

"The day before yesterday, the day I arrived from London," Susan said, trying to ignore the warmth spreading through her at the feel of his hands on hers, "I was wearing a truly elegant bonnet. I came to see your sister while I had it on, and you . . . you didn't say a word about it."

The captain, with a visible pang, admitted he had not. In his look was a disappointment that Susan well understood. He hadn't thought her so shallow as to complain about a lack of compliments to her headgear.

She continued, hoping to make all clear soon. There was so much more to this than he thought; for her the affair of the bonnet was not minor at all. She nearly despaired of explaining herself to a man, though. "Yesterday I visited your house again, this time in my most bucolic and countrified clothes. My hat had a piece missing from it, sir, and my gown was dirty from working in the garden. And you said I had never looked so pretty, or some such faradiddle.''

"I may have. What does all this mean, my darling?''

His darling! Susan gazed into his eyes, her resolution wavering. It would be something, surely, to belong to this man, whatever the terms. Yet some instinct urged her to keep trying for understanding as well as love.

"You like me because I'm a country-bred innocent," she said, feeling tears well up in her eyes. "I'm sorry, Captain. I can't engage not to change. I'm altering already from the white-gowned girl you found delightful last summer. A whole year has gone by, and time has not stood still for me.'' She lifted the hem of her skirt, though this meant breaking free from the thrilling touch of his hands. "See? A simple white morning gown, but made by Madame Hélène, the foremost modiste of the *ton*.''

Vincent stared at her, still puzzled. He honestly hadn't noticed what she had on, today or yesterday or the day before, and why she should fix on clothing at a time like this was quite beyond his understanding. "A dress?''

Susan found herself smiling. "My mother tried to teach me that clothes are very important. But I mean to speak of them only as symbols, Vincent. I have changed, as my clothes have, and you don't seem to notice or want me as I am now. Do you understand?''

"Not altogether.'' The look of disappointment was gone from his face, though, and a sneaking little smile had replaced it. "Go on. Tell me more.''

She lifted her chin. "My grandmother, for reasons of her own, tried to keep me ignorant, but I've been doing my best to change all of that. I'm not clever like your sister, but I've learned a few things in my time in London. I won't stop learning, sir, and I won't be satisfied to be left behind in the country, somebody's false ideal of goodness and gentleness and those other dreadful qualities you spoke of. I'm not a noble savage, any more than my mother was at the masked ball. I doubt if I ever was.'' She paused to take a deep breath. ''So far I've been my grandmother's experiment and my mother's foil. I must be myself from now on, not whoever you wish me to be.''

''My dear girl.'' Vincent stepped up close to put his arms around her. ''What have you been thinking?''

Susan lost the thread of her discourse completely. He was not making it easy for her to explain her doubts and worries. The trouble was, she didn't believe she cared any longer. She relaxed for one dangerous moment into his embrace. Yes, this was where she had wished to be ever since she had known him. This was where she had met him. Unable to resist, she raised her face to his in an unmistakable invitation.

Vincent was no readier than she to do the proper thing. He had been dreaming of this for months. Without further thought, he pulled her even closer and kissed her with tender longing.

What had been intended as a modest salute, a kiss that would not frighten the untried sensibilities of a maiden, soon deepened into something more. They stood locked together for a very long time.

Home, Susan thought through the haze of passion. *I have come home.*

''I won't let you go,'' Vincent murmured into her hair.

''But you must understand me first.'' Susan pulled back in his arms, though there was nothing she wished less. ''Please let me try again to tell you. I'm not who you think me.'' She paused, for the next part was a hard confession to make. ''I scarcely know yet who I am. My grandmother's rules only made me devious, not innocent. I've tried to change and become honest since I've been out from under her care, but I haven't even succeeded in that yet. Not altogether.''

''My dearest Susan, how can I prove to you that I don't want some static dream of an untried girl? That's not who you are to me. I've seen you change in the little time I've known you. We all change.''

''Can you mean that? Truly?'' Susan looked deep into his eyes.

''Of course. I ought to be angry with you, my love, for

believing that I think marriage is merely a lark with a pretty girl. If we're to grow old together, you must admit that you don't really think me so big a fool as that.''

"Oh, Vincent." Susan went into his arms again for a most satisfying reconciliation.

"See? You are changing already, and I don't mind a bit,'' he murmured. "You've grown much more abandoned in the last ten minutes. I'll simply have to marry you to keep you honest.''

"Please do." Susan stirred against him. "You've changed too, you know, since I met you.''

"I have?"

"A great deal. You seem much more carefree, somehow, than you were when I first saw you. Though you were always most exciting," she added quickly.

He smiled at the compliment. "Carefree? Hardly that. I'm still a glum old sailor. But perhaps I've come to terms, a little, with the war and the part I played.''

"You didn't like it that you were whole and others were not.'' Susan touched his face. "And to be lauded for your victories besides! How it must have pained you. I do hope you realize that it was only fate that gave you the laurels.''

"How did you know all that?" He was clearly astounded by her insight.

"Do you remember a few months ago when we went to the opera? I saw you with an injured man. A sailor from your ship, so you told me. I simply guessed what you must have been feeling. I already cared, you see.''

"You did?" Smiling broadly, he hugged her to him.

At this point Lord Delafort peeked into the room. "Well, Susan," he said as the couple sprang apart, "no need to do that for my benefit. I'm quite satisfied with the captain's suit. I merely wished to see how it was progressing. Let me go now and break it to your mother, who might take some convincing, I warn you. Best if you let the captain take you home to his sister for dinner.''

As quickly as he had come, the genial viscount was gone.

"I do so love my parents," Susan said. "I know you'll come to love them too.''

Vincent was surprised at her generosity. She had been virtually abandoned at an early age by both her parents, who, to be fair, had no failings more serious than a casual attitude which, though charming in social situations, might be less than desirable in family life.

"Do you include your grandmother in that hope?" he asked curiously.

She laughed. "How can you even ask? I owe so much to Grandmama."

"Do you really harbor no resentment for the way she raised you?"

"How could I? She had her beliefs, and she couldn't go against them. I do hope she has found out that her theories simply didn't transmit to a real human being. It must be impossible to raise a true savage." Susan sighed. "And I suppose that her straitened circumstances had much to do with her insistence on rustic simplicity."

"You know about that?" Once again Vincent was taken aback by his love's insight.

"What do *you* know?" was Susan's retort.

He smiled. "I must confess that your grandmother's very simple way of life made me suspect that she acted from necessity as well as eccentricity. I had my man of business look into the situation, hoping to find some way to help her if she and I ever became closely connected. Little did I know that we were already closely connected, as author and translator."

Susan smiled in satisfaction at this revelation of his longtime affection.

"Your grandfather left her with nothing but this house," Vincent went on. "She chose to keep the estate and has sold off everything bit by bit—art objects, furniture—to keep body and soul together. She was too proud, evidently, to ask your father for help in raising you."

"How could she do so when she had nearly forced Mama to give me up to her?" Susan shook her head. "I've suspected this before now. We keep no vehicles, have few servants, live off the produce of the estate—yes, it all makes sense. Poor Grandmama. I'm so glad she's kept this pretty room together. I suppose it will be the next to go."

"Better times are coming to her, never fear," Vincent said. "Since I know she's the author of *Lessons in Life,* the bulk of the profits on the translation will be settled on her. It's a tidy sum. Properly invested, it should make her circumstances easy."

"Thank goodness. I know Papa would make her an allowance, but this will be much more suited to Grandmama's pride."

"What is this about Grandmama's pride?" a sharp voice said from the doorway. Susan and Vincent turned around to see Mrs. Palmer framed there.

"Nothing, Grandmama," Susan said, proving that she had not yet outgrown her devious streak.

"I'll warrant you're talking over my outlandish Rousseauistic ideas, the pair of you," Mrs. Palmer said with a shrewd look. "I admit my methods have been less than a raging success. Well, go on with what you are doing, by all means."

Susan and Vincent stood frozen, quite unable to act as Mrs. Palmer suggested.

"I only came to look for my spectacles." A good-humored resignation was evident in the old lady's tones and in her keen eyes, which, when they lit upon Neptune's large black frame, became less than indulgent. "What, are you still here, sirrah?" She prodded the large animal with her foot. Years of dealing with dumb beasts gave her voice a rare authority. "These lovers wish privacy. Out with you. We'll go together."

Neptune cast one look up at his master, received a curt nod, and reluctantly got to his feet. Accompanied by the dog, Mrs. Palmer moved again to the door, spectacles in hand.

"Say what you will about my methods, Susan, my training has had its effect. What is going on here is perfectly natural," the old lady said with an emphatic nod. Then she left the room and closed the door behind her.

Vincent and Susan were laughing as they began once more to explore the fascinating new territory of each other's arms.